CW00781566

THE MATRIARCH

an erotic superhero romance

(book one of THE MATRIARCH trilogy)

by Sloane Howell

The Matriarch

THE MATRIARCH

The Matriarch Trilogy, Book 1

Sloane Howell

Copyright© 2015 Sloane Howell

All rights reserved. No part of this book may be reproduced, scanned, or distributed in any printed or electronic form without prior written permission from Sloane Howell. Please do not participate in piracy of books or other creative works.

This book is a work of fiction. While reference may be made to actual historical events or existing locations, the names, characters, places and incidents are products of the author's imagination, and any resemblance to actual persons, living or dead, business establishments, events, or locales is entirely coincidental.

WARNING: This book contains sexually explicit scenes, violence, and adult language and may be considered offensive to some readers. Please store your books wisely, away from under-aged readers. This book is a dark romance. If dark romance bothers you, this book isn't for you.

Stock Photos courtesy of shutterstock.com
Editing by Celia Aaron
Font by Pi Luo Chiu

ISBN-10: 1522782583

ISBN-13: 978-1522782582

The Matriarch

For all the mothers out there, biological or not, who are the real superheroes.

The Matriarch

The Matriarch

prologue
maggie madison

present day

Jesus Christ this guy can fuck. Shame he has to die.

I bucked my hips on Damon's stiff cock as it explored the depths of me. Veins bulged across his broad chest and his abs tensed as he tugged against the ropes I'd tied to his wrists.

He flashed a devilish grin in my direction. "You like that fucking dick?"

My hand tore through the air and slapped the shit out of the cocky son of a bitch. The bright pink finger marks on the side of his cheek brought a smile to my face. I bent over and dug my nails into his scalp, then slid my breasts up his hard pecs.

"Shut the fuck up and make me come." My voice turned to a throaty whisper. "Now, bitch."

I leaned back, grinding my pelvis into him. My tits bounced as my ass clapped into his muscular thighs and my pussy spasmed around his thick shaft.

"That's it, you dirty fucker." He filled me to the brim as my wetness dripped to the sheets. Nerve firings were building in my clit and radiating to my inner thighs. Vaulted ceilings amplified the sound of the headboard banging into the wall. The din seemed to fuel Damon as he drilled into me. The black wig on my head draped around my shoulders and danced to the rhythm of his cock.

The smell of sweaty lust lingered as the tension in my core erupted into my extremities.

"Fuck!" I shuddered on his hard prick.

The Matriarch

I convulsed as the orgasm ripped through my body. My hips jolted and I clamped down on him like a vise. Freezing on top of him, my toes curled and my thighs dug into his ribs as I struggled to breathe.

When my body released, I stared down to him. His eyes met mine.

"Shit was good, huh?" He smiled.

"It was okay."

His beaming gaze transformed to a puzzled frown. Beads of sweat dripped from his flaring nostrils and his breathing intensified. He lurched at me, eyes full of hate, powerful arms ready to inflict pain. The restraints tightened, jarring him backward. I didn't so much as flinch, fueling his rage even more.

"*Okay*? You stupid bitch!" Anger lit his eyes, but I had him trapped under me.

"Will you stop being a pussy and shut the fuck up? I'm trying to think here." I scanned the room, looking for any information that might be important.

The idiot between my thighs was no longer of use.

"You know your ass is dead talking to me that way, right? You need to suck this fucking dick off and take your ass home before I beat the shit—"

I put a finger to his lips. "Oh my god, you are a whiny little bastard aren't you?"

"You fucking bitch. I'm going to beat the fucking—"

I gripped his head and snapped his neck. Hard. I heard the familiar pop and his torso went limp, his arms dangling from the bedposts.

Leaning down, I kissed him on the forehead. "Your dick will be truly missed."

Sliding off the bed, I pulled on my tight black leather pants and a form-fitting shirt. My lacy black mask was next. I slipped it over my eyes and tied it in the back. A gothic floral design covered the majority

The Matriarch

of my face. I grabbed my steel knives and strapped them to my waist before turning to his lifeless body.

"Oh damn, sweets." I smirked. "I didn't even get you off. You were right. I really *am* a bitch."

I was right on schedule.

The bedroom door creaked when I eased it open. *Goddamn it.* On the floor below, two guards conversed, each holding a Kalashnikov. I crept swiftly down the long hallway, blending with the shadows, remaining hidden without making a sound. Just like I'd been taught.

The compound was massive and I had assholes to kill. I'd planned this job thoroughly, studying guard movements, watching the place, and hacking their security feeds.

Guard seven went on break at the same time every night, and I needed to be in position in five minutes to capitalize on that fact.

As I neared the monitoring room there was more security than usual. Every one of these fucks was a former member of the military. The Family — an unrivaled criminal enterprise backed by corporate interests — required experienced killers. The guards exceeded these requirements. Even so, the Family had its weaknesses.

Damon had been the Family's black sheep, stupid and easily manipulated. He'd been kept on the payroll as a low-level boss to stay quiet and out of Family business. It took me roughly 48 hours to seduce him, the fact that he was hot and fucked like a beast an added bonus.

More and more guards were amassing near my target. I paused against the wall as a handful walked past, their guns slung across their shoulders. They didn't see me, but they were still a problem.

Fuck. I hadn't planned on this many guards. Where the hell were they all coming from?

The Matriarch

Once they were out of sight, I weaved through the Santa Fe style estate that seemed to span for miles. I had a goal, a target, but I needed to stick to the plan.

Guard seven was still inside the monitoring room when I got there. Everything was going to hell, including this poor bastard.

Too late to turn back, I had to think on my feet. I tapped lightly on the monitoring room door. Guard seven sprang from his seat as I heard two sets of footsteps approaching around the corner. Once someone discovered the stiff prick upstairs, it wouldn't be long before the alarm sounded.

When guard seven opened the door I kicked high and hard, a sharp blade shooting from the toe of my boot and piercing his neck. I yanked the blade from the fresh wound, jammed my finger into his torn artery, and pressed my lips seductively to his as the other guards appeared.

"Get a room, Jesus." They kept walking. My ruse had worked.

When I pulled my finger from my victim, he gurgled and choked. He shuddered, clutching at his throat, gasping for air as fluid filled his lungs. I stared into his surprised eyes as he slid down the wall, crumpling to the floor in a pool of his own blood. I smiled, knowing there was one less sack of shit in the world.

Cool air from a fan washed over my cheeks as I darted into the secure room. I scanned the monitors. Each had a single female in view. My heart dropped into my stomach. The stakes of the mission were front and center in my mind as the sounds of computers and surveillance equipment buzzed around me. I leaned down to my black leather boots and pressed a button. A USB drive popped out the side with a soft click. I grabbed it and shoved it into the main computer.

The Matriarch

A bright green status bar began to fill on the central monitor. "Come on, come on, you fucker."

A siren rang through the compound. I stepped into the hallway, my head on a swivel. Footsteps hammered the ground overhead, rushing from Damon's room.

"Guess they found the asshole." I smirked.

I snapped back to the monitor. When it reached "100%" a loud buzz sounded and all the doors down the hall slid open.

Showtime, bitches.

Whimpers came from the rooms as I sprinted silently down the narrow, dimly lit corridor. Mildew and body odor filled my nostrils. It was like a rancid locker room. My shoes squeaked on the dark tiles of the modern dungeon as I stopped at each open door. Frightened eyes met mine as the prisoners cowered and no doubt expected beatings or worse.

Someone barked commands on the floor above, but I couldn't make out the words. The black soundproofed walls held in the screams, but were equally resistant to sounds coming from outside.

The rooms were holding cells for a dozen girls—all white with blonde hair. They were caged like animals waiting for slaughter. Most likely orphans or prostitutes, they'd no doubt been snatched off the streets and traded like stocks. Human trafficking was the number one moneymaker for the Family. I planned to fuck that bull market right in the ass.

"Follow me, hurry!" I yelled.

When I reached the end of the corridor I turned to verify that all twelve girls were following me. Once satisfied no one had been left behind, I led them to the end of another hallway. I stopped at a corner and shot my arm out beside me, blocking the girls from going any farther.

The Matriarch

I turned to them, their eyes wide, and pressed a finger to my lips as some of the security team flew by.

I saw the horror in the girls. The terror of captivity and torture. I recognized it because I knew it intimately.

We ran to the end of the hall. I opened a set of doors and guided us through a narrow alley. Twenty-foot-high concrete walls loomed on both sides, caging us in as surely as these girls' cells did only moments before. The alley opened to a large courtyard surrounded by a fence topped with razor wire. Our freedom sat 100 yards away, through an opening I had cut in the fence. A black van waited on the other side, hidden in the night from the massive spotlights snaking around the front of the estate.

We dashed forward, stopping at the manicured grass that filled the courtyard. A watchtower sat atop the end of each wall. Guards with fifty caliber rifles manned the spotlights. I whipped two knives from my belt and heaved them simultaneously into the air, connecting with both gunmen.

I knew what was coming as I turned to the girls. They watched as the guards toppled from their posts. "Don't say a word."

The men slammed into the ground in front of us, knives protruding from their necks, blood pulsing from the wounds.

Two of the girls began to shriek and I clamped my hands over their mouths.

"Shh!" I didn't want to hurt them, but two dead was better than all of us.

Once satisfied they were under control, I motioned to the waiting van. The girls took off. Their tattered white t-shirts fluttered in the wind as they sprinted toward the vehicle, freedom locked in their sights. But one girl froze, her senses shocked, body stiff as a board. Her face was ashen, sweat beads forming on her forehead as tremors rippled through her.

"We have to go! Now!" I shook the shit out of her.

She didn't move. Several guards appeared in the alley behind us, their guns drawn, staring in disbelief at the getaway in progress.

"*Fuck.*"

I stepped between the stricken girl and the men. The girl seemed to have snapped out of it after a couple of hard shakes, but instead of getting her shit together, she was trembling and crying uncontrollably.

"It's her!" The guards advanced.

"I don't suppose you boys are here to fuck me?" I didn't bother to hide my smile.

"Shoot them!"

They raised their automatic rifles but it was too late. I swept the back of the girl's legs, sending her tumbling to the ground in a smooth motion. I rushed back into the alley toward the armed men and sprinted up the side of the wall. I hurled three knives into the chaos. Blood exploded from three of the guards as they dropped, clutching at the weapons sunk deep in their flesh.

I pirouetted off the wall, blades extending from both boots as I twirled through the air. I sliced through one man's back, his howls of pain music to my ears. The other blade embedded and then cut through another's jugular. The blades retracted before I hammered into the ground, landing in the middle of the pack, inches from one guard's face.

"Oh hello, love." My lips pressed into his as I kicked another guard in the throat. I pulled away, biting on his lower lip before releasing it.

"Guns? Whips would have been better." I tossed him a wink and palmed two silver blades.

The Matriarch

Bodies dropped as I whipped and spun, every strike mauling a vital organ, painting a masterpiece in blood. When there was nothing but a pile of bodies I returned to the girl. She stared in disbelief. I pulled the waif into a sitting position.

When she turned to me, awe lit her blue eyes. It was the first time I'd slowed long enough for anyone to look at me. "It's you. Y-you're the Matriarch."

I heard a small army of guards approaching, the sounds of their footsteps telling me it was time to go. I threw the girl, still bewildered, over my shoulder and hauled ass toward the opening in the fence.

Bullets sliced past us as we flew through the hole and dove head first into the van. Crashing inside, I yanked the door closed.

"Go!"

The old man behind the wheel hammered the gas and we blasted down the road, disappearing into the night.

The Matriarch

part one

The Matriarch

The Matriarch

chapter one
maggie madison

fifteen years earlier

"Maggie, let's go."

I eased down the staircase. The walls were bare where our pictures once hung. The photos were all stuffed in boxes and shipped off to a storage unit god knows where. I had only been allowed to keep a few.

The house was a skeleton of what was once a body full of life and love. Two men kicked up dust while removing contents I'd always thought were permanent. The chair where Dad always sat to read. The table where we ate every family meal together.

I rubbed my eyes and glanced at the hollow rooms. The home was cold and empty as I readied myself to say goodbye.

Slouched at the shoulders and examining the floor, I dawdled toward my parents Brian and Sarah. My twelve-year-old twin brother Kyle stood next to them over the threshold.

"Don't make me go." I glared at the ground and picked at my cuticles. "I don't want to leave. Grandpa is here. What about Grandpa?"

My father knelt down, his lean, muscular frame weary. His brown eyes met mine and he brushed my hair from my cheek. His face was smooth and framed by chocolate-colored locks. His eyes locked onto mine and were less comforting than usual as his tan skin wrinkled around his mouth. His smile could light up a room but his frown could silence one just as easily. Lately, it was more of the latter.

He seemed hell bent on ruining my childhood. He was my hero and yet I could barely look at him. I

The Matriarch

clenched my fists as a tinge of fiery red seeped into my cheeks.

"We've been through this, Maggie. Grandpa understands. It's a sacrifice we have to make. People need our help. The church has never been able to get anyone placed in Golem. It might be their only chance to hear about Jesus." He had no anger, just resignation – a feeling I didn't share.

I folded my arms and stared at Mom. "You and Dad have lost it. Giving all my stuff away. This isn't fair."

I tried to fight back the tears. I failed. This was where I belonged, where we all belonged, but Mom and Dad refused to see it.

Dad held out his hand. I took it reluctantly as we stepped through the front door with nothing but a few suitcases.

Dad started the car and I wanted to jump out and run back to the house, back to where we should be. But the car moved forward. My house grew smaller as I watched through the back window. A highlight reel of happy moments played through my mind on a loop: Christmases, Thanksgivings, running through the door with my report card. Who were we giving all this up for? I didn't know, but I knew that I hated them.

Kyle had been quiet. It was as if he'd given up, accepted that this was the way things were. But he wasn't sad about it, not like I was. Why was my best friend so indifferent? He should be furious. Like me. I leered at his sandy mop of hair and playful grin.

"Aren't you mad?"

He shrugged. "Don't know."

"Won't you miss the house?"

"I guess."

Why was I the only one who cared? Why didn't anyone ask me what I thought? What I wanted? I

The Matriarch

turned to the window and folded my arms, hating my family as much as I hated the new home I'd yet to see. I occasionally sighed to remind them of my presence and the pain they were inflicting.

Ominous gray clouds littered the sky as we pulled into the airport parking lot. Kyle's eyes widened at the rows of planes symmetrically spaced at each terminal with large beige tunnels attached. When dad opened the car door for me, the hot, heavy air assaulted my face and a hint of noxious jet fuel crept down my throat. My nose twitching, I clenched my fists.

My hesitation grew with each step toward the entrance. I knew it may be my last moment in Bathory.

I leaned my seat up at the incessant urging of the uniformed woman as the engines began to roar. The plane rolled along and the foliage native to Bathory at edge of the runway caught my eye. I would miss the familiar trees. The scenery morphed to a steady green blur as the plane accelerated. The bottom dropped from under us. Waves of tingling circled through my body as I peered out at the shrinking trees. The landing gear settled under our feet with a *thunk*.

We rocketed over the expansive skyline of the city. Tall slivers of metal and glass sprouted from the ground and lingered in the clouds. The giant structures faded in the distance until they completely disappeared from view.

"Goodbye," I whispered.

The Matriarch

I jerked in my seat when the plane shook. Bags rattled overhead. Kyle's hand gripped my forearm tight.

"We're landing." He smiled.

"Did I sleep the whole time?"

"Yep."

When the plane unexpectedly wobbled again, I let out a squeal. People stared at me and looked annoyed.

My face tightened to a frown and I sneered at Kyle.

"What?" he asked.

"All you care about is riding on this stupid plane."

"So."

"Whatever."

I sat with my arms crossed, wrinkling my nose as Kyle enjoyed the ride.

"Come on Mags, seriously. We get to be the new kids. Start over. It's gonna be fun, you'll see."

"He's insane." I glared at Dad and ignored Kyle's attempts to appease me.

Kyle shrugged. "He just wants to help people."

"He needs to help his own family, not strangers we don't even know. He's driving me crazy."

Kyle wrapped his arm around me when the wheels of the plane screeched on the runway. The seatbelt dug into my waist.

"I'm here." He grinned. "We'll make it fun."

When I turned back I met his boyish grin. "Fine."

The airport was modern, with bright colored screens and clean tiles. It was like a cruel trick designed to make people travel there so Golem could trap them within its borders.

The Matriarch

My face scrunched as I looked at Kyle. He'd researched this dump before we left. "What is this place?"

"It's a separate country created within the U.S., like a reservation."

"What?"

"A long time ago it was a prison. The surrounding states sent criminals here because they didn't have any place to put them."

"Great. Dad brought us to a prison." I threw my arms in the air.

"It's not a prison. The people mixed in. Now it's a country."

I looked around. "Nope, still a prison."

Kyle chuckled.

Dad looked over at us. "Hey guys, come help with the bags. Our ride will be here any minute."

I grabbed the lightest bag there was and took off toward the door.

When we walked outside my head swiveled as I took in the view of the city. Tall, silver mountains lined the horizon to the west, their peaks like jagged blades stabbed up through the earth. Downtown was just north of the airport and a taupe, grimy haze rose above it. Dilapidated high rises and worn buildings were packed together, mirroring the cardboard shelters of the homeless that sat between them.

Kyle and I stood outside the airport, waiting for a car to take us deeper into the grubby city. Other travelers rushed around. Most of them seemed in a hurry and they rarely looked up. A filthy mist coated everything with the stench of exhaust fumes. I rubbed my arms and tried to get rid of the sooty film I imagined sticking to my skin and clothes.

I glanced at Kyle. He didn't look at me and seemed to be doing his best to avoid a conversation. I was about to say something nasty about the city, but a

The Matriarch

pale yellow cab pulled up in front of us. It rocked as one wheel jumped up over the curb and slammed back to the road. The driver, short and chubby, emerged and slammed his door. He smirked at the curb. His stained, white tank top worked hard to cover his round stomach while he examined the car for damage. His jeans were tattered and cinched to his waist but hung baggy around the legs. A toothpick hung out of his mouth and seesawed up and down when he spoke.

"Madison?"

He smelled of foul cabbage and cigarettes, and he wheezed loud enough for everyone to hear.

"Yes." Dad stepped forward holding a suitcase.

"Follow." The cabbie motioned to the trunk.

We crammed everything we could into the box on wheels. Dad strapped two suitcases to the top with weathered rope the cabbie pulled from under the seat. Faded black letters read "TAXI" under the chipped paint. Foreign symbols likely said the same underneath in starker letters, the language of Golem.

"Come, come, I take new home." The cabbie's crooked teeth showed when he smiled.

I turned to Mom and crushed her with a pitiful stare that begged her to reconsider.

"I can't believe you're doing this to me."

Tears dripped down Mom's face, landing on blonde hair that cascaded down her shoulders.

It didn't phase me. "Now you know how I feel."

I turned to the cabbie. "Can't wait." I glared at my parents with contempt as Kyle, Mom, and I piled into the back seat. I held up the broken seat belt with a show of disgust as we sped down the road.

The Matriarch

A few minutes into the ride and I hated the place even more. The roads were cracked and massive potholes tossed me like a rag doll in the back seat. Even the trees looked like they wanted to be somewhere else, sagging and drooping to the ground.

People streamed down the sides of the road, shuffling past each other, blending in with the dust that floated in the air. Depression and despair enveloped the city. The driver kept looking back and smiling unpleasantly, his rotten teeth sending shivers up my spine.

The crescent sun was impaled by the sharp mountains and disappeared slowly behind us. Lights flickered through the city as the electricity struggled to pass through the grid. I covered my nose, trying to ward off the smell permeating the air. It was sewage, but also something worse, something even more rotten. Whatever it was, it lingered, and I was afraid I would smell that way, too. Kyle didn't seem to notice. He stared out the window and grinned, as if we were starting some new adventure. I glared at him something awful, wishing he would realize how horrible this place was.

Dad tried to make friends with the driver. "Lived here long?"

"Whole life. My family were the first prisoners sent to Golem many years ago."

"Is it dangerous?" My ears perked up.

The cabbie's rotted teeth appeared in the rear view mirror, his eyes locked on me. "Can be."

"Are there places we should avoid?"

The smile turned to a serious scowl. "No where, who. You see Kiril, you disappear."

Dad gulped. "Who is Kiril?"

"Run city. Evil in veins. The politicians—" He paused to chuckle. "—are only for show. They have no power. Kiril Salzberg is boss. You know when see."

The Matriarch

Dad and Mom exchanged a look before he changed the subject. "So, what kind of things do kids do for fun here?"

"Oh, many park, school, Golem great place for kid."

The tension eased as we weaved through the streets. Downtown mirrored the rest of the city, other than one block of buildings that looked new and out of place, like they belonged in Bathory.

Dad looked back at me. I knew it was coming. He knew I liked skyscrapers. It was true, but I liked the ones in Bathory. Not the ones sitting in the middle of this dump. "Check out the buildings, Mags."

I scoffed. Pointing out a few nice things in a pile of crap was not going to win me over.

"School and church," said the driver, nodding to a small building with a peeling façade next to another with a cracked steeple.

Dad looked at me again, a hopeful smile plastered to his face. *Round two, Dad*? *Really*? "See Mags, it's not so bad." Mom stared at him and shook her head.

A small, squat school building caught my eye. It was dilapidated like everything else here, but graffiti slathered the walls. Not ornate, artistic graffiti, but black and red splatter. It was like someone tested a can on the wall before creating a masterpiece someplace else. Vines climbed the sides of the rotted wood and corrugated metal. A few shingles dotted the roof. The death trap seemed like it might collapse on someone at any moment.

"Fantastic." I huffed and leaned back against the frayed seat.

Mom shot me a look. "Be nice."

"What? I said it looks fantastic. I just hope I'm inside when it puts me out of my misery."

Kyle began to choke on the water he was sipping. Some of it came through his nose. He laughed

The Matriarch

through the pain, not by choice. Mom and Dad stared at each other and shook their heads, smiling.

"Glad I'm amusing." I folded my arms once more and sighed before glaring out the window.

Bouncing through a neighborhood, I stared at the run down shacks all crammed together, only separated by thin, rotting wood that caged in the backyards. The front yards were mostly dirt with a weed here and there.

Pulling up to our home, my jaw hit the floor. "It gets better."

The house was a fourth the size of our last and was a hideous yellow color that stood out like highlighted text. I couldn't tell if the bushes grew from inside or in front of it. A giant black tire hung from frayed rope on the tree in the front yard, like someone tried to spruce up the shack and wanted to label it 'kid friendly'.

Dad lugged our bags to the front door, Mom following.

"This ain't so bad." Kyle smiled.

He took off running toward the swing and leapt in the air, wrapping his legs around the tire. When the rope tightened, the branch snapped and crashed to the ground. Kyle tumbled toward the neighbor's yard and the tire bounced down the road.

Kyle got to his feet and made a show of dusting himself off. We all burst into laughter. He was such a goofball it was hard to stay mad at him. I was determined though. When the giggles wore off I realized this was it. This was my house, my yard, my life. I walked to the front door, defeat in every step.

I looked up at dad with a thin smile. "Whatever."

The Matriarch

The Matriarch

chapter two
maggie madison

I dragged my feet toward the kitchen of the tiny, barren house. Each step was heavier than the last as the smell of pancakes wafted to my nose. On the first day of school I would usually have a stomach full of butterflies. Today I worried about the school crushing me to death.

A familiar crucifix hung in the hallway as I walked past. I thought of at least ten things that would have been a better fit for the suitcase.

I stared at it with contempt. "Thanks a lot."

As far as I was concerned, the supposed deity hanging above my head was the reason I was stuck in this god-forsaken place. My parents attended church for a month and then suddenly uprooted my life.

Without thinking, I stuck my tongue out at the almighty (the most vulgar thing I could think of) but immediately felt lightning might strike the house. I apologized in my mind. The last thing I needed was god rooting against me.

The floorboards creaked and I felt them depress under my toes. As I eased around the corner, Mom and Dad smiled at each other in the kitchen. Pancakes sizzled on the pan as mom flipped them. I grinned at the brief glimpse into my old life.

Waves of reality crashed into me when they turned around.

"Ready for your first day?" Mom asked.

"No."

They looked at one another. It didn't matter how much they smiled, I would not like this place and they were not forgiven.

The Matriarch

"Hey Mags." Kyle tapped me on the back of the head as he zoomed by.

"Don't mess with me today."

"Ohh."

Kyle skipped into the kitchen and hugged Mom and Dad. He stole a piece of a pancake when nobody was watching. I grumbled and took my seat at the table. It was small and rickety as we huddled around it. Our plates clinked into one another.

A beast-sized bird cackled out of tune in the front yard. I glared in its direction, thinking of ways to return the torturous favor. Dad caught my hand as I reached for a stack of pancakes. He squeezed it firm.

"We say thanks to god first."

I blew a wayward strand of hair from my face. "How could I forget?"

Kyle snickered but closed his eyes. I refused to pretend to pray. I sat there and stared in disdain as Dad began.

"Lord, we thank you for this day. We pray that you bless this food and use our hands to do your work. We pray that others will find you the way we have and we can be tools to do your will. Please allow the community to accept and welcome us. Help Maggie and Kyle find friends, and that we all raise up your name in everything we do. In your name we pray. Amen."

I scoffed. Dad's foot tapped on the ground. I refused to believe in their nonsense, but decided to take it easy for a bit. I was already pushing boundaries to the limit.

I bit into a pancake, glad for a taste of home. But once the rancid taste hit my tongue, I spit it out and sputtered. "What is in these?"

"I had to adjust the recipe." Mom looked like she might cry.

The Matriarch

"They're nasty." I used my napkin to wipe the disgusting taste from my tongue.

Tears sparkled in the corner of Mom's eyes as she tried to compose herself. "I'm sorry, baby girl. I'll work on it. Okay?"

Dad's stare burned a hole into my skull as Mom brushed my hair behind my ear.

It wasn't that I wanted to be miserable. I didn't. I wanted to like the place for them. I just couldn't. It didn't matter what they said or what they did. I would never like it there. Ever.

"May I be excused?"

Dad noticed Mom's hard stare.

"Sure."

My plate rattled against the sink and I scurried toward the hall.

"I think they're great." Kyle shoveled a fork full in his mouth, syrup dangling from his chin as I left the room.

Laughter from the kitchen crept through the door while I dragged my feet, taking as long as possible to get ready for the day. The happiness in their voices raised my hackles. If we were back home I'd be walking with Kyle, excited to see all my old friends, heading to my old school. I wanted to cry. The first day of school was always my favorite. Now they had stolen it from me, along with everything else.

"Maggie let's go, I'm not waiting all day, slow poke!" Kyle yelled from the kitchen.

I plodded through the hall and made my way to the door. I mocked Kyle. "*I don't have all day, let's go.*"

Mom's hands went to her hips. "Be nice! You guys be careful. I'll see you at school."

The Matriarch

Walking down the gravel sidewalk, the dingy city and filth in the air wrapped around us. I stared at the shoddy buildings and makeshift shanties we passed.

We rounded a corner and noticed some kids huddled in a group.

"Look how filthy they are. Keep walking."

"Why?" Kyle asked.

"Because, look at them."

"Mags, they're just kids like us. What is your deal?"

"I don't know. There is just something about this place. It creeps me out."

Even though we were blocks away, I could still hear that ghastly annoying bird in our front yard. I was plotting every way possible to kill it when Kyle started talking to the kids. I nudged him. The kids looked past us. Their eyes all grew wide.

Several of them repeated that dreadful name. The name the cabbie had spoken. "Kiril."

I saw a group of fifteen men fanned out across the street. The kids quickly bent over at the waist and bowed as the men neared.

Kyle and I froze. They all wore sharp, navy blue pinstriped suits and fedoras. They also walked the same: chest out, stiff legs, chin up.

I strained my eyes to a man in the middle of the pack. "What is wrong with his face?"

Kyle stared at him. "I don't know."

One of the boys shouted something inaudible to Kyle and motioned for him to bow.

Kyle took the hint. "We should bow."

"For what?" I eyed the men.

"Just do it, okay? You heard what the cabbie said about this guy."

"I'm not bowing for a bunch of guys in weird hats. That's stupid." I shook my head.

The Matriarch

"Maggie, please, Dad would—"

"I'm not bowing." He could hear the conviction in my words. The men were just people—people of Golem, at that—and I wasn't going to bow to them. "What is that on his—" My stomach churned in knots when I realized the leader's face was wrapped in thin white linen that only showed his mouth and eyes. *Is he a mummy?* I regained my composure, intent on teaching the boys a lesson.

Kyle bent over and avoided eye contact with the men. Arms folded across my thin chest, I glared at them. One noticed and tapped another on the arm. They all stopped and stared in my direction. My knees started to wobble.

My heart dropped into my stomach but I refused to give in. Who were these guys? Why should I bow for them? My family came here to help and as far as I was concerned they should be grateful someone from the civilized world showed up in their country at all.

The man with the mummified face emerged and approached me with measured steps. He towered over me, his shadow layering on top of mine, making a monster on the pavement. His eyes were narrow and slate gray. He was death on legs, a ghost filled with pure evil. The boys quaked, but refused to raise their heads.

I stared at his hideous face, intent on standing my ground.

My bones chilled when he spoke in deep, calculated syllables.

"What's your name?"

"What's yours?" I glared at what parts of him I could see.

The corners of his mouth turned up slightly. His bandages wrinkled.

"Kiril."

"What kind of name is that?"

The Matriarch

He stared at me and cocked his head sideways. His gaze was somehow malevolent, piercing my soul like a shard of ice. He leaned in, studying my eyes, and ignored my question. "Why don't you bow?"

"Why should I?"

"Respect."

My hands trembled and his lips curled a bit more when he took notice.

"Well, I don't want to."

Kiril rose and belted out a laugh while silence surrounded him. It was the kind of laugh that haunted dreams. The men with him winced at my words.

His laughter ceased abruptly. He bent down. I picked at my raw fingers.

"You will."

His words cut to my core, eating away at my guts. He strode to the middle of the pack and continued down the street. I checked my pants to make sure they were still dry. I started to rethink my position on the lord as the boys jumped to their feet once the men were out of sight. My whole body trembled when I turned to Kyle.

"What is wrong with you?" Kyle's shook his head at me. "Are you out of your mind?"

"Forget him. What is wrong with you? Bowing for some guy in a hat. Sissy!"

The other boys looked at me like I was incredibly brave, but insane.

"We aren't going to last a week with you acting like an idiot. We are here. Get over it!"

I wanted to burst into tears when he bolted toward the school. My chest crushed against my heart. It was silly, but we had always walked to school together. He'd never left me on the street before, especially not in some strange place. I wanted to curl up in a room somewhere and never come out.

The Matriarch

chapter three
maggie madison

The odor of rotting wood and mold circulated through the schoolhouse. The taste of horrible pancakes crept up my throat. This was not how the first day of school was supposed to start. At least back home I had Kyle at my side.

Faded, crumbling paint clung to the walls and ceiling from different angles, and a dangling light fixture had me constantly looking up in fear. Random cracks snaked through the concrete floor and the stained glass mural on the wall contained about half of its original glass. The place looked like a hobo breeding ground. It had large, boarded up windows, and crusted dirt caked the floorboards.

I couldn't purge Kiril's stare from my mind. Imaginary bugs scaled over every inch of my body when I remembered his eyes, his bandaged face. Walking down the hall, I felt something tug at the straps on my backpack. I thought if I ignored it long enough it would go away.

No such luck.

I flipped around, grinding my teeth. "What!"

There was nothing but an empty hallway as my voice reverberated off the walls. I started to think I was hallucinating when I heard sniffles below. Looking down, I noticed a pudgy face and pair of soft brown eyes welled up with tears. The girl couldn't have been more than four or five years old. Her lip quivered.

If there was one thing I had a soft spot for it was kids.

"Oh my gosh, I'm so sorry. Please don't cry."

The Matriarch

I knelt down and rubbed her chubby arms. Stifling her tears, the girl still shook as I consoled her. She brushed back her thick ebony hair and revealed her pale skin. Her clothes were covered with the grotesque film that clung to everyone, but her scared, innocent face tugged at my heartstrings.

"What's your name?"

"S-s-suki."

My chest constricted as the girl stuttered. I was so caught up in myself I had frightened an innocent child. I chewed on a fingernail and examined the girl from head to toe.

"I'm Maggie."

The girl brushed her forearm across her face and wiped the tears from her eyes.

"Are you lost?" I asked.

The girl nodded, her bottom lip still quivering.

"Well, I'm sure we can find where you're supposed to be. Come here."

Suki lifted her hands to me and I hoisted her onto my hip. The backpack full of books and Suki's weight had me hunched over. Her head bounced as I adjusted her weight.

"You are *heavy*!" I bugged my eyes out at her, searching for a smile.

Suki grinned, her tears nearly gone and happy to have made a friend. I lugged Suki to the nearest classroom where other children played with toys in the corner.

"You are going to have *so* much fun today. I know your teacher and she is *awesome*."

Suki's eyes lit up. Mom walked over as sunlight peeked through the window and radiated around her casual dress and golden curls of hair.

She bent down so she was at eye level. "Who do we have here?"

"This is Suki." I smiled.

The Matriarch

Suki clung to the strap on my backpack.

"It's okay, she's my mommy and she's the best teacher I know."

Suki slid down my side and wrapped her arms around my leg, squeezing so tight my toes tingled.

"Looks like you made quite the impression." Mom smiled.

"She's just scared. I know how she feels." Mom bent down to Suki. I felt the girl's warm cheek press into my ribs.

"You know, I bet if you act big and brave, Maggie will come see you at lunchtime." Mom offered her hand to Suki.

Suki whipped her head up to me for confirmation.

I nodded. "It's true, I'll just be right across the hall."

Suki beamed and showed her adorable crooked teeth. "O...o...okay."

She released my leg and walked through the door, though she kept glancing back to me.

"Isn't she adorable?" I waved as Suki chose a toy and began pressing its buttons.

"Yes, I remember you holding my leg the exact same way." Mom ran her fingers through my hair.

She stared at the smile on my face as I turned to watch Suki make new friends. It was a smile that was no longer forced.

"I remember," I said.

"Maggie?"

"Maggie!" Kyle kicked the leg on my desk and jarred me from my imagination.

I jerked back to reality. My head flipped around to meet his face so I could lay into him.

The Matriarch

"What?"

"Thinking about Bathory?"

I realized I hadn't thought about Bathory since I met Suki. I didn't miss it quite as much. My shoulders felt lighter. The chain of weights attached to my neck disappeared. I had a new friend other than my brother, even if it was a small child.

"No. Just—" I paused. "What do you care anyway?"

"You still mad about earlier?"

"Duh."

"I was scared, okay? Did you see that guy?"

"Like I said, you're a sissy. And you left me there, by myself, in a strange city."

Kyle's head dropped. "I'm sorry."

"Just promise me you won't ever abandon me again. We have to stick together in this place."

Kyle looked up at me, serious for once in his life. He nodded. "I promise. No matter what. We got each other's backs."

I knew he meant it, but he wasn't getting off that easy.

"What do you want to do at lunch?" He grinned.

"I made a friend and I'm having lunch with her. And no, you aren't invited."

"Aww, come on."

"Fine." I glowered. "I *guess* you can eat with us. But you had better be nice."

We glanced back to Dad who stood at the chalkboard wrapping up a lesson. He dismissed us for lunch and Kyle followed me across the hall. Suki bolted through the door and into my arms.

"I hope you don't mind a smelly *boy* eating lunch with us." I pinched my nose and Suki giggled.

"Hey, I don't smell—" Kyle sniffed himself and cringed. "I mean, umm, nevermind."

The Matriarch

We strolled down the hallway. I looked up at the ceiling and the building was no longer a death trap. It had character. The cracked paint on the walls made it interesting. The rotted wood told stories of what it had seen. Kyle made faces at Suki and she laughed and snorted.

Maybe this won't be so bad after all.

The Matriarch

The Matriarch

chapter four
maggie madison

A few weeks passed and Golem grew on me. Maybe it was Suki. Kyle and I learned she was an orphan when we walked with her after school the first day. She lived in a group home. It was not uncommon for many children in the city. My heart wrenched but Suki didn't realize her situation. She always wore a contagious smile.

The drab sky lightened each day and the city seemed a little less haggard. I even grew accustomed to the smell that regularly pervaded my nostrils. The fractured streets didn't bother me as much and the trees seemed to sag less.

I still wore my bad attitude around my family, though now it was just a performance. They saw through my little act the moment I talked about Suki.

It was Saturday and the sun's heat found a way to beat down on us through the scattered clouds. Suki was visiting. We pushed her back and forth on a swing a few houses down from ours. Wisps of smoke lifted above the weathered privacy fences in the backyards of each home. I wrinkled my nose at the odor of charring meat.

"We can't even have one flippin' Saturday," I said.

Kyle laughed and pushed Suki higher. Her giggles helped me ignore the stench assaulting my nostrils. I coughed and tried to rid myself of it as I pushed Suki back toward Kyle.

"Sick?" asked Suki.

"It's that stupid meat they cook. What is that stuff?"

Suki chortled each time I gagged.

"Howse."

"Howse?"

Kyle's eyes got big and he looked away. I stared at both of them, trying to figure out what was going on.

"What is hows—wait, no. No. *No*!"

Suki laughed and snorted louder. "Dat howse!"

I turned and stared at Kyle. His head dropped and he kicked at the dirt.

"They are cooking *horse*?"

Kyle looked up at me and shrugged.

I went pale and cold sweat trickled down my face. The saliva in the back of my throat became thick and salty. I started to speak, but it was too late. I clutched my mouth, ran to the corner of the house, and vomited.

Suki clapped and laughed while I hurled my lunch.

I wiped my nose and turned to the kid. "You think that's funny?"

Kyle was trying to hold back his laughter. "Howse! Howse! Yum."

When she rubbed her little belly Kyle lost it.

"This place is full of sickos!" I fumed, fighting a smile as Suki continued her display.

"It's all she knows. Ease up a little, Mags."

"Ease up? Ease—"

My sentence was cut short when Suki pointed toward our house. "Kee-Reel!"

We glanced over as the men in the pinstriped suits strolled to our door. I nabbed Suki and we ran with Kyle to the corner of the house. Kyle shoved his hands in his pockets and stared at the dirt. He started to pace back and forth.

"What do you think they want?" Kyle asked.

I started to hyperventilate. The memory of Kiril staring into my soul sent a wave of horror coursing through my blood. Was he coming for me? Why hadn't I put my pride aside? Why hadn't I bowed?

I was petrified, but my curiosity got the best of me.

The Matriarch

"We need to get closer. I can't hear," I whispered.

"You're insane! Are you some kind of idiot?"

"Come on, sissy."

Kyle reluctantly followed with Suki as they posted up outside the nearest window. I recognized Kiril's voice. He was speaking to dad in the same evil, monotone voice I remembered.

"It's a matter of business."

"We can't afford it. Why do we have to pay this?" Dad cocked his head to the side, as if Kiril was speaking in a foreign language.

"It's a tax. The price of protection."

"Protection from who? The people we are paying the tax to?"

"Protects you from many things."

"We will have to shut down. We just can't afford it. This is extortion."

"No exceptions will be made. Everyone pays."

"We came here to help your city. Why are you doing this?"

"We didn't ask for help. That is on you. There is nothing I can do."

The men exited the door single file, Kiril at the rear. His gauze-wrapped face showed only a mouth and eyes, and he stared at me with a devilish grin.

"I'll see you soon."

The Matriarch

The Matriarch

chapter five
brian madison

It was a particularly grim Thursday when I made my way through two tall doors into a translucent, modern glass building in the heart of Golem's financial district. It sat among the decrepit high rises, juxtaposed against the cracked shelters and worn storefronts. Beggars propped against the sleek walls, panhandling for spare change or their next meal.

I marched to the front desk carrying my briefcase. My hands shook. I realized the truth in the cabbie's statements the first time I laid eyes on Kiril. He was a frightening man, someone not to be trifled with. I needed to negotiate something. There was just no way we could pay. We would have to shut down the school we'd fought so hard to open.

I attempted to steady my trembling hands. In front of me was an imposing, crescent-shaped marble desk. A young woman spun around in a chair to greet me. A headset wrapped around her straightened blonde hair to a pair of ruby red lips.

"I'm here to see Kiril."

"One moment please."

A giant man in a suit came to the front and summoned me down a hallway. A huge, jagged scar ran down his cheek like a lightning bolt to the ground. He stood at least a foot taller than me.

The hardwood floors gleamed and portraits of men in suits lined the charcoal walls. We strolled down the hall and the long corridor seemed to close in on me. The giant opened a door into a cavernous room with high, vaulted ceilings. My surroundings were all painted blood red. Kiril sat behind a

The Matriarch

mahogany desk. Large windows behind him bathed the room in sunlight. I bowed.

"Come."

Kiril had always been courteous to me. Regardless of his cordial nature, I always sensed a malevolent tone in his voice. It was as if Kiril fed on my fear. The monster's grin widened with each of my steps.

"Business to discuss?"

"Y-yes, I really want to show you our numbers so that you can see we can't pay. It's not that we are asking for a handout. It's just impossible. I've tried everything I can think of."

"This is troubling." Kiril frowned. "You must pay. I don't want to punish you. But if I don't, others will see. This is a problem."

"But we have no money. We just don't. Surely there is—"

Kiril's voice became harsh, his courteous façade fallen away. "You don't understand. You must pay. It's not an option."

Anger started to boil in my blood. I shook my head and clenched my fists. I heard my voice grow sharp as a wave of heat rushed into my cheeks. "No, no, there is no money. You don't get it."

Kiril stood and stalked around the desk, looming above me. I started to shake as his large pupils expanded and took in every detail, every ounce of my fear. The shrouds around his lips curled when he grinned. After a heavy moment that I felt lasted several beats too long, Kiril offered me his hand. I shook it reluctantly, confused.

"There's not much to say then." Kiril's skin was cold, clammy.

"So that's it?"

"That's it."

"Well, okay then. If we find some way to generate more revenue, you will be the first to know."

The Matriarch

When I exited the building, a million thoughts ran through my head. I didn't know what to make of Kiril. I did the only thing I knew. I prayed.

The Matriarch

The Matriarch

chapter six

maggie madison

Our family sat around the dinner table. I had conditioned myself to choke down whatever ingredients mom had thrown together to make the "howse" bearable.

Thoughts of Suki at the group home gnawed at my stomach. I hated that she had to stay there with no family to share terrible food with. I was thankful for my family. I chewed and swallowed, with more than a little effort, but managed it all the same.

A fist pounded on our door and rattled the picture frames on the wall. We jerked in our seats. The sun had set and we never had visitors, especially not after dark. Dad wiped his hands down his legs and gulped.

"Who in the world?" Mom said, her eyes wide.

Dad crept to the door, inhaling deep with each step. I rarely saw fear in my father. But now his knees quaked more with each stride, and I was horrified.

When he opened the door, it took only a moment before he fell back. A large fist had crashed into his jaw and sent him ricocheting into the wall. My world turned into a blur of disbelief and terror.

Mom screamed.

Streams of crimson spouted from Dad's face. I shrieked, churning my feet against the cold tile floor. A large hand yanked me up by the hair, snapping my neck back painfully. Wide knuckles dug into my skull and held me in place as I tried to claw my way free. My assailant shook me like a rag doll, demanding compliance. I looked to Kyle and Mom who'd suffered the same fate. Their screams of terror filled the small kitchen. The men turned toward the front door, now busted on its hinges.

The Matriarch

A pinwheel of smoke lingered, swirling in the air and hovering through the entry. Kiril followed. He cut through the smoke and it shifted around him. Tiny vortices spun off in random directions.

"I apologize for the interruption."

Kiril stared down to Dad, first his trembling legs, and then his bloodied face. Kiril knelt, examining him. Mom wailed and scratched at the giant bear paws holding her hostage.

"Please, just leave us alone. We don't want any trouble," Mom cried.

Kiril waved his cigar-laden hand in the air, his fingers and the smoke silencing her.

"We must have clear communication."

He sat the cigar on the tile and pulled a large serrated blade from a sheath at his hip. Glints of light sparkled along the smooth steel.

"No, please! We'll do anything!" I fought with everything I had at the hand holding me steady, scratching and clawing like a caged animal.

Kiril stared as Dad's eyes slowly opened.

"You should have paid."

Kiril pressed the blade into Dad's mouth and carved out his cheek. Blood sprayed across the wall. Dad screamed, writhing on the ground, blood slicking the floor beneath him. Kiril gripped his shirt while Dad tried to shrink away. There was nowhere to go.

Kiril leaned into his ear. "You will pay with your life and your family."

Kiril turned to me, the blade in his hand dripping blood that also ran in my veins. His pupils widened, seeming to delight in seeing all the horror they could.

"This is why you bow."

Needles pierced my skull. This couldn't be real. Couldn't be happening. The mercenary's hand fisted my hair tighter as I fought against his hold. Screams tore through the halls when Kiril sawed Dad's throat,

The Matriarch

severing his main artery and spilling his blood to the floor. Kiril wrenched the severed head free and held it up like a trophy. I went numb. I was in a tunnel. Kyle and Mom shrieked in my ears but it felt like they were a hundred feet away. Kiril dropped Dad's head on top of his lifeless body. Everything went dark.

The Matriarch

The Matriarch

chapter seven
maggie madison

I woke on a frigid concrete floor, the recent horrors shocking back to life in my mind. I searched the dark with my hands, trying to grasp anything that felt familiar, praying I was waking from a nightmare. I pawed at myself frantically, making sure I could still feel my body, and that I was still breathing.

I cried out for anyone who would listen.

It was pitch black. I held my hand in front of my face and wiggled my fingers. Nothing. *Am I dead?* The silence suffocated me – no sound, no light, not even the hint of anything beyond the ground beneath me. The moment I convinced myself I was dead, I heard a voice.

"No one will come."

"Who's that? Who's there? Where am I?"

"Doesn't matter." The girl's voice was low and somber.

It felt like a dagger plunged into my chest as I sobbed. Images of Dad's corpse raced back to my mind. Tears rolled down my cheeks and dripped from my face.

"Mom! I want my mom! Mommy!"

"Your mom can't save you from this place. Nobody can."

I swung out into the darkness to ward off the voice and its words. I was scared, broken.

Whoever was in the dark touched my hair and I clawed across the floor to escape.

"It's okay. You get used to it."

I trusted no one. "How old are you?"

"Twelve."

Had her family been killed too? Was she one of them?

"Who are you?"

"My name is Laura. It's okay. I won't hurt you."

"They, they, killed my dad."

"Kiril?"

I sobbed again at the sound of his name, reality crashing back into me.

I finally mustered enough air in my lungs and said, "Yes."

"We are his prisoners."

The girl had learned to see in the dark somehow because I felt her hand on my head once again. I pulled away.

"It's okay, I promise. It's okay." The girl sat down and wrapped her arms tight around my shoulders. My lip quivered as rivers of tears poured from my eyes. I surrendered to the stranger's arms and sobbed into her shoulder.

"Mom! I want my mommy!" I cried over and over as Laura squeezed tighter with each word and rocked back and forth.

"It's okay. Shh. It's okay," Laura said as she stroked my hair.

A loud buzz echoed through the dark and a heavy door squeaked as a man pulled it open. It was the first light I'd seen in days. It was blinding. I put my palms over my eyes, trying to shield them. I was curled in the corner, shaking and sniffling, praying I wouldn't be hurt.

"You!" A voice cut through the gloom, loud and insistent.

The Matriarch

The footsteps grew louder. A strong hand gripped me by the hair. I squirmed and shouted. The man dragged me across the floor as Laura yelled, begging him to take her instead.

"Shut up, bitch!"

He kicked Laura in the face and she flew to her back on the concrete.

"Please, god, no! Where are you taking me?"

The man didn't respond. He continued to drag me down the hallway while my feet beat against the tile, unable to gain traction. He yanked me into a room and there sat Kiril, staring inquisitively at me. The heavy hand of the guard tossed me to the floor.

"Are you enjoying your stay?"

"Where is my family?" I screamed.

"They are gone, forever."

I jumped to my feet and stormed towards him at full speed, fists and teeth clenched. I reared back to strike, but his hand shot across my face and knocked me to the ground.

My cheek burned hot, but I jumped and ran at him once more to the same result.

I clutched at my jaw as Kiril strolled over to me, taking his time before kneeling.

I sat up slowly, staring at the monster, and spat into his face.

He didn't flinch, only laughed at me, the saliva soaking into the bandages.

He leaned back down and I slapped him, hard.

When my hand met his cheek one of his hands wrapped tight around my neck, crushing my air supply. I gasped, my nails clawing into his hands. His face remained calm and collected as he watched the life start to drain from my body.

"You *will* obey."

The Matriarch

Just as I began to see fuzzy stars in my line of sight he released his grip. I crashed to the ground, clutching at my throat.

"Where is my mommy?" I asked. "Please just let me see her."

"Your family is dead. All of them. I am your family now."

"Liar!"

"You don't remember? That's right, you were unconscious when I finished."

I began to wail and begged for my brother this time. Clinging to any bit of hope that Kiril was lying to me.

"I buried them with your father." He smiled as he walked to the door and tapped on it. A guard opened the door.

I sobbed, rivers of tears soaking my shirt. I couldn't remember anything after Dad. The truth hit me all at once. "No! No! Please! Please, I just want them back! I'll do anything! Please!"

Kiril walked back toward me and grabbed me by the hair.

"They can't come back. You will pay your debt." He smiled, knowing he'd broken me. I could see it in his eyes and hear it in his voice.

He handed me off to the guard who yanked me into the hallway.

"This way." He led me farther down the nondescript, gray corridor. Every so often a moan or a scream would sound from somewhere deeper in the building.

I shuddered and wrapped my arms around myself.

He opened a door and ushered me inside before slamming it. I was alone. I looked around but it wasn't my cell and Laura wasn't there. The room was cozier and lit by lamps. A bed sat in the middle.

I walked to the bed and cried into the sheets.

The Matriarch

Thirty minutes later a door on the other side opened. Kiril entered along with an older man. They chatted in a foreign language and shook hands. Kiril led the man to me as I cowered on the bed.

"This is Mister, umm, Smith."

He nodded to the man and leaned down by my ear.

"You will do what he wants, or you will die. You will pay your father's debt. Understand?"

I froze.

Kiril walked over, opened the door, and left. The man stared at me with hunger in his eyes. He was tall and lean, a small amount of wrinkles covered his face. He had brown hair speckled with gray and hazel eyes that looked me up and down. His look grew crazed when he neared.

He reached out and touched my hair gently, then caressed the side of my face.

"Oh yes, you will do nicely."

The Matriarch

The Matriarch

chapter eight

maggie madison

seven years later

The moonlight illuminated my long, toned legs that ran up to a pair of frayed denim shorts cut above my ass. Laura and I giggled on the street corner. Odors of vomit and garbage permeated the block from the alley behind us.

A car with two teenage boys slowed as Laura teased at my blonde hair that held a few streaks of deep purple. We laughed and flirted, turning around to give the boys a better view as they ran over the curb and bounced in their seats.

Laura walked up to the car first, swaying her hips back and forth while the boys ogled her tan stomach in her cutoff t-shirt and low-riding jeans.

"Hello," she said. "What's your name?"

"Um, hi. I'm, umm, Parker. And this is Braden." Parker ran a nervous hand through his hair.

I walked around to the other boy's window, my slinky top clinging tight to my curves, highlighting my high breasts and slender frame. I propped my elbows on the window and leaned in, fully aware of the bulges in their pants.

"Whatcha up to tonight?" I smiled.

"We were, well, we were wondering..."

Laura and I grinned at each other.

"I doubt you can afford the fun we like to have." Laura tossed her hair over her shoulder.

Parker flashed a large wad of cash from his pocket. Our eyebrows rose.

"Maybe my friend was wrong." I reached over and ran my fingers through Braden's thick, dark hair.

The Matriarch

"What should we do with these two?" asked Laura.

"Hell, I don't know, but I think I want yours over there. Switch me."

"You, you, you want me?"

"Fuck yeah, you're hot." I gave him my sweetest smile.

We giggled and ran around the car to switch windows. It was an old trick. Pretend to be interested in the other guy.

I leaned in and ran my hand down Parker's leg, brushing my fingertips against his hard cock.

"Is that for me?" I whispered.

"I don't, I mean..."

"Jesus, just pull over in the alley," I looked at Laura. "Aren't they adorable when they get all nervous?"

"Yes."

I leaned down into Parker's ear and exhaled my warm breath down his neck. "You're going to have dreams about the way I fuck you."

His eyes grew wide.

"Do you have the money?" I held out my hand.

He shoved the wad of cash into my palm and I grinned.

"Meet us in the alley in five."

Parker sped across the street as we put on a show, ending with me kissing Laura full on the lips. It was obviously an act, but we learned an important lesson long ago. Men were stupid.

"I'm not upset about this at all. We'll meet our quota early tonight. Maybe we can go out later and have a drink," I said.

"Yeah, these two are actually kind of cute. Won't be some 70-year-old bag of skin who can't get hard, trying to fuck me from behind. Shit almost puts me to sleep. The young boys finish quick too."

The Matriarch

"Hell yeah they do." I gave Laura a playful slap on the ass.

The sun fell behind the buildings of Golem as our marks entered the alley. Little eddies of dust swirled into the shadows and a plastic bag floated in the air, drifting back and forth with the swift breeze that swept between the brick buildings. Pages of crumpled newspapers littered the ground, flying against the walls when cars would pass. The sound of the cars grew faint the farther we walked. A knee-high layer of fog hovered above the pavement. The boys stood there, hands shoved into their pockets as they fidgeted.

Laura grabbed Braden and led him away. I walked up to Parker who trembled.

"You're going to shake harder than that when I'm done with you." I locked my soft lips on his. I ran my hand over his chest and down to the bulge in his pants. *Wow, a decent cock.*

"How do you want me, Parker?" I ran my mouth along his neck and collarbone, brushing my lips up against his salty skin.

"I, I, I don't—"

I ran a finger up to his lips and caught a glimpse of Laura on her knees, Braden's cock disappearing in her mouth as his head tilted back toward the moon.

"Do you want to touch me?"

Parker nodded.

I reached for the bottom of my shirt and pulled it over my head. My breasts bounced lightly and the air rushed over my tight nipples, sending a chill up my arms. I backed up to Parker and pushed my ass into his crotch. I grabbed his hands and put one on each breast. He massaged me tentatively at first.

"You like my tits?"

He nodded again, completely focused on me. His cock grew even stiffer against my ass.

The Matriarch

I spun and pressed my lips to his again, digging my fingernails into his scalp with one hand and running the other down to his shaft.

"I need this fucking cock."

I unbuttoned his pants and yanked them to the ground, freeing his length from captivity.

"That's what I'm talking about." I palmed it gently.

I sank to my knees and teased his head around one of my nipples, guiding him back and forth over my breast. I flicked my tongue on the tip and his hips backed into the car.

Distant moans penetrated my ears. I glanced over to Braden plowing into Laura. Nerves fired through my inner thighs.

I took all of Parker into my mouth, sucking forcefully as his head flew back into the car.

"Shit." He moaned.

I took him into my throat and snaked my tongue around his shaft as he gripped the door handle.

I slid him from my mouth, a momentary reprieve before I dove back onto it, bobbing rapidly and stroking on his base with one hand in perfect rhythm.

He wasn't going to last long. I reached into my back pocket and pulled out a condom.

"You wanna fuck me from behind?"

"God, yes."

I bit the end of the wrapper and spit it on the ground before smoothing the condom down his big prick, teasing the head with my thumb.

I heard Laura moaning as Braden throttled her from behind. *Damn it. I picked the wrong one.*

I looked back at Parker's light blue eyes and chiseled face, deciding he was worth the trade.

I stood and lowered my shorts to the ground, revealing a bright pink thong parting my ass cheeks.

I bent over, fingers splayed on the brick wall, offering myself to him.

The Matriarch

He approached me, looking helpless and lost. I needed to make him more comfortable.

When he neared, I reached back for his dick with one hand and pulled my panties to the side with the other.

"Just do what I tell you, okay?"

"Okay."

I teased his head around me for a moment, then pressed him to my clit and stroked it back and forth.

"Holy shit." I squirmed. "You ready?"

"Okay."

I worked the tip inside my pussy and inched him into me.

"Oh my god, your cock feels so fucking good inside me." I squeezed around him.

I needed Parker to fuck me — hard. I reached back and dug my nails into his hip, pulling him into me deeper and faster.

"That's it. Fuck me hard, Parker." I moaned.

My legs began to tremble as my aching cunt clenched around him and he drilled into me from behind, harder and faster. The throbbing in my clit was too much and I finally gave in, waves of nerves fired through my hot cunt into the tips of my toes and fingers as I bucked my ass into his thighs.

"Fuck!" I gasped, becoming lightheaded in a euphoric daze.

I looked back into Parker's eyes and could tell he was about to explode.

"Stand still," I said.

He watched as I started backing my ass into his pelvis, driving his cock to the hilt over and over. Smacking echoes of wet flesh on flesh filled the alley to the rhythm of our thrusts.

"That's it. You gonna come for me?"

He closed his eyes and nodded, unable to take it anymore as he grabbed the sides of my firm ass and

The Matriarch

went all the way into me. He started to seize and convulse. His legs stiffened and he grunted as the tension in his balls unleashed into the condom.

After he shuddered one last time, his eyes opened. He grinned as he pulled out of me. I turned around and pulled the condom from his cock that was still as hard as a rock.

"Let me take care of that for you."

I went to my knees and teased him with my tongue, tasting the salty come as he squirmed. I licked the length of him and took his cock into the depths of my mouth, cleaning every inch before releasing him.

"Worth the money?"

"Fuck yes."

I looked over as Laura walked back with Braden. The boys dressed quickly and went on their way.

"What time is it?" asked Laura.

"Eight. Let's get the ol' man his money and have some fun."

"More fun than that? Jesus, I haven't fucked someone my age in forever."

"I know. That was unexpected. Who knew boys could fuck like that? Little bastard got me off." I giggled.

"No shit, Braden had a cock on him. Needed a little guidance, but once he hit the spot it was all over for me."

"Whew. All right, let's do this."

We walked down the long hallway to Kiril's office. No matter how many times I made this journey, a twinge of anxiety always ran through me. The large

The Matriarch

guard opened the door and Kiril sat at his desk, eagerly awaiting his take.

We walked up and handed him the money as he wrapped an arm around both of us.

"You are early. Very good."

"They didn't put up much of a fight." I smiled.

"Can you blame them?" he asked, cocking his head to the side. It used to make me shudder, but I had grown used to it.

"You finished early. What are you going to do?"

"Oh, we thought we might go grab a drink, if it's okay with you?"

"Fine. But first we have business to discuss."

Laura and I looked at each other. Usually we just paid him and left.

"Don't be shy. Come out here." Kiril waved his hand at a shadowy corner of the room.

A young girl appeared, walking with halting steps. I squinted at her as she emerged into the light. Her face was familiar, frightened. Tears sparkled on her cheeks as she came into view.

"Suki?" I took a step toward her.

The guard's large hands dug into my shoulders and I squealed and fought, wincing as Kiril smiled at me.

"Oh, you know her?" Kiril smiled. He seemed to relish in the fact he could hurt me with someone else from my past. "Business is expanding. You're moving to a new city. She is your replacement."

"Let her go!" I cried.

Kiril's hand connected with my cheek and I tumbled across the hardwood floor. His face steadied as he walked to me and peered deep into my eyes.

He paused with a slight grin. I looked to Suki, her knees buckling above her high white socks. My fingers tightened into fists with Kiril's breath warm in my ear.

The Matriarch

"You should have bowed," he whispered.

He gestured to the guard and I was dragged from the room kicking and screaming. My feet slid on the floor like a child trying to skate for the first time.

"Suki, no!"

Suki sobbed quietly, not daring to move.

I clawed at the floor. "Laura, please! Take care of her!"

The door slammed. I was gone.

The Matriarch

chapter nine
maggie madison

My head pounded in the dark. My palm found my forehead and I massaged the huge knot that had formed on my right temple. *I must have put up a decent fight.* A loud engine grumbled as I tried to process my surroundings. It seemed like I was in the back of a semi-truck.

Faint whispers and female whimpers sounded around me, giving me a feel for the enclosed space and cramped quarters.

"Is someone there?"

The sounds stopped.

"Yes...are you okay?" someone asked.

"Where are we going?"

"We don't know."

"Hmm." The puzzle pieces weren't fitting together.

"Are you from Golem?" I asked.

"No," the girl answered.

"I am," said another.

I peered into the pitch blackness, desperate to make out clues to my whereabouts, but was met only with the inky nothing before me. Shooting pain ripped through my head like a million fine needles, making it hard to focus.

"Where is your family?" I asked.

"I never knew my family," the same girl said.

"Me either. We were traded," said another.

"So you aren't night workers?" I asked.

Muffled giggles rang out. I didn't see the humor. *How old are these girls?*

"No, we're too young for that."

Nobody is too young for that.

The Matriarch

I cringed at the thought. I'd grown numb to it. Conditioned myself to enjoy the sex. Otherwise, I'd have ended it all long ago.

The rest of the ride was silent. I tried to form a plan. This might be my only chance to escape, to finally get away from Kiril and enslavement. I had put my past behind me, but the sight of Suki brought it back to the surface. I wanted what I had before. A normal life again.

I'd thought about escaping plenty of times before, but I didn't know Golem. I was afraid of Kiril — not that he would find me and kill me, but that he would damage me more. That he would find someone else from my past to hurt me again. He did it anyway. My obedience was for nothing. I was glad it was dark and there were no mirrors. Who had I become? I'd told myself it was the only way to survive day-to-day. Not anymore. I was done being that girl, Kiril's bitch.

But when I reached my destination I would be under Kiril's control again.

It was now or never. Escape this life or finally let it kill me along with my parents and brother.

An hour passed and I was still contemplating my next move when I heard a familiar sound. A train. The train that ran to and from Bathory. Happiness filled me for a brief second.

I had to think quick. What could I do? My mind raced but nothing processed. *Breathe.*

I took in a deep breath and collected my thoughts. "How long was I asleep?"

"Maybe two hours. It's hard to tell."

Perfect. I knew the slave runners only transported under the cover of darkness.

The Matriarch

If I could get out of the truck, I might have a chance. My family used to take drives all over the countryside. A little misdirection and I could slip out of the pack.

One, two, three...

"Oh my god, a rat! There's a rat on my leg! Get it off! Get it off!" I screamed.

The girls in the truck went crazy, pounding on the walls as I ran my hands over a few of their legs. The girls kicked and pushed, screaming and crying.

The driver slammed on the brakes and all of us flew to the front of the truck and smashed into one another before crashing back to the rear.

"It's still here! I can feel it! Get it off me!" I shrieked.

The truck came to a complete stop and a door slammed.

I kept tickling at every leg that passed to keep the frenzy alive.

The back doors of the truck flew open and three huge men scowled, holding large guns. One of them yelled, "Shut the fuck up, now!"

"Oh my god! It's still back here! It's on my legs!" I screamed from the middle of the pack. The group of girls rushed the men, landing on top of them. Surprisingly, no shots were fired.

One man yanked a girl up by the collar. "What are you doing?"

"A rat! There's a rat!" she cried, girls still spilling out of the truck too fast for the guards to count.

It's time.

I followed behind a few girls and ducked down at their backs as they leapt off the truck. I rolled to the ground and snuck around the side. The men were occupied, but I assumed at least two stayed in the front. I looked down at the white t-shirt they'd dressed me in, an easy target in the dark. I quickly peeled it off, now in shorts and a black sports bra.

I crawled to the shoulder of the road and rolled into a ditch. There was a puddle nearby and I made my way to it, caking myself in mud to get rid of my cheap perfume scent.

The girls were still screaming, but it wouldn't be long before the guards started to account for everyone. I dashed off into the woods, working up to a run once I was out of sight. A dense forest closed around me. Undergrowth scraped at my bare legs as I ran my ass off.

I sprinted for what seemed like hours, until my legs were on fire. A creek bed blocked my path, the water glinting in the moonlight.

A depression covered with some limbs caught my eye. Gasping for air, I worked my way under the large nest of branches and lay flat on my back.

I was determined to stay there as long as it took, until I was certain the men were gone. An hour passed and my eyes grew heavy. I fought to keep them open and stay alert. Before long, my vision grew darker until I finally gave in and the world faded to black.

My eyes jolted open. A man grabbed my arm. I kicked and tried to squeal, but his hand wrapped around my mouth before the sounds could escape. I flailed and bit at his hand to no avail.

"I'm not with them."

My gaze found his face. I didn't recognize him. He wasn't dressed like the guards and he wasn't armed. He was older, but his arms gripped me tight and I could feel them bulge into my ribs, sucking the

The Matriarch

oxygen from my lungs. The moonlight struck him for a moment and I saw short, cropped dark hair with bits of silver scattered throughout. Black clothes clung tight to him, and he looked to be in his forties or fifties.

"I will help," he said.

He threw me over his shoulder and ran. I had never seen anyone move with such stealth and agility. The man knew every step as he dodged trees and bushes, never slowing down, gliding through the dense brush with ease.

He suddenly twirled behind a tree. Still draped over his shoulder, all I could see was his back.

"Shh."

In the distance I heard twigs crack under foot and voices that grew louder with each second. I sucked in my breath.

I realized I'd left my white shirt on the ground, instantly alarming them to my escape.

"He will kill us. Kiril gave us specific instructions to deliver the whore."

My face grew red. I wasn't a whore, not by choice anyway.

My rescuer could sense my apprehension and gripped me tighter. I knew better than to scream, no matter how bad I wanted to. He was older but his arms were chiseled like boulders. It was too dark to make out any more distinct features, but his chest expanded and contracted in a perfect rhythm.

When the men passed, he crept in the other direction and ran up a huge hill overlooking the area. I noticed a small house on top that peeked through some trees.

He sprinted across the landscape with me on his shoulder, carrying me up the steps and through the door. The man took me to a back room where he set me down and removed a rug. He opened the

The Matriarch

floorboards like a door. I followed him down a staircase. I had no choice but to trust him. It was either him or go back to the old life, if they didn't kill me first.

I glanced around the room. He showed me to a dresser that held some random clothes I could wear. It was cozy but simple, neutral tans and grays mostly. A small bathroom was attached to the room with small, square-cut tile throughout. The carpet was thick and dark brown, and he pointed to a bed. I hadn't slept in a bed in years.

"You can sleep here. It's safe."

"What about—"

"I'll take care of it."

He disappeared back up the stairs and the door creaked shut.

I wanted to ask him questions — to know what was going on. Adrenaline was coursing through my veins. He told me to sleep but I stared at the ceiling the entire night, listening for the guards, worrying I'd be caught, and thinking about what would happen to me. If I had truly managed to escape, what was my life going to look like now?

chapter ten
maggie madison

I stretched my arms to the ceiling and my eyes slowly opened. At some point my body had given in and I'd fallen asleep.

The room had no windows and would have been pitch black if it weren't for a small light at the top of the stairs. I peered around, taking in my surroundings, getting a better look than the previous night. An antique bookshelf leaned on one wall with old leather volumes and a row of textbooks. A matching vanity with a handle missing was next to it. The attached mirror was stained with specks of rust and the image was fuzzy around the edges. A dresser sat against the far wall.

I placed my feet on the soft carpet and stood unsteadily. My thighs tensed for a moment and then relaxed as I yawned wide. The bed was small and the mattress was a hard, lumpy bit of luxury. To my left across the room was the small bathroom with a shower.

I jumped when I heard someone beat on the front door, rattling the insides of the walls in the house. The sounds underground were amplified. A shock of nerves struck my chest. When I heard a man's voice, a knot formed in my throat. I froze, unsure what to do.

Footsteps thudded overhead and a few specks of drywall fell from the ceiling onto my shoulder. My body stiffened and I stopped breathing as the volume of the voices grew.

I picked at my calloused fingers, trying to tamp down my fight or flight impulse. *Don't do it, Maggie.*

I eased up the stairs, the knot still in my throat as I neared the floorboards.

"You haven't seen a girl? Roughly 17 or 18, long legs, blonde hair?"

"No."

The visitor didn't sound convinced. Another voice rang out.

"We know she was heading this direction."

"Nobody is here."

"If we find out—"

"You tell Kiril to come see me if he has a problem."

The conversation ceased. Thoughts raced through my mind. How does he know Kiril? Who is this guy? Was I in danger?

"How do you know our boss?"

"It doesn't matter. If I see the girl, I'll let you know."

"Thank you for your time."

"No problem. I'll show you out."

They started back for the door when my foot slipped off a step and I caught myself, but not without hammering my elbow into a two-by-four that framed the house. I closed my eyes and prayed the men hadn't heard.

"You hear something?"

"No."

I stopped breathing, the blood still pounding in my ears far too loudly.

"Over there."

The footsteps were loud and rapid, pacing over my head.

"The house is old. It makes noises."

"No, I heard something, right here."

The man stomped the floor inches from my face. My eyes squinted shut and I prayed to any god that would listen they wouldn't find the door.

The Matriarch

I heard hands knocking on the wall and floor, looking for a stud, or any clue that might help them find me. I became lightheaded and thought I might pass out. I held my breath anyway.

Light footsteps trotted across the floor.

"Kaja, what are you doing in here? Come boy."

"It was just the damned dog," the other man said.

"I don't know..." More footsteps paced around above my head.

"Come on, we have a lot of ground to cover. Boss can't find out that bitch escaped or he'll have our heads."

"Sorry to trouble you, sir."

"Don't worry about it. I'll show you out."

The front door squeaked open and the sound of footsteps grew quieter before disappearing altogether. When the door closed, I gasped as my lungs filled with air.

Confused, I sat there, trying to figure out my rescuer. He had to be on my side. He wouldn't have lied to the men if he weren't. Nobody who knew Kiril would lie to his men. It was a death sentence.

I put my palm to my face and felt the mud still caked to my cheeks. I prayed it was all a bad dream as I ran back down to the bed.

The door slammed against the floor and I heard large boots pounding down the stairs. The man appeared around the corner. He had a smile on his face and his eyes were kind. Kaja followed at his heels and sniffed around the room excitedly, as if it were a treat to go downstairs.

The more I studied the stranger, the more I realized he looked like one of the men who always walked with Kiril in suits. He was older, but built well, precise in his movements. His eyes were narrow, forming a natural scowl.

The Matriarch

"It's ok. They're gone." He chuckled a bit which surprised me.

"You need a shower." He walked away, pinching his nose and smiling. "Then we can eat."

I crossed my arms over my chest. "I don't stink!"

He walked around the corner and made his way back up the staircase.

"Kaja, come."

The dog whined and stared at me, but eventually obeyed and followed his master.

I knew I liked the stranger. He reminded me of my dad. I always felt safe around Dad, until the day the monster came into our house and took everyone from me.

I raised my arm above my head and sniffed under it. My nose wrinkled and I cringed.

"Holy shit, he wasn't kidding."

The steaming water rushed over my face and my hand trembled against the tile wall. The swirling brown water slowly turned clear around my feet as it circled in the drain. *What is next*? I hadn't thought everything through before trying to escape.

Where would I go? What would I do?

Kiril's reach was vast. He always knew someone, or someone knew him. Was I going to live with this man out in the forest forever? Would he even let me? I needed to have a life at some point. What was the point of freedom if I didn't?

I held the fresh bar of soap and tried to scrub the last seven years of my life away: the abuse, the dirtiness, the forced sex, the beatings. My eyes started to burn as I remembered the things that had happened to me, the things I'd done to survive.

The Matriarch

Everything I'd suppressed and ignored, just to make it from day-to-day. It was like waking up from a nightmare I didn't realize I was living. I took a deep breath, turned off the water, and forced all the horror back inside.

My skin welcomed the cool air when I stepped from the shower. Steam lingered around the small bathroom and a fog crept across the mirror. I grabbed the two towels the man had laid out while I was sleeping.

The freezing floor numbed the bottom of my feet as I walked across the tile. I dried my hair with one towel and wrapped the other under my arms.

I noticed a pair of clothes folded for me on the bed. A small picture sat on the dresser: the man, a boy, and a woman. Was the woman his wife? What if she walked in the house and found me there, naked?

It wouldn't be the first time that had happened, but it would be the first time I was innocent of any wrongdoing.

The picture was faded.

Something had happened to him. Something bad. I could sense it. How else did this guy end up by himself in the middle of nowhere?

The clothes were anything but flattering to my figure as I tossed them on.

A heavenly, familiar smell made its way into the basement. Something I recognized from a long time ago.

"Bacon!"

I was drawn to the aroma that saturated the air. The doors above were open. When I reached the top stair, the crackling sounds against the pan were sweet music to my ears. I closed my eyes. I was briefly back home in Bathory. The taste and texture of the salty bacon crunched between my teeth while my parents smiled and I teased Kyle before school.

The Matriarch

I crashed back to reality when I rounded the corner. My mouth was watering and the man was humming, facing the stove. He turned around and smiled, nodding to my clothes.

"Sorry, it's all I had."

"Please don't apologize."

I walked up behind him and wrapped my arms around his waist. Running my hands up to his hard chest, I placed the side of my face into his back.

"You know...I haven't had a chance to properly thank you."

I felt his torso tighten as my hands started to run down his stomach and into his pants. He spun sharply and my hand flew out of his waist band. I'd never seen anyone move that fast in my life. His face was beet red and I looked down to the floor, afraid to lift my eyes.

"No!" he shouted. "Look at me!" He placed a finger to my chin and tilted my head up. "That's not your life anymore, understand?"

It was all I knew. I burst into tears, realizing what I'd done. It's not how normal people lived. It wasn't the proper way to show gratitude. I could tell he felt bad about the outburst and his face turned soft and gentle. He wrapped me in a hug and consoled me while my tears soaked into his shirt.

"I'm sorry it's all...I'm so sorry." My look begged him to forgive me.

"It's okay." He smiled and put a palm on each of my shoulders.

I managed a smile, knowing he didn't hate me.

"Okay." My bottom lip quaked.

He pulled me back into his arms and ran his hand through my hair. For the first time since I could remember, I felt safe.

He let go and placed his calloused hands back on my shoulders.

The Matriarch

"You need to eat something, okay?" he said with a large, gentle grin. "Nobody is going to take you. You don't have to be afraid here."

He walked back over to the stove and began to hum again. I sat down at the table and poured some orange juice into a glass. Memories from my childhood rushed back into my mind once more.

The man turned off the stove and lifted the pan.

"You almost made me burn the bacon. I feed people to the dogs when they make me burn the bacon." He smiled. *Was it a joke?* "Nobody makes me burn," he paused and glowered, "the *bacon*."

We both laughed. He reminded me of my dad telling corny jokes to make me feel better. I'd always faked a laugh to appease him. Still, it was comforting and I didn't feel like an outcast.

I ate and ate, barely taking time to breathe while the man sipped his coffee. I hadn't realized how hungry I was, and the flavor of the bacon was so intense I couldn't shovel it into my mouth fast enough.

I looked up and as usual he was smiling. I paused, a piece of the bacon suspended from my lip.

"It's okay. Eat. *Eat*," he said.

"What's your name?" I asked.

"Zak."

"Thank you, Zak, so much. For everything."

"You're welcome." The steam rose from his coffee.

We chatted all morning. It was mostly about me. Zak listened intently. I told him everything, from my time in Bathory to escaping the truck.

When silence finally fell and I had told every part of my sordid tale, my thoughts turned back to Zak.

"What about — wait, no, nevermind, it's not my place," I said.

"It's okay. Ask."

"Is that your family? In the pictures downstairs?"

The Matriarch

He looked at the floor. "It was."

I knew I shouldn't ask. I did it anyway. "What happened to them?"

"They were taken from me."

"I'm sorry. I shouldn't have—"

He looked sad, though he tried to play it off.

"It's okay. I just haven't talked about them in a long time."

"Kiril?"

He nodded.

"I hate that fucking prick!"

Zak chuckled and then grew serious.

"What are you afraid of?" he asked.

He was to the point. No bullshit. My eyes widened at the question. It was so simple and yet I had so many answers.

"I don't know...him finding me, controlling me. Not having a life. Not being normal. Constantly looking over my shoulder. I guess I'm just afraid of *him*."

"That's understandable. So what do you want then?"

"I want to be free. I want all of the girls to be free. I want justice for my family."

"Do you want justice or revenge?"

"Can I have both?"

He laughed, eyeing me up and down once more.

"Well, each one has different motivations. One is motivated by clear thinking, objectivity. The other feeds on emotion, rage, anger. One is good and one is bad. So it's important to distinguish."

"How do you know Kiril?" I asked.

He rose from his seat and loomed over me. I looked down, scared I'd offended him. He snatched our plates and walked to the sink. He stood there and washed them.

The Matriarch

He stared out the window, seemingly deep in thought. Kiril always stared the same way. I thought it was just to be dramatic, but it must have been something cultural. Maybe it was a way of thinking or a philosophy. Perhaps it's the way they were raised?

"We were best friends as kids. Later, I worked for him. One day, he didn't need me anymore. That was that."

"What happened to his face?"

Zak stared long and hard at me. "When we were kids he had a sister. She got up in the night and he lit a candle for her. They were poor and didn't have electricity. She tripped on her way back to the bed and caught the sheets on fire. It burned his face so bad he had to wear bandages. The same ones he still wears."

"Hmm, I expected a way more dramatic story about it."

"Their parents died in the fire. He always blamed his sister for it. He never forgave her. One day, his sister and I were playing hide-n-seek at a park. I watched while hiding in the bushes. He was sitting all alone on a bench. She went to see if he was okay. He looked around to make sure nobody was looking and strangled her to death while covering her mouth."

I wanted to throw up. "What'd you do?"

"I was too late. There was nothing I could do. He's been evil ever since the day she burned him."

"What a fucking piece of shit. I'm sorry, but I hate him."

"Yeah, you can't change the past. Only the future."

"What about your family?"

"It wasn't a cordial split when I left. He took my family and had me beaten, and thrown from the city."

"Why didn't you fight back?" I'd seen the way he moved. His lack of fear when the men came, his attitude toward Kiril. I knew he could defend himself.

The Matriarch

"I had fought enough. My whole life I was trained to kill. Learned from masters all around the world. I didn't want to do it anymore."

"So that's it? You didn't do anything?"

"Fighting is not the answer to every problem. He had already taken my family. There is a greater purpose than fighting. The ability to fight is just one small tool to accomplish a goal. It should only be used when absolutely necessary."

"What is your purpose?"

"I search for it every day. Maybe it's to find you? Who knows?" He shrugged.

I wasn't satisfied with his answer. Zak was a trained killer. Maybe if he'd offed Kiril instead of being a pussy, I'd still have my family. Instead, he just ran away.

"If you look for the real answers to questions, you'll find them. You need to rest first. Clear your emotions. Then, you will find truth."

His words resonated, but I still didn't mind wanting that son of a bitch Kiril dead. I wouldn't sleep well until he was six-feet-deep pushing up flowers. Rage still coursed through me.

"I'd have killed that piece of shit."

"Maybe. Maybe you will." He walked toward the sink. I was growing tired of his elusive responses. Sure, they sounded good, but how could I rest knowing that monster was still drawing breath? I knew Kiril wouldn't stop looking for me. He was possessive, almost single-minded in his will to dominate and own all those around him.

Zak could sense my apprehension.

"Look, get some rest. You don't have to decide everything today."

The Matriarch

chapter eleven

maggie madison

I was suspended up in the corner, watching, unable to move or speak. The blood from the girl's quaking lip stained her white t-shirt as the guard slapped her across the face once more. The sound of his hand on her cheek echoed off the walls as the other girls winced. She whimpered, cowering in the corner.

"Where is she?" he yelled.

"That's enough." Kiril glided over to her while the other girls in the dim interrogation room wept in the shadows, praying they wouldn't be next. The girl stared down, blood dripping from her lip to the floor.

Kiril lifted her chin, searching her eyes for the information he craved. He turned to the other girls and cocked his head sideways.

"Where is she?"

"We don't know," one girl said.

"We promise. We never met her," said another.

"You know *something*." He grinned widely, his purple lips showing through the gauze wrapped tight on his face.

I wanted to help them. To give myself up so they could go. But I couldn't move. I was frozen, almost like I wasn't there. They couldn't see me.

He reached to the back of the girl's head and fisted her hair, squeezing as she yelped. He retrieved his blade from his hip with his other hand. It twirled through his fingers, stopping in front of her face.

The others screamed and pleaded. The girl he held looked catatonic. Her body started to go limp in his arms and her eyes rolled back into her head as she stared at the blade.

The Matriarch

"We don't know, please!" they screamed.

He turned, seemingly enjoying their pleas and the fear in their voices, before returning to his first victim, pressing the steel into her mouth. She shrieked when he began to cut. Blood spewed across the wall as he carved out her mouth, his pupils large and his lips forming a hideous smile as he savored every cry for help.

I bolted upright in the bed, panting, as a torrent of cold sweat saturated my body.

"Zak!" I screamed. "Zak! Please!"

I slowly realized it was a dream, but it still felt real, fresh in my mind. I hadn't heard a sound when Zak's shadow cast over me. His firm hand gripped my shoulder.

"What happened? Are you okay?"

"It was him. He's torturing them." I gripped Zak tight as his arms wrapped around my shoulders. "It's because of *me*."

"It's not your fault. Just a bad dream. It'll be okay."

"How do you know?"

"Shh. It's not your fault."

"He's going to find me. He's going to kill me."

Zak turned my head so that I was looking at him.

"I won't let that happen. You're safe here. I promise."

I sobbed into his shoulder. I didn't want him to leave. I felt so defenseless. But something had to be done. For the girls, for the others held captive like I had been.

I looked Zak hard in the eye. "Teach me to fight."

He laughed at first, and then realized I wasn't kidding. His brow narrowed and his eyes grew fierce. "Why?"

"I need justice."

"Justice or revenge?"

The Matriarch

"*Justice.*"

He released me from his arms and stood. He paced the floor, back and forth, over and over. He would occasionally glance at me. I was so confused when he finally paused and walked up the stairs. *What the fuck is he doing?*

I heard the door start to creak and waited for him to close it. "We start in the morning." The door closed.

A loud horn blared and I leapt from the bed still halfway asleep. Zak stood, holding a trumpet, playing notes off key.

"I found this on the road to town a while back. Didn't know it would come in handy." He laughed like it was the funniest thing he'd ever done in his life. I wanted to knock the shit out of him.

"What fucking time is it?"

"It's time to train. Get dressed. I'll wait upstairs. Be ready in two minutes."

He disappeared up the stairs as I rushed around and threw some of the baggy clothes on. Excitement rushed through me. I finally had a goal, something to work for. I wanted freedom. I wanted to be able to defend myself. I wasn't going to fail.

Dew coated everything in my view as I walked out the front door. The sun peaked over the mountains, casting bright blues, delicate pinks, and warm oranges across the sky. In the distance, Kaja the wolf dog watched from the middle of the yard.

"What? No fucking bacon?" I asked.

Zak's eyes were serious. He was all business and in no mood for jokes as he crossed his arms. His broad

The Matriarch

shoulders stood out against the backdrop of the forest in his tight, black t-shirt and black sweatpants.

"You going to teach me how to fight?"

"No, I'm going to teach you how to run. Don't fall behind."

"Wait, you're teaching me to run?"

"You catch on quick." He flashed a smile in my direction.

I bit my lip at his subtle sarcasm so early in the morning. In a flash, he took off toward the trees without making a sound. I tore after him and quickly realized how out of shape I was. I was at a full sprint trying to keep up as he dodged every stick and leaf, anything that could make noise under his feet. He moved with little effort. I panted and beat at my chest, my lungs full of flames. He slowed so I could catch up.

He spoke to me with ease, his breathing simple and controlled.

"You can accomplish goals easily in silence."

He sped up. My legs and arms were on fire and I didn't know how much longer I could keep his pace.

"If your opponent can't hear you, can't see you...he'll never know you're there."

He crossed into the familiar woods and we cut back and forth across the hill, never down it. Fuzzy stars blurred my vision and I thought I might pass out. Zak looked deep in thought.

"Just a little farther." He glided under trees and around bushes.

I slowed, about to collapse when I caught sight of the house, fueling me to push a little harder, go a little longer.

The sun was now fully visible and the heat was taking its toll. My shirt was soaked. I managed to make it back to the house where I bent over at the waist, sucking air into my lungs, unable to speak.

The Matriarch

"Raise your head. Take in the air. You did well."

I planted my hands firmly on my hips and tried to lift my head to the sky. My chest burned like embers in a fire every time I tried to draw a breath. It seemed like hours for my heartbeat to slow as Kaja sat in the same spot, watching me with interest.

"Come inside. You need to eat." Zak was breathing fine.

I wanted to swing at him but wasn't sure I had the energy. I followed him into the house and walked to the table. The morning workout had me gross and sticky.

I sat down as he pulled some grilled chicken from the refrigerator and poured me a large glass of water.

"Eat this. The protein is good for your muscles."

He sat down at the table and stared.

"You still want justice?"

I nodded.

"Why don't you let the police in Bathory or Golem handle it?"

"Look at me. Look at the way things are. The police don't do shit." I panted, but managed a derisive stare.

"So, you are going to protect the people?"

"Someone has to." I scarfed down cold chicken. It wasn't appetizing, but it served my need. I paused occasionally to breathe.

"That's a big job for one person. You think you can do it?" He raised an eyebrow.

My face tensed, along with my fists.

He kept staring me in the eye. I could feel him logging every reaction like it was some kind of test.

"You need to become a symbol for the people. Something the criminals recognize. You have to make evil fear you. You can't do this halfway. Do it halfway and you're dead. Understand?"

I nodded.

The Matriarch

The look in his eyes made me believe it was possible, but the pain in my legs told me otherwise. I had a lot of work to do. It was either commit fully or not commit at all. It would not be easy, but I'd made up my mind.

"I want it more than anything."

He stood and stalked around the kitchen, then turned back to me. "We'll see about that."

A few weeks passed and my stamina had improved tremendously. I began to move swiftly as we ran, able to stay on his heels even though he still toyed with me.

This morning the sun rose high and hot as we ducked and spun around a tree. I chased him along the creek while he laughed, jumping from rock to rock, springing and bouncing on his toes, barely tapping the ground with just enough force to make it to his next destination.

We made our way to the house and I wasn't breathing hard at all. We finished early and my stomach was grumbling. I climbed the stairs to the front door when Zak appeared from around the side of the house. He was armed with a bow and arrow and held a live rabbit by the ears. It kicked its hind legs like it was about to draw its last breath.

"No! You are not going to shoot that rabbit."

"Not if you catch it. But rabbit is a good lunch. So we'll see."

He dropped the rabbit on the ground. It sat there, quivering.

"You can't be serious."

He drew the bow back and took aim.

"You catch it or I get to eat it."

The Matriarch

I sprinted at the rabbit and it dashed through the grass, bouncing around as I chased after it.

"You have five minutes."

"Do not fucking shoot that rabbit!"

I panted and ran as fast as I could but there was no chance. It was impossible. The rabbit was far too quick.

Snap. An arrow whistled past, piercing the rabbit and pinning it to the ground twenty paces ahead. Blood pulsed around the arrow.

I sprinted to it and dropped as it gave one last kick. Its light brown fur was stained crimson. Anger welled up inside me at the animal's suffering. Zak stalked over and grabbed the creature, still impaled on the arrow.

"You killed the rabbit," he said.

I sat on the ground, my knees digging into the dirt, fighting back tears. *When did he become such an asshole?*

Not content to let him get away with it, I stormed into the house and flung myself down at the table. Zak kept his back to me as he skinned and cleaned the rabbit, before dropping it into a pot of boiling vegetables.

My fingernails dug into my palms. "I can't believe you fucking did that, you prick!"

He was on me in two seconds, his hand on my shoulder and his voice in my ear.

"*You* did that. You weren't fast enough."

He went back to the stove and cooked the rabbit. I sat there pissed off, glaring at him any chance I got.

I refused to eat when he offered.

"Good. More for me." He ate with a wide grin.

After lunch, we went back outside and trained. Neither of us smiled or joked. When we were done, I sulked to my room.

The Matriarch

Why would he do that shit? I thought he was a nice guy.

I gripped a pillow and clutched it to my chest. The rabbit's blood was all I could see when I closed my eyes. I couldn't sleep.

I looked around the room and found the bookshelf. It was just what I needed, a book to help me forget what happened. I scanned half the titles, nothing good. They were all mathematics, economics...academic books. The rest were devoted to mediation, the art of warfare, different types of martial arts.

Fuck it.

I started to read one of them. Anything was better than the thoughts currently racing through my mind. I studied the math book first. It was basic Algebra. I remembered learning it before we had taken off for Golem.

Before long, studying the books in between workouts became an addiction. Zak took notice when I began to carry them around the house.

I studied them every day and worked the problems at night. Every day after our morning run, Zak would kill another rabbit in front of me when I couldn't catch it. I never came close. Why did he keep doing this? He could see it tortured me. I knew it was a lesson of some kind. Everything he did was calculated to draw a reaction.

I lost weight but still refused to eat the rabbit meal. I had dropped about ten pounds and could see my ribs. I couldn't concentrate for shit. Always lightheaded, with a ringing sound constantly in my ears.

My eyes were starting to cross whenever I read my books. It made it impossible to focus. I felt like I was failing at everything.

The Matriarch

I finally got so pissed off reading one night that I hurled the damn book at the wall. *Fuck.* I couldn't see straight. The ringing in my ears had my nails digging into my legs.

I got my shit together and walked over to pick up the book. I noticed a section devoted to logic and reasoning. There, in the bold text, it stated sometimes to solve a problem, one must simply look at it from a different perspective. Something in that moment, reading those words, registered within me.

The weather next morning was gorgeous and felt like spring. I loved feeling of the cool breeze wafting over my face as I cut through the forest on Zak's heels. I grew more aware each time we ran. The sounds of water flowing over the rocks and a frog croaking found its way into my ears. My senses were alive. The air smelled fresh and new, like rain was imminent, but only a few clouds hovered in the sky.

We finished our run. As expected, Zak walked around and dropped a rabbit ten yards from me. I didn't run. Zak's eyebrows arched and he lowered the bow. I pulled a carrot from my pocket and squatted down.

I set the carrot on the ground and backed a few steps away.

The rabbit's eyes darted to me and then the carrot. It inched toward it. Zak smiled.

With each second the rabbit grew more confident, trusted me more. It finally hopped to the carrot. I sat there, waiting to make my move.

The rabbit grew comfortable, looking away for a split-second. I seized my opportunity. In a flash I dove on top of it, gripping it firmly around the ribs as

The Matriarch

it squealed. "Oh, shut the hell up. I just saved your damn life."

I rose to my feet as the rabbit kicked at my arm. It hurt like hell but I wasn't letting go. I walked over to Zak and grinned from ear to ear.

"You did very good." He nodded.

"Fuck you. Your ass is eating carrots for lunch."

His laugh echoed through the trees.

"Come on. I have a good meal planned for dinner."

We walked up the steps to the house and when Zak wasn't watching I set the rabbit down in the grass. It took off in a flash.

"Don't worry. I'm a good shot. I'll get him tomorrow." He didn't even turn around.

We went inside and washed up for dinner. I sat at the table as Zak pulled out two large steaks from the refrigerator.

"We're going to eat good tonight. You've lost too much weight." He pointed to my ribs.

"When do I learn to fight?"

He lowered his eyes.

"I'll teach you when you're ready."

"How can I protect people if I can't protect myself?"

I caught his stern glare in the corner of my eye. "I'll teach you when you're ready."

"Fine."

"You really want to fight? People hit back, you know?" He chuckled.

"I've been hit my whole life."

"Not like this you haven't." He shook his head. "Not like this."

The Matriarch

chapter twelve

maggie madison

We bounced in unison as the truck rambled down the gravel road, twisting and turning through the hilly countryside. My whole body was tense. I was beginning to regret asking to learn to fight. Zak had his usual smug grin on his face. I could tell I was about to learn a lesson. It was usually a lesson in humility.

"Where are you taking me?"

"To learn to fight."

"To learn to fight." I stuck my tongue out at him with a smile.

He brushed off my silliness with a smirk.

"You better hope you have a tongue left."

I snapped back into the worn seat. Zak laughed and patted me on the head, still staring at the road.

"Don't worry. I won't let them take your tongue."

I sat there, curious and perplexed, rubbing my sweaty palms down my legs. Zak had an innate ability to always know what I was thinking.

"What book are you reading now?"

"Calculus. The plot is pretty weak. You should really update your library."

"Calculus has a great plot. Lots of plot lines."

He chuckled at his clever word play.

We veered onto the highway and weaved around a few cars. I could see the old, beaten down train on the other side of the road, heading for Bathory. The night of my escape rushed into my mind. The fear and anxiety. I thought about the girls. What was Kiril doing to them? They were probably already tortured or murdered. Thoughts of his knife in their flesh made me sick to my stomach. My lunch crept into my throat and I wiped cold sweat from my forehead.

"What do you think he did to the girls?"

"It doesn't matter. You can't change the past."

"Well it matters to me."

"You did what you had to do. Anybody would do the same."

He reached over and wiped my hair from my face. My warm cheeks were trembling. I couldn't purge the thoughts from my mind, but Zak's kind gesture kept me from hurling into his floorboard.

"They're okay. They don't know anything."

"Okay." I whimpered a little.

"Kiril is smart. He'll blame his drivers, not the girls."

I eased in my seat a bit. It made sense. The girls wouldn't know anything. It'd be pointless for him to torture them.

"So where are we going?"

His smile returned. "Don't you worry about that."

We pulled into a part of Bathory I'd never seen. It bore a close resemblance to Golem: dirt everywhere, women working the corners, children covered in filth playing in the street. If I hadn't known any better, I would have sworn I was back in that shithole.

"Where are we? I don't recognize it."

"It looks different now. Kiril expanded into Bathory."

How could one man change a city?

"The whole town?"

"Things got bad pretty quick. But just this one part. So far."

The Matriarch

He pulled down a side street. Three girls roughly my age stood on the corner. One had on tight denim jeans with a red top that rode halfway up her stomach. She acted like the ringleader. She whipped her curly brunette hair around and gave me a go-to-hell look when we passed. The three of them shouted down two boys who walked past on a cracked sidewalk.

Zak parked the truck across the street from them.

"Get out." He stared at me, his eyes and voice serious.

"I'm not getting out. Those girls are twice my size and there are three of them."

"You wanted to fight. So fight."

"They'll kill me."

He laughed.

"I hope not. You can't protect the city if you're dead."

Thanks for putting things in perspective, asshole.

"Please, let's just go. Just teach me to fight."

"That's what I'm doing. You have to learn to lose a fight before you can win."

"I'm scared."

"Good." He pointed out at the downtrodden neighborhood. "This is the place you want to protect. It's scary."

"They're going to hurt me."

"I won't let them. Didn't you take a punch from Kiril? He hits harder than those girls."

"It's different."

"You read my books right? Physics? Force is the same. Doesn't matter if it's a man or a girl."

"Ugh! Fine."

I stepped from the truck and one of the girls was already glaring at me. I turned to Zak's window, looking for any indication it was some kind of dare

The Matriarch

and he would tell me to get back in. Instead, he handed me some money.

"Go get me something to drink."

He nodded to the parking lot where the girls stood in front of a store.

I slouched as I walked toward them, head down, hoping they would ignore me. No such luck.

"Hey bitch!" The one in the red tank top stepped into the street.

I kept walking.

"Oh she's ignoring you. You better not take that bullshit."

"Hey, you little fucking whore!" The ringleader came closer. *What a cunt.* I forced my feet to keep moving, even if it put me on a collision course with trouble.

I heard footsteps and made eye contact with her. Huge mistake. The girl smiled and popped her knuckles.

"Yeah, you fucking saw me. Give me that goddamn money in your hand."

"It's not mine." My heart pounded. My hands were clammy. I could feel the bills wrinkling in my palm.

"I don't give a fuck. Give it to me or I'll take it from your scrawny ass."

My blood boiled, but I knew I had to control it. *Fighting is rarely the answer.* I tried to keep Zak's advice in my mind but the bitch kept running her mouth.

"I don't want any trouble." *Keep walking.*

"Yeah, you fucking found it though." I glanced up and all three were stalking toward me.

The girls now stood directly in my path. I had no visible escape and I didn't hide my eyes from theirs any longer. I looked back and Zak was still smiling.

I hated him for making me do this. I just wanted to go home. I wanted to knock that smug grin off his

The Matriarch

face. Then I remembered begging Zak to teach me to fight. He promised not to put me in harm's way.

I turned back and a fist slammed into my nose. My legs went to the sky and I landed flat on my back. Blood gushed down my cheeks. The pain in my nose radiated through my face and my eyes watered.

I stared up at the clouds, momentarily in a daze. The girl appeared over me and took the money from my hand.

"Thanks, cunt." She turned her back to me and faced her friends. "You see me knock that bitch the fuck out? Fucking get some of that shit you little whore!"

"Fuck you." My fists clenched and rage rushed over me.

The girls froze, then slowly turned around.

"What'd you just say?" The ringleader's face was red and her chest heaved up and down with each breath.

"I said go fuck yourself, you piece of shit!" Angry tears mixed with the blood on my face as I worked my way to my feet.

"Take the money back," Zak called from the truck.

"You shut the hell up, you old pecker fuck, or I'll lay your ass out too!" The girl leered at Zak as he chuckled.

I looked over and his eyes narrowed when they met mine.

"Use your training. You're fast."

I lowered my hips and found my center of gravity. The girls stared at me like I was insane.

"Look at this dumb little twat. Guess I'm gonna have to fuck her up twice. Make her cry again."

The ringleader lunged and I lifted on my toes and shot past her, swiping the money from her hand. I flew across the parking lot and up the steps of the store.

The Matriarch

I turned back from the top step. "Looking for this?"

The ringleader stomped her foot on the pavement. "Yo, you little bitch. Give that shit back." She glared at me, puffing her chest out as the two cunts next to her smacked their fists into their palms.

"Come take it." I laughed.

Cunt number one turned to Zak. "Your girl is motherfucking dead, prick!"

He shrugged.

Shit. Shit. Shit.

How was I going to get out of the store and past them? I hadn't thought this through when I ran my fucking mouth off. Another lesson I'm sure Zak was itching to teach. I tried to think of any means of escape as I grabbed Zak's fucking drink. I walked up and paid for the soda and pocketed the change.

I looked to the front door. The girls stood at the bottom of the steps, laughing.

"Yeah, how you gonna get out of there now? You a dead little whore." She turned to her friend and pointed at me. "This bitch dumb."

I stood frozen, examining my surroundings. The front door was the only way out.

I composed myself and sauntered through the entrance. The sun blasted my eyes but I fought through it, making sure I had my opponents in sight. A few trash barrels were to my right and the odor of stale soda, beer, and rotting food drifted across my nose as flies buzzed in my ears.

The girls were hungry for blood. My blood.

"You fucked up now, girl."

I looked to the closest barrel and an idea popped into my mind. I rolled the barrel at them. The girls darted out of the way.

While they were distracted, I made a run for the truck, my feet in perfect harmony with the ground.

The Matriarch

Zak's eyes were trained on mine when I was about fifty feet away. Two large men with ripped, tattooed muscles bulging from their white tank tops stepped in my path and I threw on the brakes. I lost my grip on the soda and it arced in the air before exploding all over the concrete.

Soda fizzed on the ground as the men stomped toward me. One of them wore a maroon bandana and he grabbed a handful of my hair. I winced at the pain in my scalp, waiting to be beaten to death. The last sounds I'd hear would be soda bubbling on the hot pavement and men screaming at me. My throat closed as the sun's blinding rays beat down on my back. I waited for the blows that usually came after I'd disobeyed. But they didn't.

I heard a truck door slam shut. I looked across the pavement to boots slamming into the street, then gazed up to his black shirt, and finally a clenched jaw that etched out Zak's terrifying face. His eyes were wide. I'd never seen anyone look as menacing as him.

When Zak spoke it was slow and with purpose. "Let her go."

"Oh, a hero. Mind your fucking business and drive off before you wind up in the hospital, old man."

Zak took a step and I felt the man's hand trembling against my scalp.

"I'm not going to tell you again," Zak said.

The man gripped my hair tighter, but I felt safer with every step Zak took.

When Zak neared, the man threw me down on my back and pain ripped through my legs.

Zak glanced down to me and spoke through gritted teeth. "Get in the truck."

I rose and limped past him.

Through his terrifying gaze, he winked at me as I hobbled past.

"Take notes."

The Matriarch

I drew a deep breath as Zak turned to them. There was a brief pause and then...

The man in the bandana lunged for Zak and he dodged him effortlessly, laughing as he flew to the pavement. The man quickly jumped to his feet. He brushed off his jeans and growled before taking a swing at Zak. He avoided it easily.

"You're *slow*." Zak chuckled as his feet shifted into position.

The thug jumped up from the pavement, jaw clenched, veins bulging in his neck. He talked a tough game, but his knees quaked underneath him. "Fuck him up!"

Both men moved in. Zak's hand blocked the first one's punch before he slapped the other man across the face. He twirled and kicked the first man in the throat before flipping back around in a smooth motion to grab the other by the wrist. A pop echoed through the street as Zak snapped the man's upper arm in half.

He shrieked. His cries of pain pierced my ears as he clutched his crooked arm. He tumbled to the pavement, writhing on the hot concrete. His accomplice sprinted away. Zak looked to the girls who stood there shuddering. The girls screamed and ran after the thug. Zak walked over to the lone guy curled up in the fetal position and still holding his arm.

Zak shook his head. "You shouldn't hit women. Only a coward would do such a thing."

He turned back to me. My knees knocked together as I tried to process what I witnessed. Zak moved faster than Kiril and hit ten times harder.

He smiled at me and looked back to the man. "First lesson in fighting: make an example out of the first person and the others will run away."

The Matriarch

We climbed in the truck and I smiled at Zak. He tapped his index finger on my temple.

"You did good. But don't forget the tools you have."

The Matriarch

The Matriarch

chapter thirteen
maggie madison

one year later

I caught Zak and Kaja in the corner of my eye as I flew around the side of the house. I cut around behind them undetected and tapped Zak on the shoulder, surprising him in the process. Kaja lifted his head and gave Zak an inquisitive look.

Zak looked down at him. "I knew."

"Hah, right!" I kept my pace.

I somersaulted across the ground, arms flying in each direction as two knives soared through the air and hit their marks.

I ran through the makeshift obstacle course of hay bales and anything else Zak could find that might trip me up. More knives flew from my hands and hit every target dead center. Zak nodded and smiled as Kaja whined and put a paw over his face.

When Zak was nearly satisfied with my performance, I veered in a different direction and his eyes widened. I sprang onto a hay bale and thrust myself into the air, flipping a cartwheel over a barrier. My foot came down and snapped a mannequin's head off. I simultaneously drew two knives from my sides and crashed to my feet in the middle of seven other makeshift dummies.

I spun around, arms nothing but a blur as blades struck every vital area Zak had marked. I was completely focused as I ran around the corner into another group of dummies for hand to hand combat.

Suddenly, a rabbit blew past my feet. Distracted and afraid I might step on it, my legs twisted up and my head smacked the dirt face first. Despite the pain, I grinned.

I sprang to my feet and started to finish the course.

Zak balled his hands into fists. "Enough!"

I halted, mustering a foul look his direction.

"What the fuck? I'm not done?"

"You're not ready. You need to put your feelings aside. This is all a big mistake." He threw his hands up and glared at me, shaking his head.

I walked over to him and looked into his eyes.

"What's the problem?" I said.

I put my hand on his shoulder, pricking him with a needle I'd palmed, and looked over at Kaja staring back at me. Zak winced but quickly recovered his glare.

"Are you afraid to let me leave? I've gotten pretty good. I should be able to take care of myself." I pulled my hand from his shoulder and dropped the needle to the ground. He smacked at his shoulder like he was warding off a bug that had just bitten him.

Zak spoke gently, but his breaths were deep and heavy. I could see a vein bulging in his neck. The same way it did anytime he grew flustered.

"Emotions will get you killed. You can't let things like a rabbit running past distract you. Of course I don't want you to go. But I certainly don't want to send you out there unprepared. I'm sorry for yelling."

"Don't be." I turned around and walked toward the house but turned back. "Actually, maybe you could just give me one more chance. Perhaps I can prove you wrong?"

"How?"

"You and me, old man. Hand to hand. I beat you and you agree I'm ready to go out into the big bad world." I smiled and winked at him.

The Matriarch

His laugh echoed through the hills and startled wolf dog.

"You want to fight me?"

"What's wrong? Scared of little ol' me?" I batted my eyelashes at him.

He mocked me. "Very afraid."

We glided over the tops of the grass out into the field, circling, arms up in striking position. Zak kept smiling. He had never actually tried to hit me before, just dodged my strikes during training, mostly to piss me off.

"Don't cry to Kaja when I pop you in the face," said Zak.

I chuckled and steadied my breathing. It was going to be hard to say goodbye to my best friend. *Focus, Maggie.*

In the blink of an eye, Zak sped toward me. I blocked his hand and countered with a strike which he also blocked. We separated and eyed each other carefully once more. In an instant there was a fury of fists and open handed chops, all blocked. Wolf dog whimpered, but neither of us looked in his direction.

Zak spun and kicked at me, hard. I dodged it and narrowed my eyes at him. Jaw tightening, I threw a jab at his midsection that he slapped away. He appeared dizzy, his reaction time slowing.

For the first time, he missed one of my hands and I connected with his jaw. He stumbled backwards and started to fall. I caught him just before he dropped. He couldn't move his legs or arms. He stared at the smile on my face.

"Feeling okay?" I asked.

"What did you do?" His eyes closed.

I lugged his heavy ass in the house as his feet dragged on the grass and up the steps. I dropped him on the couch and propped up his legs with a pillow. Wolf dog followed, whining at me.

The Matriarch

"Oh hush, he'll be fine."

Kaja sniffed around Zak's limp form.

"It'll wear off in about thirty minutes."

I smirked and rubbed Kaja behind the ears. "You saw me put his ass out, didn't you, boy?"

I stood by the stove and tossed a few scraps to Kaja, helping him form bad habits. Chicken sizzled on the pan as I flipped it over and the aroma wafted across my face.

Light groans made their way into my ears. I turned and looked at Zak as he sat up on the couch.

"Sleep okay?"

"You're funny." Zak rubbed his temples. "How long was I out?"

"Oh, it was only thirty minutes."

"Feels like hours. What'd you use?"

"A little secret I found in a book."

"Bashura?" He smiled.

"How do you know that?"

"It's my book. I've used it many times."

"Shit works."

"When did you get me?"

"Remember this?" I shut the stove off, walked over, and placed a hand on his shoulder.

I flashed him a quick wink with my hand still on him.

The corners of his mouth curled into a wide grin.

"The rabbit?" He looked puzzled. "You tripped over it on purpose? Why?"

"You are too fucking cautious. I'd be here forever if it were up to you. Part of me thinks you don't want me to leave. I've been doing little things for weeks to

The Matriarch

piss you off. To the point you finally dismissed the whole idea of me going out on my own."

Beaming at me with pride, he walked toward his bedroom. "You're ready. Follow me."

I followed Zak into the one room I'd never been. I was often curious, but never entered it, out of respect.

Pictures of an older couple hung on one wall. I assumed they were his parents. I looked over at the bed and there was a masquerade style mask on it. It was a gorgeous, black gothic design with lace filigree that flowed around the face.

"It was my mom's. It was made for a customary celebration in Golem. The tradition was lost over time."

He turned back to me.

"You must be a symbol for the people. You must protect them. In nature, there is no greater protector than a mother."

He looked like he might just shed a tear as he stalled in the middle of the room and stared at a picture of his mom on the wall.

"A mother," he said. "A mother is the greatest protector in world. She makes children feel safe. In the ancient world, the mother was the leader. She was the matriarch of society." He stared deep into my eyes. "You will be the mother for the kids who don't have one."

A giant wave of heat ballooned in my chest as he took the mask and placed it over my head. My hair flowed out the sides and fell on my lean, muscular shoulders.

"Now you're ready."

I wrapped my arms around him and he gripped me tight, holding me close to his solid chest. I pulled back a little and looked up at him through the mask.

"Thank you. For everything."

His warm palms pressed into my cheeks.

The Matriarch

"You're welcome." His face beamed as he stared at me. "I'm proud of you."

We sat around the dinner table, both of us picking at our food. My leg twitched. Zak looked up at me.

"What's wrong?"

I tried to play it off. "What?"

He stared back at me. I knew the look. "Just nervous. Going out on my own."

"There's a bag under the table for you. There's money to help you get started." He smiled.

"You don't have to—"

"It's done."

I knew better than to argue.

"What's your plan?"

"I'm going to go to get an education. Have a normal life during the day."

"Really? And what are you going to do in this 'normal life'?"

"Business. Finance."

"Well. I think you'll be very good at that."

"It will give me tools other than my fists to fight Kiril."

"How so?"

"I can interrupt his infrastructure, buy companies, give him legal problems. Are you sure you read the business books?"

Zak sighed. "Money is boring. You don't need money if you know how to hunt rabbit."

The Matriarch

chapter fourteen
maggie madison

A knock at the door jarred me from my sleep. I must've been napping hard. *Who the hell is here?* Nobody ever came to the house. I stretched my arms above me and yawned. Rising from the bed, I heard voices through the ceiling. I closed my eyes and focused on the sounds.

Then I heard *his* voice. My fingers began to shake and the room closed in on me.

"Zak."

I'd never forget that moment. All the air in my lungs escaped me and I gasped, praying my brain was playing a cruel trick. The voice grew louder. Footsteps pounded the floorboards above and I could hear him clearly. *Kiril.*

I crept up the stairs, positioning to strike if it came to that. *How did he find us? Why was he here?*

I watched through the small hole I'd drilled in the floor. Zak knew it was there, and backed slowly into view. He never looked to me but I saw his index finger wag on the side of his leg, warning me to stay hidden.

How the fuck does he expect me to sit here and not do anything?

"Why are you here?"

"To visit an old friend."

I'd had enough at this point. Zak's eyes were trained on Kiril's bandages, staring at him with contempt. His neck was tense and his hands balled up into fists. It was no exercise. This is what I'd trained for. Zak's lessons played over and over through my mind. *Justice not revenge.*

The Matriarch

"We had a deal. You don't look for me. You don't bother me."

"You don't watch the news, friend? You didn't hear? Things change."

I closed my eyes and focused, making out the position of three other men. One was near the door, probably to watch wolf dog. I could hear his familiar panting. The other two were just out of view.

"What has changed?"

"The United States. I made a deal."

Zak's face tensed even further, his breathing labored, and his index finger wagged at me once more.

"What deal? What about our arrangement? I should've known better than to trust the word of a coward."

Kiril chuckled. "It was a business deal. A closed border is no good for Golem. There is much prosperity on this side." The bandages around his lips turned up to a smile. "Oh, I made one other deal with them."

"What's that?"

"This." Kiril sank his serrated blade into Zak's throat. Blood gushed from his mouth and arterial spray painted the wall. I bit my forearm. Hard.

Kiril slowly pulled the blade out and held Zak by the back of his hair.

"It was a personal matter." Kiril let Zak crumple to the floor.

His lifeless gaze stared at me through the hole in the floor. My teeth dug into my flesh as rage coursed silently into my arm. Blood dripped to the stairs.

I heard wolf dog struggle and growl. Kiril walked toward him, leaving my field of vision. I heard the knife whistle through the air and then a whimper. Kaja went silent and a thud echoed through the room.

The Matriarch

A moment later the door closed and a vehicle retreated down the dirt road. Silence.

I threw open the door as soon as I was certain they were gone. *Why hadn't I done something?* I should have ignored Zak's warnings. What if his signals were calls for help?

I dove on top of Zak, running my hands over his cheeks, bawling. My tears and blood dripped onto him, and I caressed his face. My one friend, my mentor, the one who had saved me from a life of prostitution and doing anything I could to survive. Kiril had already taken my blood. Now he'd taken a piece of my soul, too. I screamed with rage until my voice failed and turned into deep sobs.

I ran my hands through his hair and kissed his cheek before grabbing a pillow off the couch. I set his head on top of it, covering my mouth with my other hand.

Wolf dog lay by the door, a single gash of red over his heart. My hand still covered my mouth and salty tears streamed down onto my lips as I walked to him. I knelt next to him and stroked his fur, waiting for him to spring back to life. Eventually, I used my thumb and index finger to close his eyelids.

"Rest easy, boys."

I leaned against a shovel at the edge of the tree line. Zak and wolf dog were lying on the ground in front of me. I'd cleaned both of them up. Zak wore a traditional business suit from Golem that I had pressed. I grabbed the shovel and walked a few paces from them.

I struggled to get the words out.

The Matriarch

"One last training exercise with my boys watching?"

I sniffed and rubbed my eyes on my shoulder as the shovel jammed into the Earth.

"How to honor those you love."

I finished the holes and my spirit finally broke. I fell to my knees and wept uncontrollably into the graves. Crawling over to them, I ran my fingers along each of their heads.

"I love you so much...both of you...and..." I started to choke on my words but managed to stutter through them. "I'm going to m-miss you both so much. So very much. I'm going to make you so proud of me."

I stood and hoisted wolf dog up into my arms and kissed his fur, pressing my face into it to smell him one last time before placing him in the ground. Then I picked up Zak's heavy body. My muscles strained but I fought through it, intent on setting him gently next to wolf dog. When I finished, I said one final goodbye and covered them with dirt.

I packed the graves down with the shovel, staring around at the forest and the house. It was quiet and serene, lifeless now. I wiped the tears from my face and picked up my bag, the mask dangling from its side. Anger raged in my blood.

"Justice my ass."

I walked toward the truck packed with the rest of my belongings. The lace from the mask flipped in the wind as I climbed in and fired up the engine.

"Time to go home."

The Matriarch

part two

The Matriarch

The Matriarch

present day

THE BATHORY DAILY NEWS
MATRIARCH PROVES THORN IN THE SIDE
OF "THE FAMILY" ONCE MORE

BY: JIM BRISTOL

BATHORY CITY - The masked vigilante crime fighter known as "The Matriarch" has struck again. Reports are that she killed nearly a dozen men and freed as many as 10 captives from a Family compound. Sources indicate that the crime fighter — known also as "Protector", "Temptress," and "Black Mantis" seduced Damon Sabbath to gain entrance to the heavily guarded location.
Investigators remain quiet as they collect information, but with the rumors of police collusion and political corruption, citizens seem to have embraced this real-life superhero as one of their own. Salzberg Industries, the rumored business arm of the Family, has denied knowledge of the captives or the break-in. The CEO, Kiril Salzberg, was unavailable for comment, but the web site had the following statement:

"Salzberg Industries, in order to protect the proprietary nature of its operations, and due to the private status of the company regarding the laws that govern how legal entities operate, does not disclose information of its holdings to the public. We strive to create jobs for working people, provide products and opportunities to the public in order to foster an environment necessary to maximize the

The Matriarch

*standard of living for all citizens, help to build a
thriving middle class, and serve the poor citizens of
our nation through various charities and private
foundations. Any rumors that Salzberg Industries
has ties to illegal or unsavory ventures are simply
that — rumors. These allegations are libelous and
patently false."*

A source described the scene at the compound as "a
complete bloodbath" while another stated that, "it
was like a whirlwind of knives and kicks and she was
gone, nothing left but a pile of bodies."

The identity of "The Matriarch" is still unknown.
According to authorities, she is listed as number one
on their list of top ten most wanted criminals. The
identities of the girls and the manner in which they
escaped is also unknown. Anyone with information is
asked to contact Detective Mike Sharpa at the
Bathory City Police Department.

The Matriarch

chapter fifteen
robert banks

"How long until it's complete?" Kiril's voice was so cold it made my skin crawl.

I pushed my glasses up my nose, fingers twitching. My right arm trembled as I lowered it from my face. I'd worked for Kiril the last five years in his secure lab back in Golem.

"It's difficult to say. We have a lot to do. Controls, review, rigorous studying of side effects."

"This is a top priority. It needs to be done, soon."

We stared through the observation window that had tortured me the past five years. Young girls were hooked to IVs. Some of the girls vomited, some had skin lesions. It was horrifying, unethical, wrong. Kiril made it known he cared little for the cost, as long as the goal was reached. The girls he trafficked were cheap test subjects who yielded immediate results.

I never thought that my training — studying to make lives better — could have led me down this dark, twisted path.

"What are they capable of now?" His soulless eyes burned into my skull.

"Follow me."

We walked down a long corridor. My heart raced every time I heard Kiril breathe through the shrouded mask. I couldn't pinpoint what it was about him that evoked such dread. He could have been a scholar with his naturally scientific mind of inquiry. Completely lucid at all times. The fact that he was sane made him even more frightening. His wrapped face didn't help.

He knew exactly what he was doing, and that scared the hell out of me. We stepped into an elevator

The Matriarch

and my heart dropped into my stomach. I glanced to his face and wondered what traumatic event created such a monster.

After the brief trip down, the door couldn't open fast enough and I sped through it, pretending to be in a hurry.

We moved briskly down another long, cold hallway that was bright white, the tiles squeaking under our shoes. We turned into a training room with weight equipment and a sparring mat. A girl stood with an employee near a large punching bag. I nodded to the employee, who stepped away.

The 14-year-old girl stared at Kiril and me with her pink, bloodshot eyes.

The employee nodded to her. The girl twirled and screamed. She exploded the training bag with her lower leg.

Dust fragments and debris rained down around us, powdering the floor. Once everything settled, the girl stood staring, her chest heaving up and down in sharp, fluid contractions.

Kiril grinned as we looked up to a large monitor that read 1.2 tons.

"That's the force on the bag." My eyes darted to his.

"Is it good?"

"The average elite fighter punches with roughly 775 pounds of force. Her kick was 2,400 pounds."

Kiril's smile grew when the girl grasped her stomach and screamed in agony. She fell to the floor and vomit splattered on the mat. She started to convulse. The employee called for medics as Kiril strode to her and knelt down. He cocked his head sideways and gazed into her pinpoint pupils.

She was barely breathing and bubbles were coming out of her nose as the medics rushed to her.

The Matriarch

"You're making a great sacrifice." The medics hauled her off on a stretcher as the monster turned to me.

"Why were her eyes so small?"

"The serum, in its current state, heightens senses dramatically. The body naturally reacts and her pupils contract to limit the light they take in. Otherwise, she wouldn't be able to see."

"Ahh." Kiril's head tilted back and he nodded to me. "Fix the problem. I have a meeting. I want this done soon." He turned and walked across the mat and disappeared through the door.

The Matriarch

The Matriarch

chapter sixteen
jack meer

Kiril always looked out of place at our strategy meetings. I glanced around at the nervous men in suits sitting at the conference table. Kiril surrounded himself with the brightest minds in finance, marketing, and operations. We all twitched as he breathed through the linens, none of us daring to look him in the eye.

Mark Taylor sat next to me. He was VP of Marketing. "You have to tell him," he whispered.

"He's going to kill me." My hands trembled on my legs as I looked at the mummy, afraid of what would happen when I broke the news. I gulped and raised my voice. "Mr. Salzberg." Kiril turned slowly and looked in my direction.

"Yes?"

"I'm umm...I'm afraid I have some bad news."

"What's that?"

"Three of the small pharmaceutical companies we were courting were acquired earlier this morning."

Kiril's head perked up.

"Is that so?"

"Yes, sir. I'm sorry. We're working to find out what went down. None of them were actively seeking outside capital. We don't know how this happened. Our department is baffled."

"Yes...it is, baffling."

There was an awkward silence. I wasn't sure how to respond.

"We had term sheets ready to present and were informed just before our meeting that they had accepted offers. The offers were for controlling portions."

"Who acquired them?"

"They wouldn't comment. But our due diligence teams observed high-level employees of Balfour Capital leaving their buildings this morning."

Kiril's fists clenched, but his demeanor remained calm.

"See what you can do. These companies are of importance."

"Y-yes sir."

Kiril rose to his feet and disappeared down the hall as two large men followed. One of them reappeared in the door. "Meer. Come with me."

I was led down the hall toward Kiril's office. I'd heard stories of the shit Kiril did behind closed doors. None of it was ever confirmed. I knew I never wanted to find out, yet here I was.

I turned the corner into the mummy's office and he stood there staring at the wall. Pictures hung all around. It was surprisingly professional, not the torture chamber I'd envisioned.

I watched him at the wall, seemingly deep in thought. His arm raised from his side and drove a hole through the sheet rock. A crack hurtled for the ceiling. My knees quaked under me. I'd never seen anything like it.

He walked to me slowly, composing himself.

"I'm sorry." I tried to sound respectable but came off as a total pussy. I was scared. There was no hiding it. He knew it and so did I.

"I want to know *everything*."

I started to speak when his hand shot out and clamped around my neck. My legs kicked but didn't find the floor.

"How did this happen?" His face was only inches from mine. I looked in his eyes and saw only death.

I clutched at my throat, unable to speak. My eyes moved wildly around the room.

The Matriarch

"I-I don't know." I struggled to get the words out. Kiril released his grip. My feet rammed into the floor.

"It is your job to know!"

"They ran the acquisition through shell corps, there was no way—"

"There is always a way. We have to clean up this mess."

"How?"

Kiril stared at me with his head tilted, like I was some strange sort of bug.

He smiled slowly. "Who do we know at the courthouse?"

"There is one on the payroll. What do you want me to do?"

"Get a copy of the documents. Lawyers will find a loophole. Do your job!" He collected himself. I could tell he didn't like to get emotional. "We will find leverage and lean on the owner. Fix this mistake you've made."

I winced.

"Look, this isn't our off books business. It will be difficult to maintain legitimacy—"

"You don't understand. We must have these companies."

Kiril kept information tightly compartmentalized and it sometimes made my job difficult.

"Get it done."

"Yes sir." I was still shaking, on the verge of pissing my pants. I looked over at the pictures of Kiril's family. I'd never been in his office before. Nobody went in his office.

"You see my family?"

I nodded.

"Family is a strong motivator for action. You have a family?"

I knew better than to lie. I nodded slowly.

The Matriarch

"I will visit your family. I will break their bodies, one by one." He reached down and took one of my fingers in his hand. I couldn't look at him. My face went numb.

"Right in front you while you watch, helpless. Understand?"

I nodded. Pain ripped through my arm as he snapped my finger sideways. I clutched my index finger and fell to my knees, wailing.

Kiril leaned down and tilted my head up to him, fingers pressed into my chin.

"Make it happen."

chapter seventeen
maggie madison

I strutted down the street in a short, charcoal pencil skirt and red blouse, drawing stares as I passed through the crowd. The wind blew strands of my dyed brunette hair in front of the glasses I now wore. People recognized me from news coverage and magazine articles.

My love for downtown Bathory never ceased. I soaked in the city as it played with my senses: the smell of hot dogs from street carts, trash piled on the curbs, the roar of the overhead trains that zipped above, and the rumbling of the ground as they passed. This was home.

I walked between two vents in the sidewalk, steam billowing from them on each side, stopping briefly to look at my phone for the time. I glanced around the buildings, searching for an address above a glass door or bolted to the wall. The city had charisma built into every detail. The buildings were mostly brick, many with murals painted on the sides.

I spotted my destination across the street and weaved through yellow taxis and blaring horns, arms flailing out of windows. I turned and faced the glass doors of a small holistic pharmacy. The business intelligence department of my company suggested it as a possible acquisition. It wasn't a priority, but I knew Kiril would be watching. It was chess with him, and I knew his surveillance team would report back.

Two garbage workers ogled my ass as I walked past. I swayed it a little for them, just to be nice.

I composed myself and walked through the front door. Bells on the door chimed when I entered. I feigned a startle at the sound. My story was that I

hadn't slept in days and my nightly activities kept my
adrenaline constantly pumping. It wouldn't be hard
to keep a straight face, considering it was the truth.
The doctors had tried everything to help. Ambien
didn't work, Lunesta was a fucking joke, perhaps
something natural might give me some relief, or at
least a reason to be in the store.

"Something I can help you find, miss?"

I turned and froze, staring into a pair of warm,
emerald eyes. He was tall with mussed brown hair.
He could barely see me through the shelves, but I
could see all of him. He wore a green apron wrapped
around a set of broad, sturdy shoulders. A welcoming
smile formed on his chiseled jawline, revealing a
sparkling set of white teeth.

Holy hell. I snapped out of my daze.

"Just looking."

He walked around the corner. I turned to face him
but something changed. His brow narrowed and his
personality grew cold.

"Oh." He scoffed.

What the fuck did I do?

"Place isn't for sale." He walked briskly back
around the counter and crossed his arms over his
chest.

"What makes you think I want to buy this place?" I
stared around the shop as if it were a complete
shithole.

He chuckled and looked at me with one side of his
mouth quirked up. I wasn't fooling him.

I clenched my fists and my jaw tightened. Nobody
was going to treat me like this. "I don't have all day.
Do you have anything for sleep?"

"You *really* want something?"

"I'm looking for something natural. My doctor
prescribed Ambien, but it makes me feel weird. You
have anything like that? Or are you just a stock boy?"

The Matriarch

He completely ignored my insult and it made my jaw tighten even more.

"Yeah, fix it with a pill." He paused and looked me up and down again. It made my heart race, but I was still nice and pissed.

He dropped his arms, opening up to me a bit. "Sorry, can't help myself, greedy pharma companies. They want to fix everything with a pill when nature has the answer. You should know. Don't you own three or four of them?"

Fucker knows who I am. No wonder. Actually it's nine, asshole.

"I'll just go someplace else. Sorry to bother you."

I turned on my stiletto heel.

"Wait. Just. Wait a second."

I tried not to smile as he walked around the counter. I wanted to tell him how wrong he was. How he shouldn't judge people. But I knew he was right. I'd ignored things for the good of my companies. Things I knew that happened. It wasn't always what was best for the consumer, but what was best for the bottom line. It was necessary for the overall good, but I couldn't explain that to him. I admired his passion.

"Have you heard of melatonin?" He stared at me as I ogled his muscular frame.

"No." It was a lie, but I wanted to hear him tell me about it. I hadn't tried it yet, so maybe it'd work and he could be my hero. *What the fuck? Snap out of it, Maggie.*

"You need a natural source of it. We have some in capsules. It looks like a pill, but it's naturally extracted and in its original form. Follow me."

His ribs grazed my back as he shuffled by and my face began to tingle. I followed him like a puppy on a leash, admiring the view of his ass in his tight jeans.

"So, do you own the place?"

He glanced back at me and smirked. "Really?"

The Matriarch

"Okay, fine. No business. Got it."

He stopped and turned so abruptly I almost bumped into him. He was throwing me off my game.

"Cody Powell." He offered a hand. "Not that you didn't know that already."

I reached for it and his touch was surprisingly soft and inviting. I stood there a moment, my hand lingering longer than it should.

"Rebekah Balfour. So, you know who I am, do you?"

"I do. What I don't know is what you people want with this place."

"People?"

"Yeah, suddenly there is this huge interest in a small pharmacy that barely breaks even." I frowned and started to ask more questions before he interrupted me. "Here it is."

He handed me a small bottle that read 'organic' on it with various medical information wrapped around the eco-friendly label. *Look at this hippie shit. Fuck it. I'll try anything if it gets me to sleep.*

"Thank you."

I was still jittery and on edge. It bothered me though I didn't know why. I didn't know why my heart raced every time a word came from his lips. I didn't know why I couldn't stop staring at his mouth. What I did know was that I understood his passion. His love for the family-owned business. His loyalty. I didn't like that he thought of me as some vulture, trying to strip his company for a quick buck.

"Look, I think we started off all wrong here. Did I come here to scope out your business? Honestly, yes. Did I intend to buy it? Most likely not. But I am curious now because I know that Kiril is the other 'people' you are talking about. I can't let him get your company."

His muscles relaxed and he looked relieved.

The Matriarch

"You don't have to worry. Like I said, it's not for sale. But thank you."

I stood stationary, still drawn to his lips and eyes. I tried to focus, but every time he spoke the sounds barely registered.

"Yeah...I mean, umm, no, thank you," I paused at his puzzled look, "For the medicine, thank you for the medicine."

He smiled down at me, clearly aware of the fact he was making me nervous.

"No problem."

When I walked through the door and into the street, I turned my head back and caught him watching me. He gave me a quick wink and my heart beat like a drum. Butterflies raced in my stomach. I caught my reflection in a window and my face was pink as a carnation. *Fuck, that was one beautiful man.*

I snaked around the private drive to my house in my brand new black Tesla Model S. The engine screamed as I accelerated into a sharp turn. My torso shifted to the side and pushed my back into the seat at an angle. My eyes focused like lasers on the road. Raw energy coursed through my veins. I smirked.

Perks of running a billion dollar company. Gotta keep up appearances.

I didn't mind having nice things. I worked hard for them after I left my old life behind. Harder than anyone knew. I aced the high school equivalency test under an alias and worked my ass off to be top of my class in college. I made my first million three years out of school, and after a few savvy investments I now owned one of the largest VC firms in the world. If I

The Matriarch

was going to fuck bad guys up at night I could drive whatever I wanted to. I was Rebekah Balfour. Maggie died along with Zak and Kaja.

Speeding through the hillside country in my new toy did nothing to rid Cody from my mind. Thoughts of him coupled with the power under my hood sent a warmth between my thighs. I gripped the steering wheel, taking turns wiping each of my sweaty palms down my skirt. Pebbles and dust flew from the ground behind the rear tires as I maneuvered a tight corner, sending the tall reeds lining the road into a frenzy.

I slowed around a corner and turned up the long drive to my secluded mansion. It was a modern piece of architecture. Huge curved glass windows molded with the hills in the backdrop that overlooked the city and its majestic skyline.

I tapped a few buttons on the flashing screen and the garage door opened. I pulled through the single opening into a showroom that housed many vehicles. A Porsche Spider, '67 Shelby GT 500, a Lamborghini Gallardo, an Audi SUV fully loaded, and a few others that sparkled from the track lighting suspended above them.

I drove into the empty space designated for the Tesla and stepped from the car, running my hand along its curves, feeling the power and beauty under my fingers.

"What do ya think of 'er, Mags?"

"Amazing."

The old, familiar man stepped from the shadows, his face lined with wrinkles and his thin, silvery hair shimmering in the light. He was the only man on the planet who knew my real name.

"She would have made our getaway a little easier than that ridiculous van." He chuckled.

The Matriarch

"I know. Too bad we couldn't strap all the girls to this beast. How are they?"

"Oh, they'll be fine. They seem to have taken a liking to me." He grinned. "All these young ladies aren't the most terrible view in the world."

"You old perv." I leaned in to hug him. "Grandpa?"

"Yeah?"

"Nothing—forgot what I was going to say. Go get some rest. I'll make dinner."

He laughed as he walked away.

"Dinner? You? That's some funny shit. It's already on the table."

Beautiful young girls scantily clad in my workout clothes filled the dining room.

"Grandpa! Did you even show them any normal clothes?"

"Of course not. A young woman has to express herself. Those legs won't last forever!" He looked around at the twelve pairs of legs strutting around the dining room.

Some of the girls snickered at his goofy smile.

I shook my head as I walked up to the table. The girls crowded around, all intent on thanking me for having them in my home.

"What?" Grandpa smiled again and shrugged, feigning innocence.

"Grammy would kick your ass."

"Oh, she'd want this ol' man to be happy."

He was the polar opposite of my father. Dad was straight-laced and as pure as they came. Grandpa cursed like a sailor, drank, and shouted. Still, he had a moral compass about him that had been passed to my father and ultimately to me. If he'd known what

The Matriarch

was going on in Golem he would have burned the place down. He still beat himself up constantly for heeding Dad's wishes and letting us leave Bathory, even though I forgave him long ago.

"You're bad."

"If I'm going to risk this pretty face taking bullets, by god, I'm going to be rewarded." He turned to the girls. "Ain't that right?"

"We don't mind, really," said one of the girls. "We told him we just wanted something comfortable to wear."

"Well, we'll work on finding you schools and getting you back on your feet as soon as possible. Won't we, *Grandpa*?"

"Oh hell yeah, you girls are gonna be just fine."

He said it jokingly but I knew he meant every word. He was just as committed as I was. They didn't have anything else in the world. Grandpa was a family man and it broke his heart when my father up and moved us.

I'd begged Dad to let me stay with him, something Grandpa once told me he wished he'd taken me up on. At the time though, he insisted Kyle and I go to keep the family together.

I tilted my head up to Grandpa when I saw tacos on my plate.

"What?" he asked.

"I have a—umm—date tonight."

"You need protein, Mags. Kicking ass takes protein. Shit everyone knows that," he whispered where the girls couldn't hear.

"I'm not eating this."

"Hey, more for me and my new girlfriends." He playfully wrapped his arm around one of the smiling girls.

"I'll just eat after. I have to get ready."

"Be down in a few."

The Matriarch

I stepped into my walk-in closet that was the size of a normal living room. Business suits, evening gowns, and accessories lined the walls. I walked to a display of shoes. "Hello, girls." It ran floor to ceiling covered in heels and designer boots. Another perk of running a huge company.

I pressed my palm against a flat panel display and it scanned my hand. It rotated in three dimensions before flashing green. The door slid to reveal a hidden staircase. I wound down in a spiral, my hand running along the cold rail into a hidden room.

"Lights."

The lights flickered on and then dimmed slightly, adjusting to my eyes. My black suit was laid out on a table, and my knives shimmered, strung along a leather belt strap. I looked to my mask, lying in the middle of it, and then my boots with retractable blades set out in front of my carrying bag.

My fingers slid along the blades, making sure they'd been properly sharpened.

Multiple wigs hung on the wall along with a low-cut, black dress and pair of matching pumps.

"Everything should be in order." I turned to Grandpa making his way down the steps.

"Thank you."

He looked me in the face and his leathery palms clutched my cheeks.

"Be careful." Concern accentuated the wrinkles on his weathered face.

"I always am."

"I had a few tweaks added." His eyes lit up as he grabbed my top.

"Oh yeah?"

The Matriarch

"Had thermal options added to your suit. Built in climate control, connects to some bullshit called Bluetooth. In case it gets cold or warm out. Anti-moisture synthetics, to wick rain and perspiration."

"Nice."

He gripped me with a bear hug that squeezed the oxygen from my lungs.

"Come home in one piece, baby girl."

"I promise."

"I love you, sweetie."

"I love you too, Grandpa."

The Matriarch

chapter eighteen
maggie madison

"Well, you are a kinky fucker aren't you?" I climbed on top of William Greinke in his leather office chair, straddling him as I pulled playfully at his tie. His eyes grew huge and his cock stiffened in his slacks. I reached back for my hair tie that held the wig in a ponytail, releasing it as I shook my head. Waves of auburn teased at his face.

I reached down and ran my hand along his trembling leg, inching my fingers toward his cock, then ran my palm the length of him.

"Oh my." I raised my brows, wrapping him up in my fingers and stroking gently back and forth.

"Now, this is a dick." I slowly unbuckled his belt and yanked it from his slacks. "So you want to fuck me on your desk? Or fuck me in this chair? How do you want me?"

I lifted up from him, exhaling down his neck as I pulled away. I turned around as he sat slouched in his chair, ogling every inch of me.

"Stroke that fucking dick for me," I said over my shoulder.

He reached to his cock, rubbing back and forth on it over his slacks. His thumb teased at the head as he stared at my ass.

I slid my skin-tight, black dress up, slapping my ass lightly. I glanced back to log every reaction while my head swiveled, taking in my surroundings.

I worked my hands under my dress, putting on a show, and pulled down a lacy black thong. I let it drop to the floor pretending it was an accident. "Oops."

The Matriarch

I covered my mouth with my hand, showing him the whites of my eyes as I turned back around. I went to my knees, crawling toward him on the ground.

Both my hands ran up his legs over his slacks, digging my nails in, my eyes locked on his. "I don't know if you can handle this pussy." I reached a hand between my legs and hovered my mouth over his hard prick, breathing on it and teasing his inner thighs.

I moaned, my index finger stroking my tiny bump. It swelled at my touch. I pulled his slacks down to his ankles, marveling at the cock that sprang free and swayed back and forth in the air.

I gripped at the base of it with my free hand, slipping two fingers inside my slick, aching cunt, and slowly inched them deeper. I wanted him bad, for the sake of the mission of course.

Eyeing his cock, I licked my lips and exhaled on his tip and down the shaft, pressing my tongue to his balls. Pulling my fingers from my slick folds, I let go of his dick, stood, and kissed him hard and deep, before biting at his lower lip.

I plunged my fingers into his mouth, forcing them into his cheek. His tongue swirled, sucking my juices from them. I playfully slapped the side of his cheek with my free hand. "You like how that pussy tastes?"

He nodded.

I sprawled to my back on the floor, grinding my hips up and down in the air, circling my fingers around my entrance.

"I said stroke that dick for me." I moaned and panted, watching him watch me.

He wrapped his fingers around his prick and stroked, increasing the intensity every few seconds, knuckles turning pale.

I worked two fingers inside and my eyes rolled back. "I want your cock so fucking bad. I want it so

The Matriarch

bad, baby. I can feel it inside me. Oh my god." I let out a squeal.

"Come and get it." I looked up and he was pumping his cock hard and steady, staring at me with hungry eyes.

I paused for a moment, shifting back up to my knees, gaping at the length he held in his hand. "I think I will."

I slapped his hand from his cock and took the tip in my mouth, sucking his head without warning, and slapped it on my tongue. I plunged him into the depths of my throat, hands at my sides, doe eyed watching his head crash back into the chair.

I bobbed on him, saliva streaming down his shaft and my chin, coating his balls, gagging myself on the pulsing cock jammed in my mouth.

I held all of him in for a moment, my lips pressed against his pelvis at the base, before releasing him and panting for air.

"Can't handle that dick?" He smirked at me.

Wrong move, bitch.

I grinned and slammed my mouth down once more, his head teasing the back of my throat. I shook my mouth on the base of his shaft like a hooked fish.

"Holy fuck." His head flew back to the ceiling.

I released him momentarily as his eyes opened, and then spit all over it, staring his big prick down, thinking of all the dirty things I wanted to do to it. Then I took him all the way in my mouth once more, swirling my tongue around him as I went up and down on his prick. I felt the tension rise quickly in his balls against my chin.

I released his dick and slapped it, hard. Knocking it back and forth in the air as he winced. "Not before you fuck me."

The glint in his eyes held excitement and fear.

"You really are a naughty bitch."

The Matriarch

"You have no fucking idea. No idea, at all."

My soft thighs straddled his muscular hips. I ripped his shirt apart, buttons rattling across the desk like shrapnel. A carved up six-pack appeared as I turned around and pressed my tight ass against his throbbing cock.

I slid my cheeks up and down, spreading them with my hands and letting his shaft tease across my puckered asshole.

"You want this pussy bad, don't you?"

"Fuck yes."

"How hard you gonna fuck me?"

"I'm gonna drill your fucking cunt." His confidence grew. I liked it.

"Oh yeah? Fucking do it then, pussy!"

I turned and slapped him, straddling him and hiking one of my feet up on the desk. I gripped around his tight shaft and lowcred my pussy to him, hovering over the tip. I eased his head inside, my mid-section shuddering as he went into me.

Fuck me, it's huge.

I knew he wouldn't last long the second I sat on him. He filled my wet cunt as I circled my fingers around my clit. A sigh escaped my lips.

"That's it, right there." I lowered my leg and wrapped my arms around his neck.

I bounced my ass on his thighs, drilling my pussy to the hilt with his stiff cock.

An orgasm was building deep in my core as I sped up the tempo. I bounced harder and faster as he leaned back. I pressed my forehead into his and stared into his eyes.

"Fuck me, baby." I gasped.

Neurons fired through my body. I rocked my hips back and forth, feeling every inch inside me as I clamped around him, body tingling in a daze.

The Matriarch

I shook for a moment and came on top of him, clawing at his pecs as I jolted one last time.

The grin on my face was reciprocated in his.

"You done fucking me or what?" I playfully slapped him once more.

It was all the goading he needed.

"You want more?"

"Did you come on my fucking tits yet?"

His eyes grew large. He slapped my ass, leaving two big red hand prints, and gripped my thighs. My pussy clenched at the stings, and my heart raced against him. He stood up as I spread my legs wide around his hips.

He maneuvered his hands under my ass and got a firm grip, holding me in the air as he hammered into me. My head flew back. His pelvis slapped into my legs, drilling me in time with my screams as I felt his hard prick jackhammering into the depths of me. My fingernails dug deep into his arms, fueling him to speed up.

My voice began to vibrate as he rammed his cock in and out of me. My pussy was drenched and hot. Smacking sounds echoed through the room.

I squealed louder and faster as the bottom of my ass slapped into his thighs as his legs stiffened.

"You gonna come for me?" I barely got the words out.

He nodded.

I yanked my top down, letting my breasts bounce in rhythm as he went into me a few more times before slipping his cock out. I dropped to my knees, squeezing my tits together between my arms as he furiously stroked his cock.

He increased the tempo of his hand. I stared into his eyes as his body went stiff. I could see his load bulging in the head of his cock as he let out a grunt. The first wave shot across both my tits and my erect

The Matriarch

nipples. The warmth of his come on my skin had my eyes wide open. I smiled at him while he continued to grunt and stroke, some of it landing on my neckline.

A strand of come dangled from the tip and I caught it with my tongue, wrapping my lips around the head of his cock. I gulped down his last few salty drops.

"Well, that was fun." I giggled.

He stood there in a euphoric daze, slowly regaining his consciousness.

"Jesus Christ." He looked at me like I was all his fantasies wrapped into one.

"Well, be a fucking gentleman and go get me something to clean this off with." I stared down to my tits.

He paused for a moment. I sensed apprehension as he shrugged and walked from the room.

I flipped to my feet and pulled a thumb drive from my purse. I jammed it into his computer and pressed a button on the side, staring down at my come-covered chest.

Messy bastard. Goddamn, he can fuck though.

It hadn't taken much convincing to get him to bring me here. All I had to do was bat my eyelashes and say, "Wouldn't it be fun to fuck in your office? I'll make it worth your while."

The thumb drive flashed green and I swiped it from the computer. It slipped through my fingers and rattled against the floorboard near the door.

"Son of a fucking bitch." My heart raced, thumping into me.

I started toward it and froze, sitting back down in his office chair.

He walked through the door, looking worried, carrying some tissues from the restroom.

"This was all I could find." He buttoned up his shirt (what buttons were left) and looked around the

The Matriarch

room, before handing me the tissues. I wiped the load off my chest and tossed them in the waste basket.

He turned his head to the corner where the green light from the thumb drive cast a faint glow against the wall.

Fuck. I sprang from the chair and kissed him as he buckled his pants.

"We really shouldn't be in here." He pulled away from my mouth and stared around.

I yanked his head back to mine as he started to look in the direction of the flash drive. "Don't fucking pull away from me." I kissed him slowly, one eyebrow raised as I stared at it in the corner.

"Really. We have to go. Now."

"Ugh, fine. You're no fun once you blow your fucking load."

He laughed as I grabbed my purse and adjusted my skirt down my ass.

I walked to the door, careful to block his view.

"What is that?" My heart practically stopped. I did not want to kill this motherfucker in his office. But I would if it came to it. He stared into my eyes. The flash drive was a few feet away.

Fuck me!

"What?" I did my best not to look nervous or tremble.

He walked over to me with a serious look on his face. I saw pictures of his family on the wall. *Guess they won't get to say bye to their nosy daddy.* I hoped with everything in me he wasn't heading toward that drive. My hands grew clammy. My heart sped up against my ribs.

Inches from my face, he looked me up and down.

I stopped breathing.

"The sexiest fucking ass I've ever seen." His hand slapped my right cheek in his palm. I feigned surprise and dropped my purse over the drive.

The Matriarch

"Oh, you think you can handle that shit again?" I was up by his ear as he squeezed my ass a little harder before releasing it.

I bent down and grabbed my panties from the floor. I sighed as as relief rushed over me. I stood and placed them in his hand.

"A souvenir."

He stared at them as I bent over and picked up my purse, shuffling the thumb drive inside of it. I couldn't get to the elevator doors fast enough as I strutted away, rocking my ass back and forth. Holding my thong in his hand, he stared, a huge smile spread over his face. He followed me like a puppy after his favorite toy.

Cars raced by outside the window as I woke in a strange apartment. A heavy, sweaty arm was draped around me. It tightened against my ribs as I tried to escape its clutches. I paused for a moment, exhaling lightly, and slowly peeled a finger at a time from my waist. I set it on the pillow next to me.

"The shit I do for this city." I smirked.

I hopped out of bed without making a sound, pulling my dress back on before rising to catch a glimpse of my disheveled red wig in the mirror. I shuddered at my appearance. *Aren't you a looker, Jesus.*

William adjusted in the bed, snoring loud, taking the breath from my lungs as I tiptoed across the room and slipped out the door.

Sunlight overwhelmed my eyes as I fumbled through my bag for a pair of sunglasses. I made my way down the stoop of the apartment building.

The Matriarch

The nearest street sign eluded me for some reason and I was turned around. Having drivers had spoiled me. Walking by in suits and everyday clothes, people hustled children to the bus stop, running late for meetings. They sneered at me. I looked down and realized I looked like a street whore. It didn't bother me much. I was used to the stares. I grew up with them.

The usual urban smells swirled around me. I looked up to some clouds approaching the city from the West and scratched at my scalp. I hated wearing the fucking wigs and thought the price paid should include a 'no itch' guarantee.

Making my way around the corner to an alley, I found a dumpster. I scanned the area for anyone who might be watching before pulling the wig off and letting my brunette hair cascade down my shoulders. I tossed it in the trash and caught a glimpse of myself in a window.

"Well, it's an improvement I guess."

I made my way a few blocks, keeping my head down, praying nobody recognized me.

Walking across the street, I passed a mother scolding her child as they walked. I could still hear them behind me when I froze in my tracks and the child ran straight into the back of my legs, buckling me at the knees.

"Sorry, sorry. Are you okay?" I asked as I stared down at the young boy as his mother apologized to me. I hoped he wouldn't get in more trouble than he was already in.

I shimmied my minidress down farther and glanced up. Reality crashed back into me and I remembered why I'd suddenly stopped. Cody was walking down the sidewalk toward me.

Shit!

The Matriarch

The sunlight hit his face from the side, casting shadows along the line of his jaw. He ran his fingers through his hair and locked his eyes on mine.

I flipped my head to the side, pretending to be looking across the street at something else. Not fast enough.

"Rebekah?" I could feel his eyes on me and my hooker outfit.

There was no way out. I turned and smiled as if nothing was amiss about my slutty dress and disastrous hair.

"Hey." *Eloquent, Maggie.*

He chuckled for a second, his eyes darting to my ensemble. "Long night?"

I didn't know what it was about the apron wrapped around his frame, but I wanted to rip it off him. I could do it too, easily. If he only knew what I was capable of.

But there was something about the apron. It made him innocent and playful, young at heart. It took years off of his age, as if his boyish charm didn't make him seem young enough already.

"How did the melatonin work?"

"Oh, you know...It was great. I've been sleeping great." I played with my hair like a little schoolgirl. *Knock that shit off, Maggie.*

He smiled a little, completely unconvinced. I knew I looked like I hadn't slept in days and I said 'great' far more times than any normal person who was indeed, 'great'.

"I see." He stood there, ripping my breath away with his emerald eyes.

We both stood awkwardly as my hands searched my hips for familiar pockets, only to be met with the thin material of the dress. My mind blanked, wiped clean, unable to process anything that could be considered a thought.

The Matriarch

When I finally managed to speak, he did too, and our words jumbled together. We both paused.

"Sorry, go ahead." Cody's hand ran through his hair once more.

"No, no. You first."

"Okay. I want to apologize for being rude in the shop the other day. Rough morning, and I just...I took it out on you. I'm sorry."

He thought that was being rude? Jesus, where is this guy from?

"I actually thought you were nice. I mean, you knew why I was there." I giggled like a little bitch. It drove me insane.

"Well I still felt awful when you left. I was pretty harsh." His face turned pink and his hands fumbled in his pockets. "Maybe I can make it up to you?"

"It's really not necessary." I wanted desperately to be somewhere else, and at the same time I didn't. I clutched my arms around me, trying to cover up my outfit.

His smile faded, like I took the life out of him. It was like taking a punch to the stomach. I wanted him to smile again. To smile at me.

"Well, what did you have in mind?"

His mouth turned up to a grin and happiness flooded my veins.

"What are you doing tonight?"

"Me?" *Me? Who am I right now?*

He looked around playfully at all the people ignoring our awkward encounter on the sidewalk.

"Umm, yeah. You. What is Rebekah Balfour doing tonight?"

I smiled and relaxed, trying to remember if I had anything planned. My body tensed up and it made me uncomfortable.

"Sorry, just, it really was a long night. I'm not doing much at all."

The Matriarch

"Would you like to have dinner with me?"

My mind went in a million different directions. Was he asking me out on a date? Had I ever even been on a real date? What would I wear? What was I supposed to do? How was I supposed to respond? I frowned.

"It's okay, seriously. I didn't mean to blindside you. It was a long shot anyway. Beautiful billionaire and street merchant. Can't fault a guy for trying, right?"

"Yes." The words escaped my lips before my brain convinced me otherwise.

His eyes sparkled and his face lit up.

"Yes. That sounds like fun." *What are you doing, Maggie?*

My answer was apparently unexpected. Cody fidgeted with his hands, sliding them down his apron, pretending to straighten it. I was regaining my composure at the expense of his awkwardness.

"One condition, Mr. Street Merchant."

"What's that?"

"Can we please go somewhere low key?"

"Afraid to be seen with the peasant boy?"

"Oh my god, no!" I squeaked and heat rushed to my cheeks. "No, I'm sorry, that sounded so — I just want to be able to talk, without people constantly interrupting us."

"I get it. You've never dated a celebrity before. You're worried I won't give you enough attention. I get that a lot." His sense of humor charmed my inner girl once again.

He tilted his head up and assumed an unconvincing model pose. I laughed, almost to the point of snorting, but managed to compose myself and play along. My eyes and voice grew serious in tone, mocking him.

"Ohh, no. I definitely haven't. You're my first."

The Matriarch

"Why don't we stay in and I'll cook for you? That work?"

I stared.

"You? Cook?"

"What? A man can't cook? That's sexist you know? It's the 21st century."

"This is true. That sounds wonderful, actually. Here's my number. Give me a call this afternoon."

I handed him a card from my purse and winked before walking away. My ass swayed in the little dress and my heels clacked on the sidewalk. Suddenly, I was striding with confidence.

When I reached the end of the block, I looked in my peripheral vision and saw Cody standing there, still holding my card and looking at my number. I blushed as I turned the corner and my hand covered my mouth while I giggled.

The Matriarch

The Matriarch

chapter nineteen
maggie madison

I got home from work and rushed around my closet, pacing back and forth, sweating more than any woman should. "I don't know what the fuck I'm doing. I'm freaking out!"

Grandpa sat in a chair, laughing at my predicament, seemingly enjoying how nervous I was. I could tell he was excited to see me go on my first real date.

"I see that." His crooked smile beamed from his face.

I walked over to him with a mean-spirited look that softened as I neared. I bent down and put my hands on his shoulders. "Please, Grampy. I need your help. I really want this to go well."

"Ohh, I suppose I can teach you some game."

I stood up as he rose from his seat. "Game? Where in the hell did you hear that?"

"Shit Mags, I gots all the game. You jus' watch 'n learn."

He strutted around and I felt like a child again. My heart grew warm. I calmed down and started to breathe without soaking every garment I put on my body.

He placed his palms on my cheeks, staring into my frightened eyes.

"It's going to be fine, baby girl. He's just a person. You're just a person. Nothing more. Not everything is as complicated as you make it out to be."

I stared at the ground, hating feeling like this, vulnerable.

"But what if he doesn't like me? What about all my secrets? My past? It *is* complicated. I'm wasting his time."

"He knows he asked out a billionaire tycoon finance genius. Surely he doesn't expect things to be simple."

"I guess."

"Mags? He asked *you* out. The boy likes *you*."

I smiled and he wrapped his arms around me.

"I'm sorry you didn't get to do this sooner. Your life wasn't supposed to be this way. It shouldn't be this way for anyone."

"Stop it, you're going to make me—"

I pulled back from his hug and saw his welled up eyes.

"You bastard." I wiped my eyes, mascara running down the sides of my nose. We both smiled through the tears and laughed before hugging again. "I'm going to have to redo my makeup, you asshole."

He leaned forward and kissed my forehead. "Just remember, even when they're older, boys don't ask out girls they don't like."

"Thank you." I hugged him again, gripping my fingers into his back, nuzzling my chin on his shoulder.

He started to walk from the closet. He looked around at all the clothes inside, baffled that I couldn't choose something to wear.

"One more thing...Keep it in your pants, Mags. It's not a mission. Real men need to earn it."

My mouth gaped open. I never spoke about my sexual exploits to him out of respect, but he was far from ignorant. Childish, yes. But he wasn't stupid. This was the first time he had ever mentioned it.

"Grandpa!"

The Matriarch

For some reason what he said resonated. I had only ever used sex as a tool. It was always to gain something, control someone. It was all I knew.

I swerved around a corner in the Model S, drawing stares at every turn.

"Let's try out this 'Ludicrous Speed' shit."

I hammered the pedal. My back rammed into the seat while the electrical engines screamed in the front and rear of the car. My eyes were wide, an intense tingling rippling up through my stomach and into my chest.

"Fuck me! That's the shit right there."

The large flat screen in the dash showed me the way to Cody's. He sounded apprehensive on the phone, but the last thing I wanted to do was have my first date come cook at my house. I was trying to go over everything possible in my mind that would make me seem more girly. Fucking, killing, and finance didn't leave a lot of room to explore my day to day romantic emotions. I was turning tricks for Kiril when most girls went on their first date, went to prom, lost their virginity. It made me hate that piece of shit more.

I veered into a private parking garage of a high rise building in downtown Bathory. I stared up at the huge buildings jutting from the ground. They looked the same as they did when I was a child. Even now, I still gazed at them.

I started to open the door handle and it pulled away before I could grip it. My instincts kicked in and I grabbed the wrist of whomever was trying to get into my car.

"Relax! It's just me!" Cody gripped his wrist.

The Matriarch

I let go and watched him shake his hand in the air like a limp noodle.

"I'm so sorry. Oh my gosh. Cody, I'm—"

"Holy crap, you are strong...and fast — Jesus." His smile set me at ease.

Crap? He's cute.

"I just...I thought you were trying to break into my car."

He reached his hand out to take mine, leading me away.

"I just wanted to open the door for you."

"How did you even know I was down here?"

He stared at me then darted his eyes to the car and back.

"Right, right, sorry. It's my new baby."

"It's...really nice." He didn't sound overly impressed. "I like that these have electric motors. Great for the environment."

"This car can go 0 to 60 in 2.8 seconds, but yeah, I suppose the environment is important too."

He grinned and shook his head at me.

"You definitely have a way with words. Come on. Dinner is going to burn."

I walked up next to him and took his arm. He looked confused.

"What's the problem? Unless you were full of shit about being a gentleman?"

He stood there dumbfounded.

"You have a mouth on you...All apologies."

He led me through the entry into the lobby over to the elevators. Some people in the building stared as we disappeared through the doors.

The elevator lingered, taking its time, and I didn't know how to start a first date conversation. I gave speeches at work all the time. I'd always been good at seducing men. But now, nothing.

The Matriarch

We reached Cody's floor after what seemed like an hour in the elevator and walked to the door of his condo. He fiddled in his pocket for keys and finally got the door open. We passed through a small entryway and into the main living area. It was nice and clean. I could smell fresh vegetables and what I thought was chicken baking in the oven.

I ran my hand along the cool black leather of his sofa while he walked into the kitchen. He moved to the stove and pulled out an apron, draping it over his shoulders and tying it behind him.

"You and your aprons." I glanced around to modern picture frames of him and family. The walls were taupe, several plants standing in vivid flower pots or suspended from the ceiling.

"I know. They're part of my wardrobe these days."

I walked through the kitchen, observing everything around me. There was a small cherry pub table with four stools and a center island with a black granite top. The kitchen was a mixture of stainless appliances and a dark mahogany wood that looked like it had been custom installed.

I walked up to see what Cody was cooking and felt waves of heat from the stove wrap around my legs.

"I feel naked without one on anymore." He smiled as he finished tying the apron in the back.

All I heard was naked and immediately began to picture Cody's six-foot-one muscular swimmer's frame underneath his layers of clothes and the apron. I lost track of my thoughts for a moment, staring at him, the urge to rip his clothes off lingering in the back of my mind.

"I need to finish up a few things in here. Why don't you go watch some TV? Sit down and relax."

I snapped out of my lustful daydream.

"Huh? Oh yeah. That sounds great. Sorry, long day."

The Matriarch

He smiled.

"Well, you look fantastic for having such a rough day."

I stared down at myself and didn't really see anything special. A crimson wrap dress with a v-neck and black stilettos. Cody seemed to like it though.

"Well, thank you."

He followed behind and grabbed a remote while I walked into the living room. When he pressed the power button there was live coverage of a breaking news story.

A reporter stood in the foreground, cars ablaze behind him. Teens ransacked stores, spraying them with paint. They didn't appear to steal, only destroy. They wore mohawks and their arms were covered in tattoos. White and black makeup concealed their face, painted like skulls, dark shadows around their eyes.

The reporter stood silent for a moment, watching the carnage and then slowly lifted the microphone to his mouth.

"We are live in the streets of Warchester where riots broke out earlier today. A movement has taken over the streets, calling themselves the G3n3rat1on of Ka0s. The rioting began sometime around one p.m. after messages went out to their Twitter and Facebook followers. It followed the Supreme Court ruling on the controversial internet privacy laws that have been a subject of intense debate. The regulations granted the Federal Government unprecedented reach. Law enforcement had not taken previous threats seriously, and have since been overwhelmed. We are told they are a regional

The Matriarch

movement with a loyal following comprised mainly of members in their teens and twenties. Their leader issued a public statement today."

A recording came on the TV as we stared. The eerie voice rang from the speakers.

"We, the G3n3rat10n of Ka0s, are deeply saddened by the choices made by the leaders of our country. The government feels it can reach into our homes and siphon any information it deems necessary at any given moment. We call on our members and others who oppose this fascist despotism, to take a stand for freedom and liberty. This type of intrusive power is not to be trusted in the hands of these Robespierres who seek to favor the wealthy, impoverish the poor, and create slaves of the middle class. Will you stand up to fight tyranny? Or will you slowly watch your freedoms erode? They have heard our warnings. They have heard our demands. The only recourse is violence. You will hear from us, you will fear us, you will not rule us."

I turned slowly to Cody who still stared at the screen in disbelief.

"Can you believe this shit?" I looked at Cody and he began to shake his head.

"I mean, it's awful. But...he has a point. That ruling was absurd."

My face filled with heat. I had to constantly remind myself that I had an identity to protect, which meant a billion dollar enterprise that had to be guarded.

"That ruling was to protect citizens." I folded my arms and shot him an evil gaze.

"Hah! More like protect the pocketbooks of the clowns running this country and the—"

"The what?" I shot him a look and he bit at his lip.

"Nothing." He shook his head once more and walked back to the table.

The Matriarch

"You were going to say the rich. You were going to say me? Weren't you?"

I knew I should let it go but my face was on fire. How could he not see things from my side? Did he think all the rich cared about was money? What about people they employed? What about jobs they created?

"No, you're different, but—"

"But what?"

"Well, rich people have a lot to lose when those at the bottom threaten their livelihood."

I turned back to the TV as a teen laughed in the camera, lit a bottle on fire, and tossed it through the window of a large bank. The Molotov cocktail exploded in the lobby as he danced in the street. He took out a spray can and painted a big anarchy symbol on the side of the wall.

"And this is the answer?" I pointed to the screen.

"I didn't say that. Look, can we just eat? I thought we were on a date?"

I pushed a few strands of hair from my face and began to calm down. I should've been doing something, but I had no idea what. My phone began to ring and I held up a hand to Cody as I took the call.

"Everyone is safe? We are not under any threats? Okay, good."

I turned back to him.

"Okay, okay. Sorry. I just worry for my employees. I want to make sure they're okay."

I sat down at the table, curious to see what Cody had cooked for us.

"It's fine."

He walked over to me and sat down.

"I wouldn't have asked you out if I thought you were some corporate monster."

He always said the right things to make me smile.

The Matriarch

I arched an eyebrow. "You haven't seen me in a board meeting."

"Hah."

He walked over and smiled as he pulled something heavenly from the oven. He returned and sat it on the table in front of us.

"A man who can cook. You're a rare one."

"Shh, you haven't tasted it yet. I'm sure I botched it somehow."

He pulled out a bottle of white wine and poured two glasses.

"It smells perfect. This is perfect." I grabbed the remote and shut off the television.

"If you had served red wine with fish I might have doubted you." I laughed at my joke, not expecting him to catch on.

"Okay, Sean Connery." My face lit up at his response.

"A Bond fan?"

"Umm, yeah. I have them all on Blu-ray."

I leaned over and whispered in his ear. "You want to drive his car? I can arrange it."

"Shut your mouth, woman. Don't tease me."

"I have one of his Aston Martin DB5s from Goldfinger. It's in my garage."

His eyes were intense. "That's the sexiest thing a woman has ever said to me."

He held up his glass as I clinked mine into it, both of us staring at each other as we took a sip. I cut into the chicken and took a bite as it melted in my mouth.

"This shit is insane." My mouth was still full of food but I didn't care.

Cody chuckled for a second.

"I'm glad you like it. It helps if you chew."

"Shut up." My mouth was still full as I punched at his arm.

The Matriarch

"So, tell me about you." I stared into his eyes. "Tell me about Cody." The wine was lowering my inhibitions and I worried I was being too flirty and forward.

"Well, Ms. Balfour."

"So professional, I like it. Continue, sir."

"I'm 29, and well, let's see. I went to culinary school and graduated. I love to cook. I had plans to open a restaurant when my parents were in a car accident and became disabled."

"Oh, I'm—"

He cut me off. "It's okay. It was a while back. Anyway, they are at an assisted living facility. They're okay and all. I took over running their business."

"Go on, tell me more."

"Well, I have a brother and sister. Nieces and nephews. Yes, I spoil them to no end."

I took another sip of wine and motioned with my hand for him to continue.

"Do you own the shop outright?"

"Well, the family lawyer had us divide the company so that it would take two of us to sell. I'm a bit worried because we are doing better than we ever have. If anyone knew, they might go to my brother and sister. I sometimes worry they are itching to sell the place."

He looked me up and down. "Is this why you came on the date? You working me for information?" He was joking but I felt bad. It did kind of look that way.

"I wouldn't do that, Cody. I promise."

He smiled. "Well, let's see. I love cooking for people. I also enjoy doing volunteer work and I love kids. I've had one serious relationship, ever. The shop doesn't give me much time to date."

I smiled at him and took another bite. I could let him cook for me all damn day. We finished eating and Cody cleared the plates, washing the dishes while

The Matriarch

I sat at the table. It was relaxing. He was easy to talk to. I looked to the clock and realized three hours had passed. In that time, I had forgotten about the daily responsibilities that usually filled my mind: running the company and protecting the city. For a brief second I felt like a normal girl, who liked a boy, and was lost in the moment. I swooned and gagged simultaneously.

It was getting late. Tomorrow would be a long day, and I was nervous about the uprising.

I pushed back from the table. "I've had a great time, but I really have to go."

"Yeah, it's getting late. You know? I don't think you told me anything about you."

"Oh, I guess I didn't. It's okay though, really. This has been perfect. I don't really do this, well, ever."

"Next time I want to hear all about you."

"Deal."

Cody stood up and yawned. I eyed his body while his eyes were closed and his arms stretched into the air. "So when is next time?" I asked.

His eyes opened and cut right through my armor. "Soon, I hope."

He walked me to the door and tried to ignore my incessant pleas that he did not need to accompany me down to my car. He finally conceded the offer after he realized there was no chance of changing my mind. He opened the door and our eyes locked, faces inches apart.

"I'm serious, when are we doing this again?" I asked. *Get your shit together, Mags. Stop being so desperate.*

I looked down at the floor and then lifted my head to meet his kind eyes. Everything came rushing back: the adrenaline, butterflies, my stomach twisting in knots. I hoped he felt the same.

The Matriarch

"What time are you getting up?" He joked. This bastard just said all the right things to me. I laughed as my body tingled. Cody grinned.

"Five a.m."

"So yeah, about that...it doesn't really work for my schedule so...maybe a different time?"

I pushed his shoulder at his teasing, but not without feeling how solid his upper body was. We both stared at one another, completely silent.

Cody's hand moved a strand of hair behind my ear. His palm lingered a moment longer and caressed the side of my face. I was melting. My heart rate increased. My breathing grew shallow.

Everything around me faded as he leaned in. His soft lips pressed into mine and I became weightless, floating on a cloud. His free hand went to my hip and then the small of my back as his tongue sank into my mouth, kissing me long and hard. *Fuck*. I was lightheaded and warm. I yearned for any bit of pain to let me know it was real. He finally released me, and I stared up into his green eyes once more.

"Call me." I winked.

An inexplicable feeling rippled through my entire body as I strode down the hallway. My face was bright pink and warm. I had a constant urge to squeal and giggle. Excitement, mystery, intrigue, euphoria, hope, happiness: none were strong enough words to describe my feelings. I turned the corner and caught him staring at me. My heart fluttered as I pressed the button on the elevator.

Even after the dinner and the kiss that took my breath away, I couldn't shake a worry that had lodged itself in the pit of my stomach. *This will not end well.*

The Matriarch

chapter twenty
chief justice ramirez

Clouds blocked the stars over the Capitol skyline and a chill wind bit at me, reminding me it was almost autumn. I crossed between two buildings after leaving my office. It was one in the morning and the wife and kids would not forgive me for losing track of time again.

I strolled behind a building, tossing two empty Starbucks cups in a dumpster.

"Hello, Your Honor." I froze and did a one-eighty. The voice sent a chill of horror through my body.

"Who is that?" I kept turning, brick buildings swirling in my vision, but nobody was there.

Footsteps echoed through the shadows and a metallic noise clanked to my ears, like a lead pipe tapping on bricks. My hands started to shake, knees quaking, knocking into one another.

"Oh, just a young man." The voice was raspy and cold as the night. A silhouette emerged from the shadows. A streetlight illuminated a face covered in pale white makeup.

I started to run but the sounds in the shadows froze me dead in my tracks. Goosebumps sprouted on my forearms and the hair on my neck stood at attention.

"What do you want?" I stared as his face came into view, painted like a skull, eyeing me like a hunter after its prey. A large "A" with a circle partially around it was on one cheek. His purple hair formed sharp spikes, pointing in all directions.

"To send a message."

More metallic clanking sounds shot down the alley, as if there were an army behind the ghoul with

The Matriarch

the painted face. Laughter and voices chimed in but only the lone man was visible.

"I have a wife and children." My voice quavered.

"I know. And so do others." He moved closer. My legs began to wobble as the haunted face now stood inches away. His irises were pale white.

My fear turned to anger. "You're nothing but a punk criminal."

The man stood there and stared up at the street light.

"No, Your Honor. The criminals—" He reached out and ran his hand along the lapel of my jacket. "—they wear suits." His hand wrapped around my throat, crushing my wind pipe.

My eyes were wide. I could barely breathe as I saw at least thirty men surrounding me from the shadows. I squirmed and clawed at him, trying to break free, but his hand wrenched tighter around my throat. A group of his thugs stepped out into the light.

"You see, we are born with inalienable rights in this country." He squeezed my throat tighter and his fingers crushed my wind pipe completely. "A right to privacy."

I squirmed and his hand clamped around my neck with more force.

"Some of us, well, we think that's pretty important." He nodded, halfway laughing as he watched me paw at his grip.

My eyes began to close and he released me. Frigid air burned as it rushed into my lungs. I coughed and spat on the ground, clutching my throat.

"Who, who are you?" I managed to speak while gasping for air. "You're him aren't you? The nutjob leader? Kaos?"

"That's the rumor." Kaos stalked away, taking a large steel blade by the handle from one of the other men.

The Matriarch

Unadulterated fear shot through my veins, into my chest, causing my heart to race. I began to claw at the ground, kicking my legs at the pavement, trying to scoot across the cement. My back slammed into a pair of legs. I stared up at 20 more goons standing behind Kaos with their arms all folded. Their skeletal faces were further masked by scowls.

"These are just kids. You're brain washing them. They don't know any better."

"Oh, they know plenty. It's you who sold out to the dollar, to corporate interests. You sold these men into indentured servitude. For what?"

He towered over me, pulled a piece of paper from his pocket and slapped at it with the large blade, laughing.

"A lake house in 2007? Private school for, what, what's this say here?" Kaos turned to the man next to him.

"Oh, Jimmy. Little Jimbo. Good for him." He leaned down into my face. "Education is, umm, *very* very important. Oh, and Beatrice. Who names their kid *Beatrice*? Are you trying to get that girl's ass kicked at school every day?"

"It's a family name." I snarled, sure I was as good as dead. "Where did you get this information?"

"Oh, well. It's not so fun when someone else goes through your personal information, now is it, *Judge*?" He smiled as the moonlight passed through some clouds and cast a spotlight on a set of bright white teeth.

"What else? Let's see, a prized horse named Renfro." He paused and started to cough, choking on his laughs. "Five hundred — does, does, does that say thousand?" He handed the paper to the other man who stared at me with a terrifying gaze and nodded his head.

The Matriarch

"Five hundred thousand dollars. *For a horse*." He screamed in my face as the blade pressed to my cheek. "Oh, pardon me, Your Honor. I have a temper sometimes." His voice was back to a calm tone.

"H-how do you know all that?"

"You see, judge—" He shook his head back and forth. "—We are the next generation of this country. Unlike your own, we embrace change. We adapt, we learn things, and we grew up with technology. We are proficient at using it. While you and your old rich fucking buddies moan about your smart phones, and plug away your personal shit into 1s and 0s that we — well, we know how to find it."

Kaos smiled, scratching the blade on his own cheek. "Well, we can't hang out here all night, Your Honor. Change is in the air and we are busy men. Can you smell it?"

He inhaled deeply as I shrank away. "We do have one last question. Was it all worth it? The umm, the umm, the money and the horse and the house and the school?"

I looked down at the ground, a sob welling up in my throat. "No."

"I didn't think so. But you see, death is a strong — what's a good word — umm, well, it's a good way to make people change behavior. You see, if we let you live, nobody will find out about this. You'll be back to selling my brothers out for tickets to a private box at the Nationals' game, while their families *starve*."

One of his goons grabbed my right forearm and Kaos pushed the blade into my palm. Blood poured from the wound. Kaos cupped his free hand over my mouth. I screamed for help into his hand and the cold bastard grinned wider. Pain radiated up my arm and into my shoulder. He twisted the blade as it drilled through my hand. I kicked and fought, but it only

The Matriarch

made it worse. He finally pulled it out and wiped the blood from both sides of the blade on my shirt.

"We'll see how many opinions you write with that hand now. Oh wait, we're, we're going to kill you. I guess that was completely unnecessary." His laugh was a terrifying melody that echoed down the walls of the alley. "So sorry, Your Honor."

Kaos put the blade to his own throat and looked at me.

"You see, I would have taken this blade to myself a long time ago, but you took that right away from me before I was ever born."

He handed the knife back to one of his goons and started to walk away. He paused momentarily and then turned back to me and walked over. He bent down in front of me, staring into my eyes like he was searching for my soul.

His hand reared back at an intense speed and I winced, covering my face. Kaos reached into my pocket for my phone.

"We wouldn't want to leave you with this, now. Would we? You might try to call and warn someone."

He punched a few buttons on my phone and then held it up and smiled really big as the flash went off. He tapped the screen a few more times and handed the phone to one of the men holding a lead pipe.

"Stay here with him. Wait for further instruction." His voice sounded normal, as if he hadn't just butchered me in front of an audience.

"What are you doing? Where are you going?"

"Oh, we'll be in touch. Very soon."

My eyes were purple, my nose cracked and slanted as the men continued to beat me relentlessly in the

The Matriarch

corner of the alley. The pain had faded long ago. I was limp, broken. A lead pipe whistled through the air and smashed into my already shattered knee cap once more. I barely flinched at the blow as my body slouched against the wall. Only one eye hung open. Everything was blurry. Sounds mixed together. My ears rang and my body felt disconnected, torn apart. It sent pangs of nausea to my stomach.

Some punk song started to blare from my phone in one of their pockets. He pulled it out and chuckled. He placed it in my palm and it fell to the ground as I tried to hold it.

The man laughed harder.

"Got some real problems, motherfucker?"

He held it up in front of my lazy eye. I barely made out Kaos's smiling picture flashing on the screen for a video call. The goon accepted the call and Kaos appeared on the screen. The dim green light illuminated his skull makeup. Rustling bushes sounded like static coming from the phone speaker.

"Oh, hey there judge. You're looking good." He laughed. I wanted to die. "Check this out. I think you'll enjoy what technology can do. Thanks a lot Internet." He snickered, holding the phone out to a mailbox with my address stenciled on it.

I began to squirm and attempted to scream, but loud, muffled gurgles were all that escaped my lips.

Kaos flipped the phone back around to his face and pressed a finger to his lips. "The phone is on mute. Nobody can hear you. Now if you'll excuse me—" He held the blade up to the camera and ran it through his spiked hair. "—I have some guests to entertain."

The phone went blank and I flopped around like a fish out of water.

I mumbled a few inaudible words and the men leaned in, trying to make them out. I tried to speak

The Matriarch

again but the words didn't sound right. My mouth didn't work.

"I think he just said, 'kill me'." The goon looked to the other.

They looked into my eyes and huge grins covered their faces.

"In time, Your Honor."

The Matriarch

The Matriarch

THE BATHORY DAILY NEWS

SUPREME COURT JUSTICE TORTURED, KILLED

BY: JIM BRISTOL

CAPITOL CITY - It is a day of mourning in the nation's capital today as word of Justice Ramirez's death and the murder of his family spread through town. Prominent lawmakers, lobbyists, and other government workers held moments of silence as they reflected on the 20 years of service the former judge gave the city. The president issued a statement and ordered that flags be flown at half-mast.

"This senseless act of violence and the riots spurred on by enemies of the state are not the way a healthy democracy functions. You can rest assured that we are devoting every resource we have to apprehending these terrorists and holding them accountable for their actions. Our thoughts and prayers are with the Ramirez family and others who have suffered at the hands of this group."

Sources who wished to remain anonymous tell us that Ramirez left his office sometime after midnight and was murdered two blocks away. Preliminary autopsy reports show that he was severely beaten and stabbed before he was killed. Residents in the area woke to a horrifying sight the next morning as he was erected on a cross, his corpse crucified next to a streetlight at Fifth and Main Street downtown. The following message was hung over his head:

The Matriarch

01001010011101010111001101110100011010010110 0
0110110010101001001
0111001101010011011001010111001001110110011001
0101100100

It reads "Justice Is Served" in binary code, the low-level language in which microprocessors are given instructions. Authorities who responded to Ramirez's house described the scene as something out of a horror movie. His wife and two children were tortured and their bodies mutilated, along with a five hundred thousand dollar prize horse. G3n3rat1on of Ka0s, a rogue hacktivist group, have claimed responsibility for the murders on their website and social media accounts, calling them a "wake up call" to the country and a "defense of liberty." Ka0s, the leader of the group, has asserted that they are "just getting started" and that "no leader who directly infringes on a citizen's right to privacy and freedom is safe from their reach."

The Matriarch

chapter twenty one

blake jackson

"Bring him to me." Kiril stared at the security guard.

"Sir." The guard turned and hustled down the hallway.

"How did this happen?" Kiril turned to me.

"We are still looking into it." I stared at the wall, avoiding his gaze.

"What was compromised?"

"We are still investigating that as well."

"What do you know?" He loomed over me. I gulped. The amount of money he paid me wasn't enough for the fear I encountered at work every day. But nobody ever quit. That was a death sentence. As Chief Technology Officer, I knew far too much about his security and the sophistication of the network that communicated his secret activities.

"As of now we know data was extracted from a secured hard drive and left the premises." My voice cracked.

Kiril pressed the tip of his fedora up to reveal a bit more of the bandages on his face.

"Any Family business?"

I looked at the ground.

"So yes?"

"It-it is possible, yes."

"That is very troubling."

My hands were shaking. I couldn't believe this fucker brought some whore to the office. My life was at risk. I'd heard the stories about people who fucked up. It never ended well. They just disappeared.

The guard shoved William through the door and when he saw Kiril he turned to run. The guard froze him in his tracks and he turned back, pale as a ghost.

"Thank you for joining us." Kiril looked at me then back to William.

"S-sir."

"This is our CTO, Blake Jackson. He has questions for you."

"We believe data was extracted from the secured drive at your workstation. Any idea how this could happen?" I knew exactly how it happened. We'd seen the recording.

"What? *No*. That's impossible."

"Is it?" Kiril inched toward him. I felt a little sorry for William.

"*No*. This is outrageous. I would never—"

Kiril slammed William's back to the ground and sank a knee in his throat. William coughed hard, gasping for air.

Kiril wrapped his fingers around William's throat and brought him to his feet as he stood. Kiril slid his victim up the wall. William's legs dangled beneath.

"Who were you with?"

"Nobody, I swear—"

His lips turned pale blue as Kiril squeezed him harder.

"Who did you bring here?"

"A woman. Just some whore. I fucked her in the office, but then we left. I swear."

"What was her name?" His voice rang off the walls.

"Ger—Gret—uhh, Gretchen. We were only here for thirty minutes tops, I swear."

Kiril signaled to the guard who pulled up a security photograph of the red-headed woman on Will's computer monitor.

The Matriarch

"Her?" He pointed at the monitor as William squinted his eyes, peering at the screen.

"Yeah, that's her."

"Did you leave her alone?"

"No—"

Sweat dripped from his pores as he shuddered in front of Kiril.

"Okay, okay. I left for a minute to go to the bathroom, but that's it."

Kiril nodded to the security guard who clicked the mouse. It showed the woman crouched over. She was alone, inserting a thumb drive into the computer.

"That *bitch*." Will clenched his fists.

"You were reckless. You endangered my business." Kiril backed him into the corner of the office. Will cowered against the wall.

"Please. I didn't know, I swear."

Kiril turned to me. "Many secrets were on that computer. Was it connected to the network?"

I nodded to him, unable to watch.

"How did she know it was this hard drive?"

"That is a good question, sir." I shrugged, still wincing at Will.

"Investigate. Find out."

A streak of urine ran down the inner leg of Will's khakis as Kiril turned and faced him.

"It's good that you fear me." Kiril snarled.

He drew two knives from his waist beneath his suit coat and twirled them in his fingers before bringing them to a halt on Will's neck. Blood oozed around the tip of the blades that barely penetrated his skin.

"You *should* fear me." Kiril cocked his head sideways and stared into William's eyes, exhaling inches from his face.

Blood sprayed across the room as he ripped the blades across Will's neck and pinned his chest against

The Matriarch

the wall with his hand. Will's white dress shirt saturated with crimson as he bled out in front of everyone. I shuddered, afraid I might vomit as I turned my head to avoid seeing Will's corpse. Kiril released him and the body slid down the wall and collapsed on the floor.

He spun the blades and holstered them, turning to the guard.

"Get him out of here."

Kiril sauntered toward me, my eyes hidden by my palms.

"Find out what happened."

"Y-yes sir."

The security guard grabbed his walkie talkie while Kiril strode out of the room.

"Yes. Need body removal, room 248."

The Matriarch

chapter twenty two

maggie madison

I sat in front of my keyboard, rummaging through the directory full of PDF files and images, all legal documents and meticulous notes.

"No, no, no." The light from my computer was giving me a headache and frustrating the shit out of me.

"Hey Mags, didn't even hear you come in. How was your date?" Grandpa's voice always made me smile. But I was too tired to respond.

I had my elbow propped on the desk, face in my palm.

"Not well?" grandpa asked.

"What? No, the date was amazing. I got a goodnight kiss." I swooned in my chair for a second and realized what I was doing.

Grandpa's eyebrows arched.

"And before you ask, I was a good girl. Just a kiss."

"Well, what the hell then? Why do you look like someone killed your...favorite pair of shoes or something?" It got a laugh out of me. *I do love my shoes.*

"Going through the drive from the other night. There is so much data."

"Ahh, the paper chase."

"He is trying to buy Cody's business. Cody has no idea. Shit is getting complicated already."

"What's it say?"

"I don't know. I need to have one of the scientists look at it. All kinds of research studies and paperwork for a term sheet, angel investing, ran through a dummy corp. Why the hell would he want a hippie medicine business?"

The Matriarch

The documents were all marked 'secret' as I scrolled through.

"He's offering ten times what that business is worth, and it has Cody's brother and sister's name on the legal documents. They own fifty-one percent of the company."

"Look at that shit." Grandpa's eyes bugged out as he pointed at the screen.

I followed his finger and my own eyebrows raised. A picture of the human anatomy filled the monitor. There were formulas and scientific jargon covering the page. I didn't understand it, but it was obviously a genetic experiment of some kind.

"What the fuck is he up to?" My mind raced, trying to figure out the puzzle. I'd have been lying if I said I wasn't a little excited at what I'd uncovered.

"He's bad news. Always has been," said Grandpa.

My eyes burned from looking at the computer for so long. Grandpa placed his hands on my shoulders and rubbed them softly. He looked down at me, his fingers trembling, concern in his eyes.

"I know...Holy shit, here we go, look."

Kiril had come a long way since his life of crime in Golem, but it was all about to catch up with him. He tried to appear legit but the files contained all of the correspondence between him and The Family. They discussed everything: drugs, extortion, trafficking of humans, racketeering, bookmaking. The sophisticated money laundering system they had in place was all documented with flowcharts and contingencies.

"That is powerful shit. I suggest you tread carefully." I could feel Grandpa's stare in the back of my head as I heard his words.

"I know...I know."

The Matriarch

The headquarters of Jackson Pharmaceuticals sat just outside of the downtown skyline, directly adjacent to a major interstate. I steered the Model S into a parking space at the front of the large manufacturing plant and tapped on my phone as the gadgets in the car shut down. I stared at the large glass rotating doors and the company logo chiseled out of granite. A soft cool breeze tossed my hair aside when I opened the door and stepped from the car.

A curved stainless steel archway greeted me as I passed through the revolving doors and stopped at security. A guard in uniform holding a black wand awaited me. I sat my purse and keys on a conveyor belt and walked through the metal detector, pausing as the guard waved the wand around me. Everyone had to be scanned, due to the proprietary research that took place in the labs. He motioned me past.

A man in a white lab coat stood waiting as I grabbed my things and walked to him.

"Sorry to bother you, Dr. Ranosz. I'm sure you're busy."

"No, no, come with me. We always look forward to you visiting." He glanced to my heels clacking on the marble floor down a long corridor. Offices and large meeting rooms flanked us on both sides. "Besides, you usually have something interesting."

Balfour Capital owned a substantial percentage of Jackson and I sat on their board of directors. I knew he was kissing my ass and feigning interest, but I needed to pick his brain.

He showed me to a lab. It was frigid and filled with expensive microscopes and centrifuges lining the pristine, stainless steel surfaces against the wall. A long dry erase board with notes and equations

The Matriarch

spanned one side of the room. Formaldehyde and bleach enveloped my nose and I swore I could feel it on my skin. I pulled out the thumb drive and he brought up the files on his laptop.

After a few moments of study punctuated with "ohs" and head scratching, he finally formulated a thought. "These are formulas for biologic processes. Anabolic in nature. Wow. This is cutting edge stuff." His excitement grew as he studied the documents. "DNA and RNA splicing, protein instructions..."

"Does it look functional?"

"Not at this time. It's highly unethical. This type of research is in its infancy, certainly not even close to a human testing phase. Where did you get this?"

I glowered and he knew better than to press further.

"Understood."

"Hypothetically, why would someone with this info be after a natural medicine store?"

"Well, assuming they are testing on humans and trying to mitigate side effects, they may be searching for natural supplements. The body can sometimes absorb them better, more efficiently. If they can find natural ways to combat the side effects of a developed drug, they can administer them simultaneously and mitigate risk. I have to warn you though, this level of chemical would make someone capable of seemingly superhuman feats of strength and agility. The effects on a human would be...well, highly variable, and extreme. Possibly fatal."

"Thank you, doctor."

"Anytime."

"As always, I trust you'll exercise discretion with what we've discussed?"

"Absolutely, Ms. Balfour. I'm always glad to help."

What did Kiril want with this drug? An army of super soldiers? I wasn't sure what disturbed me

The Matriarch

more: him with an army, or him testing it on children.

The Matriarch

The Matriarch

THE BATHORY DAILY NEWS

KIRIL ARRESTED: CONNECTIONS TO THE FAMILY, UNLAWFUL GENETIC TESTING REVEALED

BY: JIM BRISTOL

BATHORY CITY - Documents released to this paper show that the CEO of Salzberg Industries has deep connections to The Family and planned to build an army of super soldiers. The thumb drive, released by Kaos, contains a cache of legal documents and scientific research.

Kiril has spent the better part of a decade distancing himself from shady organizations and criminal activity, appearing to do legitimate business through various corporations. New information reveals illegal activity to be a significant source of income, funneling through various shell corporations and complicated money laundering schemes involving charitable enterprises. Most disturbing was the scientific research being carried out on orphans and impoverished children, and the associated documents that indicated the plan to build an army of super soldiers. Further motives are still unknown.

Kaos released the following statement:

"We continue to fight for the poor, expose corruption, liberate humans and reveal their ability to remain autonomous in their decision making. Freedom is a cherished right, and while many may not agree with our violent methods of attaining our goals, they must still hold these values and ways of

The Matriarch

life dear. Kiril is a self-serving criminal, a parasite who feeds on those less fortunate, much like our elected officials and business leaders. There is no room in a liberated society for any of these vile, sub-human creatures."

Police served warrants at Salzberg Industries early this morning and took him into custody without incident. His trial date and formal charges have not yet been released. We will continue to update you as this story progresses.

chapter twenty three

maggie madison

"What the hell? Where did he get that information?" I stared at Grandpa.

"I don't know, but look at his eyes."

I glanced up to the picture of Kaos paused on the screen. His eyes were lifeless, his face hidden behind the layers of pale makeup. It sent a shudder up my spine.

"He makes me cringe."

"That is a dangerous man, Mags."

"He's another thug. Just like the rest of them."

"Don't underestimate a man focused on an idea. Men corrupted by greed, power; they can be manipulated. That man is pure evil. He doesn't feel a goddamn thing."

I'd been unable to obtain any information on Kaos. He came out of nowhere and had a huge following. I'd exhausted all my resources trying to locate IP addresses, search databases not available to the public, contacts within various criminal enterprises. Nothing. It all led one place, a dead end.

"At least that other fucker is behind bars."

Grandpa sipped a cup of coffee. "Not enough of them if you ask me."

"It's one problem off my plate for now."

"Oh, is the Matriarch gonna take a day off? Wanna hang out with the ol' man?"

"I wish. Have a hot date."

"Oh." He perked up. "With apron boy?"

I turned away and blushed.

"Maybe."

Grandpa leaned down and placed a hand on my shoulder.

The Matriarch

"Good for you, baby girl. You deserve it."

"I love you." I smiled.

"Oh, I love you too, sweetie." He hugged me tightly around the neck and gave me a peck on the cheek.

Large skyscrapers surrounded us on all sides as I sat in the park with Cody. He'd promised me a picnic. Birdsong rained down from the trees and children squealed at a playground in the distance. I couldn't stop staring into his emerald green eyes as he constantly brushed his copper mop of hair from his face.

"What is this? No-apron Wednesday?" I giggled.

He bent down and kissed me on the cheek. Stubble dotted his jawline and brushed against me as he pulled away. My arms and legs tingled at his touch.

"Maybe."

We sat next to each other on the cloth blanket. I ran my hand through the needles of the familiar grass, remembering the feeling when I came here as a child. Opening the basket, Cody pulled out some fruit and an assortment of cheeses.

"Where's the—"

He silenced me with a finger to my lips, pulling out a bottle of wine and two glasses.

"You think of everything don't you?"

"I try," he said. "Here, I grew this in my greenhouse."

I eyed the bottle of wine, but allowed him to feed me a strawberry to amuse him. Sweet flavors filled my mouth as it melted into my tongue. I wasn't a big fan of fruit, or vegetables for that matter, but it was by far the best strawberry I'd ever tasted. I

The Matriarch

immediately motioned for him to give me another before I'd finished the first.

"So good." My mouth was full as I spoke and Cody laughed.

"All organic. None of that crap from the grocery store."

He always seemed to take pride in everything he did, down to the very fine details. I admired him for that. He didn't think of things as chores, or tasks that needed to be completed. Everything had his own personal touch and care infused into it.

"Wine?"

I'd completely forgotten about it already.

I nodded. "You trying to get me day drunk? Take advantage of me?"

"Yes." He grinned. *That fucking grin of his.*

He sat down on his side, elbow digging in the ground, and propped his head with his hand as he poured my glass with the other. I couldn't stop staring at his face.

"Now, you were going to tell me about you this time."

I tensed up and he took notice.

"You don't have to."

"It was that obvious, huh?"

"A bit." He looked down at the blanket.

I hated this. I'd been dreading the moment, hoping he wouldn't bring it up. Telling him the truth was impossible, but I didn't want to lie either. My throat constricted. I tried to get a few words out.

"Just one memory. A good one. Surely you have one?"

My eyes went to the sky and then back to him.

"Okay, I've got one. It probably doesn't seem like a big deal, but it was a day just like today, in this park. Me and my family were having a picnic too. Nothing special happened or anything like that. It was just me

The Matriarch

and my brother playing, looking back at our parents. They looked like the two of us, on a blanket. It was just a really good day."

"So do you talk to them often?"

"Who?"

"Your parents or your brother? Sounds like you were close."

It all rushed back. I couldn't breathe and my eyes welled up. I'd worked long and hard to form a barrier to my past and he was crashing through it. He was getting close. Too close.

"I'm sorry. I'm sorry, you don't have to answer that. Shit."

Heat flooded into my cheeks and I wanted to tell him everything. I just couldn't. Grandpa and I never discussed them. The sky was closing in on me and it was like I was being forced into a tiny box. My clammy hands pawed at my legs.

"I'm so sorry." I jumped to my feet and took off around the corner, leaving Cody in a daze. I glanced over my shoulder and saw Cody sitting, mouth agape, staring at me as I ran away.

I flew around the corner and up the road, drawing looks from strangers as I sprinted across the street.

I fished in my pocket for my cell phone and tapped at the screen.

"Mags?"

"Yeah, it's me, can you come pick me up?" I clutched my chest.

"Be right there." The phone grew silent for a second and I could still hear him breathing. "Where is there?"

"I'll text you."

When he hung up I sent him the address. Fifteen minutes later he pulled up the road.

I'd calmed a little but my airway still felt constricted. The harder I tried to breathe the worse it

The Matriarch

became. I stepped into the car, obviously a wreck and hurting.

"Where is that apron wearing pussy? I'll fuck his shit up!"

I panted heavily and attempted to muster some words. I grabbed Grandpa's shoulder and pulled my face into it.

He gripped the steering wheel tight, still ready to hand Cody an ass whipping.

"He didn't do anything. It's me."

He grabbed me around the neck and I pressed the side of my face to his chest. He caressed my hair.

"What happened?"

"He just — he asked about Mom and Dad and Kyle and I just lost it. I just got up and ran away. I tried to talk but I couldn't."

My head raised and I saw Grandpa's bright red face.

"I'm broken. I'm so messed up. It was just a wave of guilt and horror. We never talk about them."

"I'm so sorry, sweetheart. I know. We should talk about them more."

My torso trembled. Every repressed memory, every feeling, every emotion surfaced at once after years of being pushed way down. I hated myself for letting it get to me. I hated myself for liking Cody so much.

"I ruined it. He hates me now. I just ran away."

"No, shh. No, baby girl. He doesn't hate you. I promise."

"I can't tell him the truth. And I want to so bad, Grampy. I don't want to lie to him. I want to be with him. He's perfect and treats me good."

"He better." Grandpa mumbled under his breath but kept his eyes fixed on me.

Pain shot into my chest like a dagger digging down into my guts once more.

The Matriarch

"I did something awful this morning. Something he'll hate me for."

Grandpa knew the tone in my voice. It was the tone I used when I did something he wouldn't approve of.

"What'd you do?"

"Something terrible."

I didn't want to tell him and he wasn't forcing the issue. He ran his fingers through my hair and stared at me again.

"Look at me, Mags. I know you two haven't been dating all that long, but if he really cares about you, it won't matter. You might fight or argue, but if cares about you, he'll forgive you."

I nodded.

I opened the car door and stepped out, composing myself in the street and drawing in a huge breath. Relief rushed through me. I knew Grandpa was right. I just needed to hear him say it.

"Thank you."

"What the hell? You have me drive out here and don't need a ride?" His cheeks were rosy again and he smiled with a huge set of teeth.

"I need to go back." I grinned.

"I know. Get out of here."

"I love you."

"Love you too, Mags."

I closed the door and Grandpa hammered the pedal. The tires smoked and squealed on the pavement as the car howled down the road.

"You son of a—" I stood there wide-eyed.

A hand was in the air through the rear window and waved goodbye.

I smiled as I wandered back to the park. It was one of the longest walks of my life. I'd only been gone about twenty minutes but it seemed like an eternity.

The Matriarch

When I walked back into the park Cody sat on the blanket. His face was in both palms. I took another deep breath before heading over.

I stopped ten feet behind him as he stared out at some kids playing.

"I'm sorry."

His head whipped around and he smiled before growing serious. I started toward him and he leapt from the ground and ran to me.

"No, no, it's okay. I'm sorry for asking questions and—"

My lips interrupted him and my fingernails ran along his scalp, nestling my palm on the side of his neck. I pulled back and stared into those beautiful green eyes.

"You didn't do anything wrong, my life is just...well, it's complicated."

"If you ever do want to talk about it. I'm here. But you don't have to say anything you don't want."

"Thank you."

He pushed my hair back from my face. I grinned.

"You're beautiful. You're a beautiful person." He kept smiling at me. Why was he making me fall so hard for him? It was not a good idea.

The ridge of my nose began to tingle.

His eyes were still locked on mine. "You need to know that."

The Matriarch

The Matriarch

chapter twenty four
john salenger

We walked up to the prison in our federal uniforms. Everything was legit. All the fine details double and triple checked. That's how our leader operated.

I had joined for a cause. It pained me to wear this government uniform but it was for the mission. Kaos was changing the country for the better. Sometimes you gotta break some eggs to make an omelet.

"You ready?"

Brandon looked at his watch and nodded. "Let's do it."

We walked to the front door, my heart beating a million miles an hour. I'd feel better about everything once our badges worked. Two large officers stood guard. It was all simple if everything went according to plan.

We were both vets. Served our country with honor and distinction. Sold out by politicians. Sure, we were angry. Angry as fuck. Our own representatives had thrown us under the bus for their own gain.

The guard halted us when we neared.

"Inmate transport." I steadied my hands as he eyed my badge. They nodded at our federal credentials and motioned us through.

"What's the bag for?" The guard eyed Brandon. He would've eyed him more if he knew what we were about to do. Who we were.

"We have our own restraints. It's precautionary."

"Carry on." The guard was stern but his hands twitched the second he'd seen we were feds.

Once inside the layout was just as we'd been told. Two doors up on the left is where we needed to go.

The Matriarch

We strode down the expansive hall with solid white walls and tile. Our boots squeezed against the shiny surface. We got to the door and stopped. Brandon looked in all directions. "Clear."

We opened the door to the utility closet and snuck in, closing the door behind us. I pulled a flashlight from the bag and clicked it on. Light filled the room. Racks of cleaning supplies were on two sides. "Here it is."

He pulled a handle and moved the temp wall. Inside was an expanse roughly four feet wide with pipes running overhead. He nodded in the direction we needed to go. "Yeah, that's it."

We ran between the walls, ducking down to avoid hitting our heads on the metal cylinders above us. It was all too easy. Adrenaline coursed through my veins. Who would have thought? This is how I would make a difference. Serve my country.

We got to the spot and B worked his magic. He was once a demolitions expert in the Army. He pulled the beige blocks of soft plastic from the bag and stuck them to the wall, eyeing his watch carefully. One fuck up and he'd kill everyone inside. He pushed in metal pins with wires attached to them and we moved beyond the blast radius, flat against the wall like we were trained.

The wall was cold on my back as my eyes pinched shut. I clawed at the frigid surface behind me. B eyed his watch, his finger on the button.

"Two, one—"

My ears were ringing and debris filled the air. I never even heard the explosion.

We ducked through the hole. Alarms grew louder as my hearing returned.

"Come on!" I motioned to Kiril. He was as terrifying as he'd been described with his bandages.

The Matriarch

Two poor bastards were on the ground in jump suits, not moving. I don't know if he killed them or we did.

Kiril followed through the hole and into the narrow passage. We hauled ass to the closet door we came through just moments before.

"Hold out your hands."

Kiril offered his hands I pulled out a set of silver handcuffs and clapped them on his wrists. B held his ear close to the door when we got there, listening to the other side.

"Clear."

He opened it as flashlight haze shined through the big ass hole we just blew in the wall back behind us. We stepped into the hallway as guards hauled ass towards Kiril's cell. We beat at our clothes to get the dust and debris off. Kiril's jumpsuit was easy to wipe off, thank god. I cringed at his face while my hands swiped at the orange material.

When we reached the end there was an office. Inside a guard sat on the other side of a large pane of glass. He was shaken all to shit and on the phone with someone.

I rapped hard on the glass to get his attention. "Transfer to federal facility." I kept my voice calm and stern but my knees were shaking like a motherfucker.

"I didn't hear anything about him leaving. We just went into lockdown."

"Check the database. These orders are from the attorney general." I saw B eyeing his watch when nobody was watching. Kiril stood as if nothing important were happening. Steady as a rock.

"I don't give a fuck who the orders came from. Nobody leaves."

B pulled a sidearm with a silencer and double tapped him as glass rained down to the floor. Kiril smiled at the blood.

The Matriarch

I jumped over the counter and kicked the corpse in his chair. He rolled up against the wall as I hit the button to disengage the locks.

We ran Kiril through the door. An unmarked white van without windows sat running out front as promised. I opened the door and Kiril stepped in as we slammed it shut behind him and crawled into the front.

As we drove away, I looked in the rear view mirror. There in the back sat Kaos with a devilish smile on his face.

.

The Matriarch

chapter twenty five

maggie madison

I picked at the salad with my fork, unable to pierce the lettuce I'd been stabbing for the past forty-five seconds while staring at Cody. I'd never been so vulnerable to a man's stare, his green eyes always studying me, learning more about me.

Garlic and basil wafted into my nose and I looked around the Italian restaurant. It was family-owned and tucked in the corner of a shopping center. The owners had greeted Cody like family at the door when we'd arrived. Pictures with various celebrities were plastered along a wall. I'd never heard of the place. Sepia-stained concrete floors ran beneath our feet and amplified the smallest sounds. Everything was wrapped in maroon and cream checkered linens, even the silverware. It gave the place an upscale feel for a hole-in-the-wall joint.

"How was your day?" Cody's grin ate through my armor of feelings as usual.

"Long." My eyelashes fluttered.

What was it about him? His eyes, or facial features, or movements? He was so young at heart, but still rugged and strong. He was nice and gentle to everyone he came into contact with. Worry still struck me every time I was around him. I knew it couldn't last, but I didn't want to give it up.

I could kill just about anyone in the room with my bare hands, but he still made me feel safe. Cody was truly an enigma. A fucking hot one.

"Well, it probably wasn't longer than any other day." He leaned back with a grin on his face, proud of his witty comeback.

The Matriarch

"Time is relative." I fidgeted with my fork some more and mumbled. "Smart-ass."

"What was that?"

"Huh?" I grinned.

"You said something. What was it?"

"I said *smart-ass*."

He reached over and took my fork, replacing it with his hand as I felt the smallest of vibrations in his fingertips.

"You can call me a smart-ass out loud."

My face flushed and I uncrossed my feet under the table and stood to lean in a little closer, and then closer, until I was only a foot from his face, still standing on my side of the table.

"Smart-ass." I winked.

I kept trying to figure him out. To figure out this whole ordeal. Where was it going? What were we doing? I knew one thing. I'd never felt like this about anyone before. Butterflies were constantly in my stomach. I was too nervous to talk. Hell, to breathe. I judged every move that I made. Played everything in my head over and over.

My little wink just now was the first time I'd felt successful flirting with Cody. Yet the awkwardness drew me in, made me want him more. I slowly moved back down to my chair, still staring at his sculpted face when my ass barely missed the edge of my chair and I went straight to the floor, shrieking on the way down.

The next five seconds were the longest of my life, sitting there on the cold concrete. I wanted to make a run for it, but Cody was in my face before I could take a breath.

"Are you okay?" His face was serious, but I could tell he was holding back a laugh.

I sat there, flat on my ass, mortified as people gawked at me with their mouths open. I looked up

The Matriarch

and my eyes met his again. I froze. Words tried to form but they couldn't escape my lips.

Cody stared back at me, his hand in my hair.

At the same time we both smiled. I started to giggle and it turned into full-blown laughter. Cody stared briefly before chuckling with me.

He leaned down and kissed me on the forehead, helping me to my feet. I covered my mouth and it didn't help. I couldn't tell if it was actually funny at this point or the only way my body knew how to cope with the utter embarrassment. Every time I tried to speak I laughed harder.

Cody looked around the room and could see people snickering.

"It's okay folks, nothing to see over here." He grinned.

The waiter came over to check on us and Cody handed him his credit card.

"Please get us out of here." He locked his eyes on mine.

I still held my hand over my mouth. My face was beet red but I was able to speak.

"I just, I cannot—"

Cody wrapped his arm around my waist. "Well, that's probably enough small talk for one evening."

I leaned up near his ear. "Thank you."

He placed his hands on my cheeks, pushed my head back, and stared in my eyes. "You're perfect."

Everything else faded when he told me that.

Held up by puppet strings, I stood there, floating on air.

The waiter hurried over, cutting my moment in the clouds short.

"Here you are, sir. Just the drinks."

"Oh my god. We didn't even order yet?" I could feel how red my cheeks were.

The Matriarch

"Don't worry. I know something that suits you better." He chuckled like he had a plan.

I stood in the street, elbow resting on the stainless steel hot dog cart as Cody tucked a third napkin into my blouse.

"Can I eat yet?" I stared at him, trying not to giggle.

"Almost done Rebekah-proofing you. Just one more second here, and — done!" He took a step back as I held my hot dog away from my body. Three napkins sprouted from my neckline and covered my top.

"It's about time. Thought I was going to starve to death!"

"There's ketchup on that thing. Better safe than sorry." He pointed at my hot dog.

He snickered as I took a bite.

"Sorry, I know it's not the greatest place for a dinner date."

"Are you kidding me? This thing is awesome." I was talking with my mouth full of food again. *Shit*. I covered my mouth. "Sorry."

He stared at me adoringly. "You just eat what you want whenever you want. Don't you? I swear it's like you don't know where your next meal is going to come from — I mean, I didn't mean it like that, just—"

"I wasn't born rich you know?"

We walked down the sidewalk while people passed, staring and giggling.

Cody shrugged. "No, I didn't."

The Matriarch

"I'm sorry. I still haven't told you much about me." I took another man-sized bite and caught myself chewing with my mouth open.

"It's okay. You don't have to."

"No, no. I'm fine. I was born here in Bathory. Lived here until I was 12."

Cody nodded. He rubbed his palms down his jeans. Hell, I'd be nervous too if I were him. I'd run off and left him last time. I was secretive and he seemed to respect that.

"My parents started taking us to church because they found god. Whatever that means. Before I knew it, we were moving to Golem to *help* people."

I finished off the hot dog and tossed the container in a garbage can along with my bib fashioned from napkins.

"I, umm, lost my family. Grew up on the streets until I was 19."

I didn't want to lie but there was no way I could tell the whole truth.

"Wow, I can't imagine. I'm sorry you had to go through that." He reached for my shoulder and pulled me close to him.

"You don't have to say anything else. It's okay."

I nudged him back to get a glimpse of his face.

"I want to tell you everything. It's just hard."
Goddamn it. You're going to get hurt letting him in. You're going to hurt him, too.

He pulled me back to his chest and placed his hand on my cheek.

"It's okay, I promise." He snaked his fingers through my hair.

I could see him racking his brain for anything to take my mind off things.

His eyes lit up. "Follow me. I want to show you something."

The Matriarch

His hand slid down my forearm. Our fingers interlocked as he pulled me toward the end of the street. The crisp air rushed over my cheeks.

We made our way down the street. A few people stood outside the buildings smoking. The smoke stung my nose and reminded me of Golem. Strangely, I missed it a little.

A few blocks down we turned and passed Cody's store. Rounding the corner, I could see we were heading to a clear building a little way off the main thoroughfare. Bright lights fought to shine through the plastic windows as we made our way to it.

"Is this yours?"

"Yep."

Vivid colors encapsulated me as I walked through the door, spinning to take it all in. Breathtaking tropical vines snaked up the walls: wisteria, blue sky, and coral. Huge blooming violets, birds of paradise, hibiscus, and calla lilies filled in the lighter greens with bright colors. I stopped to breathe in the natural bouquet.

"I don't get to show it off much. A lot of it is used for the business. Some for fun."

He walked over and picked a rich purple orchid and placed it in my hand.

My heart leapt from my chest. I'd never been given a flower before. My eyes closed as I pressed it to my face and took in the sweet smell.

"I love it."

"It suits you."

"The flower?" I stood there puzzled. How could a flower suit somebody?

"Yes."

"Why?"

He took my hand and walked over to the rest of the orchids.

The Matriarch

"Well, orchids are beautiful." He pushed my hair back. My spine tingled at his touch as I fought the urge to melt to the floor.

"But, they are very complex. Complicated. Delicate."

His words drew me closer to him. I wanted to hear him talk about everything.

"If they aren't treated properly, they die easily. But if you give them the attention they deserve and treat them right, they are absolutely stunning. They thrive."

He had me. I was overwhelmed by the beauty of this place, by him most of all.

I sat the orchid down on a table and walked to him. Our eyes locked, both oblivious to the world. He leaned down as my hand found his chest. His lively heart thumped against my palm.

"I'm not good at this."

"At what?"

"Being a girl."

He laughed.

"I'm serious."

He smiled at me once more.

I placed my palms back on his cheeks. "You don't understand. Nobody has ever said those kinds of things to me."

The air left his lungs as I watched him understand the truth in my words. I could see in his eyes that he felt bad for judging me too soon. If only he knew what I'd done. He'd know he was right to hate me from the start. But I couldn't tell him. Not now anyway. All I wanted was to be in his arms and it made me sick to my stomach. It meant compromising everything I'd worked for, everything I was. I still didn't care.

The Matriarch

"I'm telling you now." He leaned in closer. My eyes squeezed shut as he moved to my lips. My hands pressed into his chest again and I leaned to his ear.

"I've never dated anyone."

"It's okay." He moved closer.

"I don't know what I'm doing."

"It's okay."

I started to say something else and his index finger pressed to my lips. He moved his finger. His soft, warm lips replaced it, and I tingled as they pressed against mine. Time stood still. My lips ghosted across his. One of my hands went to his shoulder, the other to his neck.

Our mouths parted into a slow, full, passionate kiss, velvet tongues intertwining. My face heated. My fingertips teased at the small hairs on his neck. His muscular hands shifted from my hips and wrapped around the small of my back, pulling me tight as our mouths remained locked on one another.

A tingling crept between my thighs and my knees began to tremble. Cody worked down my neck. I tilted my head back to the greenhouse ceiling, barely able to make out the stars through the translucent panes. The heat on my neck sprouted goosebumps on my skin. I sighed and ran my fingers through his hair.

He worked his way up, nibbling from collarbone to earlobe, stimulating every tiny nerve along the way. I ran my hand along the defined ridges of his shoulders. My nails traced his upper back as he increased the tempo, breathing heavily.

My eyes shot open and rolled back as he exhaled down my throat. Synapses fired and ripped through my body as my back arched into him. My thighs contracted. I saw the orchids and replayed Cody's voice in my mind, comparing me to the gorgeous, delicate flower. I was anything but a delicate flower. But tonight, for him, I would be.

The Matriarch

I gripped Cody's head, pulling it backward as I returned the favor, kissing down his neck and over his collarbone before biting softly on his ear. The side of my face nuzzled against his prominent cheek bones. My hips pressed into him and I felt his arousal growing. Mine was unavoidable as I panted into his ear, tasting his salty neck.

"Is this too fast?" he asked.

My face was on fire and the greenhouse was steaming up.

"I don't know. Do you want to stop?"

"God, no. Should we?"

"I don't know, should we?" I prayed he would take control.

His hands slid to my ass, gripping it firmly as a squeal escaped my lips.

"I don't think we should." His stubble teased my neckline.

His powerful fingers dug into my ass, yanking me into him. My senses were overloaded as his hard length pressed against my clit. He lifted me off the ground and I wrapped my legs around his hips. He sat me on top of the table, our lips locking once more as his erection bulged against me through layers of clothes. I gasped and pulled his face to mine.

We kissed hard and long, his tongue sinking into my mouth and dancing with mine. He paused, looking into my eyes.

"I want to go slow. I want to enjoy you as long as possible."

My heart melted along with my panties.

He reached behind him, pulling his shirt over his head, revealing a lean, chiseled frame that looked like a sculpture. Defined planes and muscles in all the right places, his abs were cut like square pieces of a puzzle. I didn't know how long I would be able to

The Matriarch

hold out as my fingernails grazed the ridges of his back, teasing him as he kissed down my nape.

His hands made their way to my breasts, squeezing my erect nipples between his fingers in rhythm with my moans. My arms lifted as he pulled my blouse over my head. He unclasped my bra and let it fall to the floor. His mouth explored my body and he brushed his knuckles against my warm skin, studying every inch I revealed.

I squeezed the inside of my arms into my breasts and they wrapped around his face. He eyed me intently, his hands gripping me, kneading my soft flesh. He laid me back on the table, working his way to my mouth. Our tongues swirled. In a torrent of ecstasy, I clawed at his back, digging my nails into hard muscle. Gripping my breasts firmly, his mouth dove to one, sucking forcefully as my head and arms arched backwards and my fingers gripped the back of the table.

I moaned as he spread my legs and pressed his hard length against me. His tongue circled around my tight nipple before lightly biting, tasting me as my breathing grew louder.

His grip remained on my breasts as his cock pressed against my pussy. I couldn't think anymore. All I could feel was him. His fingers worked lightly around my tight nipples and my breathing erupted in labored bursts. Waves of ecstasy shot from every limb, every angle into my clit.

He kissed down my stomach, every touch making me shudder. One of his hands slid to my inner thigh as his mouth hovered a fraction of an inch over my pants.

I'd never been this hot in my life, clawing at the table as his lips brushed against my tense pussy, perfectly pacing every move that he made.

The Matriarch

He looked up to my eyes, seemingly asking for my approval before his hands gripped at my waistline and pulled my pants down as I raised my hips from the table. My thighs quivered as the fabric slid down, leaving me in nothing but a pair of black lace panties cut halfway up the ass. Every touch sent chills through me as he moved back up my legs from the floor, getting to know my body intimately as I squeezed my breasts.

"Oh my god." I cooed as his stubble scratched past my knee and his tongue slid up my glistening thighs, tasting everything along the way.

"Do you want me to stop?"

I took a handful of his hair and pulled him closer to where I needed him, answering his question.

He pushed my panties aside and circled the tip of his stiff tongue around me, spreading my lips with his fingers and making contact with my clit.

I jolted on the table at his touch, tides of energy building inside me that I tried to hold back. He pressed his lips around my clit and began to suck it, working his tongue in lazy circles. My thighs instinctively squeezed, tremoring around his face as I quaked on his lips.

"Oh god." I put my hand to my mouth and moaned into it.

My fingers dug into his scalp, grasping the back of head as he fought back. I panted and moaned, harder and faster as he intensified the pattern, circling his tongue around me as I dripped down his chin. I lifted my head far enough to see my wetness on his jawline. He looked up at me.

"Fuck!"

Right when I was about to erupt, he slowed his pace, bringing me back down.

"Are you close?" He murmured against my hot skin.

The Matriarch

I glared at him and yanked his hair, pulling him back into me as hard as I could.

He gave in, stroking his tongue rapidly over me as the table began to shake. I knew he could feel my orgasm on the tip of his tongue. He slipped two fingers in to the hilt, angling them up and circling them rapidly over the ridge they found deep inside of me. He buried his face into my pussy and sucked my clit, his tongue frantically working it over.

I tried to scream but all I could do was gasp. My stiff legs locked around his face. "Fuck, *Cody*." I shook violently and my hips arched off the table as I came on his fingers, bucking my hips wildly with the electrical jolts that shocked my core. His mouth followed me, his tongue locked onto my clit.

Time stood still and my vision was a blur. A moment passed and everything came back into focus. Cody slowly slid his fingers out of me and breathed lightly on my swollen lips, watching me shudder as a chill ripped through my body.

"Just making sure you're alive." His eyes studied me.

My chest rose and fell in heaving breaths. I was totally spent.

Working up to my stomach, he kissed around my belly button, staring up into my eyes as the world returned to me. Breathing heavily, I lay there and tried to piece myself back together. I grinned.

I pulled him up to me and claimed his mouth. My breasts pressed into his chest and his hands ran through my hair. If there was a more perfect place to be, I didn't know where it was.

My fingers started working to his pants and he blocked them with his hand as he leaned away. He pushed a few sweaty strands of hair from my face and looked deep into my eyes.

The Matriarch

"It's about you tonight." He pulled me up to his chest and picked my naked body up off of the table as I wrapped myself up in him. Our lips met again.

"I want you so fucking bad right now." I was in his ear, hot and heavy. It sent his erection into the stratosphere when my naked body squeezed around him.

"I want you more. But I don't want to rush things. I want everything about it to be perfect."

My heart thumped and I nuzzled my cheek on his shoulder. Nobody had ever made a night completely about me.

He sat me down and watched me put my clothes back on. I saw his brain churning, the angst building inside of him.

"Wanna get some air?" I smiled.

"Yes!" The words couldn't escape his lips fast enough.

Fully clothed, we walked from the steamy building. The panes around the table were fogged up. The cool night air struck our sweaty bodies, providing momentary relief.

"I think I might walk back to my place. Cool off a bit." My shields were down as his eyes cut into me.

I didn't want to leave his side, but I knew it was probably a good idea. I leaned my cheek into his arm. He turned into me and we kissed. This time soft and light.

"Call me tomorrow?" I asked.

"Of course."

We occasionally glanced at the other as we walked separate ways down the empty street. My legs were jelly. My mind spinning. Every cell in my body was stimulated, satisfied. An endless loop of every moment cycled through my brain, analyzing what I should have said or done.

The Matriarch

Two blocks down, my head turned and I caught his eyes. We both froze, staring at one another for a brief moment.

Then it happened.

chapter twenty six

maggie madison

The squeal of tires screeching pierced my ears. A solid black van fishtailed around the corner behind Cody. He spun around to face the van as it slid to a halt. Two giant men in masks darted from the doors. He tried to bolt but it was too late.

"Run!" Cody stared at me helpless as they wrestled him through the van door.

I took off toward where I'd parked my car earlier. I clicked a button and the door flew open on the Tesla.

I jumped in and hammered the pedal, tearing down the road, leaving two smoldering black stripes on the pavement.

Taking a sharp corner, I felt the raw power of the car rush through my body. The back wheels flew out from under me but quickly corrected back to parallel. Adrenaline pounded in my veins, crazy thoughts coursed through my mind. A pair of red tail lights a half-mile ahead glowed bright in the darkness. It had to be them.

The car flew through gears, the tachometer angrily bouncing back and forth in rhythm with the screaming engines. The whites of my knuckles showed as I gripped tight on the steering wheel. I hammered through a red light, almost taking out an elderly man with a cane. He waved it crazily in the air, giving me the finger with the other hand.

"Sorry!"

I gained on them quickly, plotting my next move, when the van disappeared down the other side of a small hill.

"Fuck!"

A gust of wind mauled pedestrians as the Tesla blew past them, kicking up swirls of dust in its wake. When I cleared the hill I noticed the van on a service road. The Tesla started to accelerate when a blast sent me ducking below the steering wheel. A bullet pinged off the hood.

"Oh fuck you!" I slammed on the brakes. The barrage of fire rang out as I tried to look out the window, making sure I was between the lines on the road. Bullets screamed past me, one spider webbing the windshield before the men stopped to reload. I activated the 'ludicrous speed' option and jetted forward in the car, heart pounding against my ribs, fingers tight on the wheel.

I spotted an exit to the service road and whipped the car behind the van, obscuring their line of fire. The van weaved in and out of cars quickly, trying to shake me. At the last second they cut down a side road. I barely missed plowing through the exit sign as I followed in pursuit.

My gut wrenched as they began to slow. *What the fuck?*

"Oh shit!"

The side door to the van flew open and a man leaned out.

"Fuck, fuck, fuck!" I threw on the brakes.

The man strapped a military grade bazooka to his shoulder as I redlined in reverse. Smoke billowed up into the night sky from my tires. He loaded a large exploding mortar, and my throat started to close. Finally, the tires gripped and the Tesla flew backwards, throwing my chest against the steering wheel.

The man pressed a button, smiling at me, another holding tight to him around the waist. In an instant, I bailed out the door like a tumble weed, rolling into a ditch. A bright orange flame sprayed from the back of

The Matriarch

the launcher. The mortar howled through the air, connecting with its target as the Tesla shot straight up. White hot shrapnel fell around me. The frame of the car slammed back into the pavement. Flames and smoke mushroomed up into the night sky. Stumbling around in a daze, unable to hear through the ringing, I watched the red tail lights disappear around a corner.

The Matriarch

The Matriarch

chapter twenty seven
cody powell

When we arrived at a lab the men were less than cordial, pulling me like a dog on a leash. I was dragged into a building as I fought against their holds.

"Don't fight. It'll only get worse." One of the masked men dug his fingers into my shoulder and walked me through a door.

They kicked me to the hallway floor if I didn't walk at just the right pace. What the hell? Why was I here? Thirty minutes ago was one of the greatest nights of my life. In a flash it was my worst nightmare.

Equipment and monitors lined the walls of the room I was pulled into. The men cinched me to a chair with zip ties.

"Where am I? What do you want?"

A guard's hand smashed the side of my face. I tasted blood.

After a few minutes a door opened. More guards entered. All of them were dressed in military style tactical gear. Kiril strode in behind them. He sauntered over and eyed me up and down. I sat there, staring at the mummy. Kiril's head canted slightly as he sized me up.

"Shall we begin?"

His voice made me nauseous. Made my bones rattle. I'd seen him in the news and his picture in newspapers, but hearing his voice in person, under these circumstances — I wanted to vomit.

"Begin what?"

"Negotiations."

Sweat trickled down my cheek. My head was on a swivel. I felt the ties dig into my arms as I fought

The Matriarch

against them, trying to see if there was any give. "Negotiations?"

"Perhaps coercion is the appropriate word. You have something that I want."

"What's that?" I knew what it was.

"Your company."

I laughed for a moment as if he couldn't possibly be serious. My eyes darted around the room to see if I had any hopes of escape. I glanced back to Kiril's cold eyes and large black pupils.

"What do you want with my company?"

"It doesn't matter." He rose to his feet, pacing slowly with his hands behind his back. "You're going to sell it to me, regardless."

"Umm, no."

"That's unfortunate."

"Well, I'm sorry you feel—"

"For you." He cut me off mid-sentence and looked away, nodding. The two large guards approached, smiling and cracking their knuckles.

Their muscles bulged from their guard uniforms and they seemed to delight in the pain they were about to dish out. I strained against the ties holding my arms. My skin was raw and started to bleed through the burns. Kiril backed out of their way.

A guard's fist smashed my jaw like a sack of bricks. My head snapped sideways and spewed blood to the tile floor. The first stepped back and the other forward. When my head rotated back I was pummeled with another blow, this one harder than the first. Pain radiated through my jaw and shoulder, then back up to my temple. My groans echoed off the walls.

Kiril appeared in front of me. His lips curled to a smile, seemingly enjoying the spectacle.

"You change your mind?"

The Matriarch

I sat there, vision hazy, the taste of copper in my mouth. Blood dripped off my nose and soaked into my shirt. My jaw had to be broken. I panted, looking up to Kiril. Sweat mixed with blood as I tasted salty metal on my tongue.

"It's not for sale."

When Kiril nodded the men unleashed hell on me, hammering my head, jaw, and ribs. I grunted louder as each blow shocked me with more pain than the previous. My sweaty arms tensed as the restraints held me down for my beating. Kiril snapped his fingers and one of the large men stopped his punch mid-swing. The men stepped away.

Kiril walked to another man standing in the corner and retrieved some papers.

"I have the contract right here. Just sign it. Make it easy on yourself."

Head hanging limp, face bloody and bruised, I winced each time I tried to turn my torso. Blood oozed from my nose and I felt like I was moments from passing out.

Kiril waved the legal documents in front of me and offered a pen.

My head tilted up.

"No." It was all I could muster before my head dropped back toward the floor. I had to look up to see what was going on in the room.

The men started to come forward but Kiril held his hand up to stop them. He grabbed my chin and looked into my eyes.

"You would die for your company?"

I stared back at him and felt blood pooling in the corner of my mouth. Without thinking, I spat the blood at Kiril's face, speckling it with red blots that soaked into his bandages. He didn't flinch. The tension in the room grew palpable.

The Matriarch

He reached into his pocket and pulled out a long steel blade, flipping it through the air effortlessly. He aimed the blade at my face, pressing it inside of my mouth, cold steel on my tongue as it shifted to my cheek.

His stare, painted with my blood, horrified me. I was as good as dead.

"You *will* sign these."

chapter twenty eight

maggie madison

I burst through the front door and ran past Grandpa. He was reading a Sports Illustrated swimsuit edition. "What in the..."

"No time!" I flew up the stairs.

My feet barely registered a sound as I zipped across the marble floor. I stripped as I went, tossing my shirt and yanking my pants off. I made my way through the closet, my palm slapping against the security display before gliding down the spiral staircase. At the last second I leapt, landing hard on the balls of my feet. My head lifted and I stared at the Matriarch outfit, glowing from the ambient light overhead.

I threw on a wig and straightened it on my head. I pulled on the thin, elastic body armor and strapped my blades across my waist. Grandpa eased down the steps.

"Is this a good idea?"

"Not now. Kiril has him."

I nudged Grandpa out of the way, readying my go bag.

"You need to step back and take a breath. Reason this out."

"I don't have time!" I ran toward the garage and straddled a jet black motorcycle. I turned the key, firing it up. The engine howled with each turn of my wrist.

Grandpa stood in front me shouting. I couldn't make out his words.

"What?"

"It's voice activated, the suit!"

He walked around to me and I nodded.

The Matriarch

"Be careful!"

His arms wrapped around me and I squeezed his trembling shoulders. I mouthed the words 'I promise' as the door raised.

The tires lurched under me and I rocketed down the driveway, disappearing into the turns of the hills.

I flew around the curves, leaning into each one as the chill night air hammered my torso and the side of my legs. "Room temperature."

A warmth crept along the curves of my body, ankles to neck. "Kick ass." I could get used to this shit. *Thanks Grandpa.*

I sped past cars, weaving in and out of traffic. The skyline was lit up and grew in front of me. My heart drummed as anger coursed through my blood. I hated being unprepared, but the thought of losing Cody outweighed my concerns. Sweat began to cool on my cheeks as the breeze rushed over them. An hour ago was the most intimate moment of my life and now he was gone. For what? His family's company? Not happening.

Nearing Kiril's lab, I slowed to the speed limit, and then to a silent roll. This is where he had to be, judging by the direction they were headed.

Large, snaking spotlights swept across the grounds and in front of the security detail. I parked up the road and hid the bike behind some bushes. Merging with the shadows, I searched my brain for any plan that would let me get Cody out without making a scene.

The place looked business as usual as I crept fluidly from tree to tree, momentarily transported back to the field with Zak. My mind flashed through all of the lessons, but at the forefront remained Kiril's blade running into my mentor while I sat helpless under the floorboards. Relaxing my jaw, I suppressed my rage, meditating on the task at hand.

The Matriarch

Keeping watch over the sleek silver building, I eyed the two guards at the side entrance. I'd been near the place before but never at night. Security was heavy and cameras at every corner.

I tight roped along a wall, picking up a rock and tossing it over the guards' heads. It clanked on the ground and rattled to a stop. Spinning around, weapons hoisted, the men stared into the empty street.

I gripped my blades and sprung from the shadows, thrusting sharp steel into one man's back and ripping the blade up as crimson spewed from his mouth. My other knife sliced the second man's neck. Arterial spray painted the wall.

I dragged their bodies into the shadows, swiping one of their badges and sneaking through the gate.

Careful not to attract attention, I navigated the side of the building, clinging to the wall. When I reached the door I held up the guard's badge and waited for a buzz. The lock unlatched and I turned the knob, easing inside.

I was sure there'd be surveillance as I eyed the long hallway with doors adjacent on each side. A camera in the corner pointed down the hall confirmed my suspicions. I leapt in the air and sliced the connected wires.

My head was whipping back and forth as I lurked down the hall, ears at attention, listening for any clues. I looked both directions when I reached the end of the hall. There was muffled speech and then I heard a man groaning. It grew louder as I neared a door on the right. This was it. I heard Cody mumbling, but couldn't make out his words.

With a deep breath, I pushed the door open.

The Matriarch

It was horror. His blade in Cody's mouth, Kiril grinned at me. I saw my father, then Zak, and then stared at Cody. Heat radiated from my skin as the suit tried to cool me down.

There were guards everywhere in the room. One of them started to call for help on a radio. I gripped a throwing knife and hurled it into his skull as his walkie talkie dropped from his mouth. His body slammed to the ground on top of it. "Tell your friends only pussies call for help."

"You came." Kiril pulled his knife from Cody's beaten face. "I like your outfit. It's cute." Cody's eyes were swollen and his face was battered. His lips were turning purple and crusted blood clung to the neck of his shirt. My fists clenched, but my face remained calm.

"I always wear black to a funeral." I smirked.

Kiril raised his hand to the other guards and five of them rushed me. I turned back to the wall, planted a foot, and vaulted into the air vertical over them. I hung suspended as three knives soared from my hands. Three bodies fell lifeless. I drew my two large blades from my belt, landing with both feet firm on the ground. I flipped around, slicing through the fourth at the neck as he gurgled blood and collapsed. I spun with a roundhouse for the remaining piece of shit. The blade from my boot gashed open his back. I flipped around with my trusted steel in hand and severed his arm in half.

The bloody stump sat on the floor as I strolled to Kiril, holstering my knife. A shriek rang through the building when the guard spotted half of his arm a few feet away from him.

"Should tell your dog not to bark at night. That shit's rude."

The Matriarch

"I'll make a note." His gauze wrapped lips turned up to a grin.

When I neared, he held up a finger, wagging it back and forth.

"Not yet." I glanced to Cody's unconscious body. His torso was slumped over and held up by his wrists.

Kiril signaled a guard and all the doors in the room opened. Fifteen men ran inside forming a barrier.

"Foreplay?" I winked at him.

He nodded, looked at his men, then back to me. All hell broke loose.

I whipped my knives back out as the stampede ensued. The room looked like a horror film. I was a blur, a wild cyclone dodging strikes and carving up anything in my path. Men dropped all around me and blood rained down as Kiril smiled, eyeing every maneuver carefully. I kicked the blade in my boot into a man's thigh when a gun appeared over my shoulder. I turned and stared down the barrel, laughing at it.

"Should've brought handcuffs. That shit gets me hot."

My head darted sideways and I kicked straight up into his chin, the blade from my boot ramming into the roof of his mouth. He projectile vomited blood to the floor and fell face first. I grabbed his back as he hit the ground, cartwheeling over him, and kicked through a man's ribs. The blade impaled his heart and I ripped my foot from his chest cavity as his soul went to meet whatever fucking god he prayed to. Kiril eyed me with amusement, standing amidst a pile of death, completely unscathed.

When I turned to face him all I saw was the bottom of a shoe. Everything went black as a shooting pain pierced my skull.

The Matriarch

The Matriarch

chapter twenty nine

maggie madison

I slowly opened my eyes. My pulse beat in my temples. Whose foot was that? It was the hardest blow I'd ever taken. Careful not to move too quickly, I raised my head with caution. My mouth dropped open as the stabbing pain shifted to my abdomen.

Suki glowered next to Kiril, her arms folded. I was overcome with confusion, unsure if it was from the blow to the head or eyeing Suki standing there.

Kiril nodded and Suki turned and left the room. My arms burst in a rage, recoiling back into the chair. The ties bore into my wrists. I yanked and wrestled against the restraints, quickly realizing it was useless. Cody's limp body sat next to me, still unconscious, held up by ties now wrapped around his chest. I saw his lungs contract and he occasionally let out small groans.

Kiril beamed with pride, taking his time, savoring the moment. He bent over to me, his eyes the only thing I could make out. The rest of him hidden behind layers of linen.

"Your fighting skills are impressive. Where'd you learn them?"

"Fuck you."

He sighed.

He could unmask me at any second, revealing my identity. I couldn't let that happen. The fear was worse than knowing he could kill me at any moment. I knew Kiril wouldn't make it easy for me. He would torture me first, or worse, he would torture Cody in front of me. I couldn't let him know that I knew him.

"Do you know this man?" He nodded to Cody.

"No."

The Matriarch

"It's not wise to lie to me." I wanted to knock him the fuck out, but I had to remain calm. I had to find a way out of this chair.

"I don't know who the fuck that is. Why don't you just take my mask off and get it over with?"

Kiril leaned back down in my face.

"I don't need to take it off. Nobody cares who is underneath. They'll only care that you're gone. So tell me...why did you come if you don't know him?"

He unsheathed his knife. I swallowed hard, cursing myself for showing the slightest reaction.

"I like blood." I smiled.

"Well please enjoy." He pressed the knife back inside of Cody's mouth, staring at me and smiling as I tried not to give in.

He pressed the blade against the corner of Cody's mouth and began to saw toward his ear. Blood spewed down Cody's chin as he moaned. I lost it. I started beating my back into the chair, fighting against the restraints with all my might, grunting and heaving heavy breaths.

"Ahh, so you do care?"

"Zak should have let you fucking burn to death. You fucking coward!"

Kiril's hand tore through the air, smashing the side of my face. It was like he owned me again. His other hand gripped my neck so tight I couldn't scream.

"What do you know?" He growled through his gritted teeth.

I looked over at Cody. The open wound spilled blood from the cut halfway up his cheek. I hated myself for saying Zak's name like that, giving Kiril additional information about me. But it felt good knowing I could get to his ass.

I tried to speak. He loosened his grip to hear what I had to say.

The Matriarch

"I know you're a bitch. And I know you're hideous under that mask. And I know you killed your sister because you're a fucking pussy."

I braced myself for the onslaught that ensued. His fists were like solid boulders, driving me back and forth, shaking me like a convict in an electric chair. The pain was nearly unbearable, but I wouldn't let him break me. Not here. Not ever. If I was going to die, I would die with the satisfaction of knowing I cut him, deep.

"Don't you talk about her! Ever!" He screeched in my face. Gripping a fistful of hair, he lifted me and the chair to his face.

"Yeah. You don't talk so much now. Do you? You think I didn't recognize your mask? I know it's from Golem. You're not as clever as you think."

He dropped me, turned his back, and walked a few steps.

My faint chuckle began building to a rhythmic laugh. He turned back, fists clenched, jaw tightening under the mask. I spit a mouthful of blood. It splattered the floor. I began laughing hysterically. Kiril strolled back. His phony laugh tried to mock mine.

"Yes, it's very funny. Isn't it?"

I nodded, smiling at him.

He cocked back his fist and pummeled my face. My body went limp next to Cody. I could still hear and could barely see as Cody shook in and out of consciousness. He had a brief moment of lucidity as he stared at me and his eyes rolled to Kiril.

"Don't you worry. I'll finish her off soon."

The Matriarch

My vision slowly sharpened. A surgical table had been wheeled in and Cody was strapped to it.

Kiril walked in with a man in a white lab coat and they approached the table.

"What are you doing?" They ignored me.

Kiril walked over and crouched next to me. He was up to something.

"We are going to turn your friend into a woman since he bleeds like one. What's the correct term? Castration?" His chuckle in my ear sent chills down my spine. I raged against the ties still holding me down.

I thrashed in the chair as it skidded on the tiles. Blood dripped from my nose.

Kiril walked back over to the doctor, both nodding to each other. They unbuckled Cody's pants. I screamed and pleaded.

"Don't worry. I'll kill you soon enough for the world to see. But him—" He nodded to Cody. "—we'll let him live, as a woman of course."

The doctor drew on Cody with a marker as he groaned.

Kiril stared at me, savoring every reaction. The doctor pulled out a scalpel. I was helpless. There was nothing I could do.

The doctor moved the scalpel down to one of his marks. Kiril's eyes widened. I turned my head, unable to watch.

A blast shook the walls and ceiling. A shockwave of drywall and dust pelted everyone. My ears throbbed and I frantically turned my head, trying to see through the dirty haze. Men wandered around confused. A glow emanated through the dust cloud. I heard faint pops that grew louder as my hearing returned. Bodies dropped as gunfire echoed through the room.

The Matriarch

I saw a man in a black ski mask, mowing down guards with two handguns. An AK-47 was strapped to his back. Kiril fled as the man ran over and pulled out a large knife, cutting me free.

I fell to my face trying to get to Cody. My legs were completely numb as my blood migrated south. I recovered and cut Cody free. Kiril and Suki filed back into the room.

"Run!" I stared at my rescuer.

The man in the mask pointed his guns, ready for a shootout. I pulled him to my face and nodded at Cody. "Get him out of here! I'll take care of them."

The man was hesitant but threw Cody over his shoulder. They ran to the hole in the wall.

I looked to them. "Wait. Where are you taking him?"

"Don't worry, we'll be waiting for you." Something in his voice sounded familiar, but I didn't have time to think.

He looked at me once more for a moment before disappearing.

I flipped around. My goal was to buy Cody and the man enough time to escape. Kiril snapped his fingers and the wall of men parted. Suki strode between them.

"Time to die." He grinned.

Suki walked through the group of guards. Her tennis shoes squeaked on the floor. A pair of baggy, navy pants hung from her waist and a maroon lycra top clung to her chest and arms. She popped her neck to the side with her fist, glaring at me. Hints of her childhood innocence hid behind a mask of rage.

We circled, staring at one another, waiting for someone to strike. It was time.

Suki shrieked, lunging at me. I dodged her kick, spinning away unscathed. I'd never seen anyone kick that hard, not even Zak. Kiril was unamused.

The Matriarch

"Kill her."

Suki feinted left and came back across the top, rocking me with a right cross. It sent me rolling across the floor. Her leg hammered down from above, but I rolled just as her foot crashed to the floor where my head had been. A crack screamed across the tile. I hopped to my feet, wincing. Suki unleashed a fury of jabs that I blocked with my elbows. Pain ripped through my arms and midsection, making it difficult to breathe.

How the fuck does she hit so hard? I tried to dance around, bouncing side to side, fighting through my cracked ribs. Suki swung at me. I grabbed her arm and leaped up to her shoulder, wrapping my legs around her neck and locking her in an arm bar as we crashed to the ground.

It was over, nobody escaped the arm bar. Pulling on her arm was like trying to bend iron. Suki's bicep flexed and her elbow bent. *What the fuck?* Her free hand swung, clobbering my mouth. Blood gushed as I flew across the floor before flipping to my feet. I panted as blood oozed from a gash inside my cheek. Heaving breaths in deep waves, I bent over at the waist.

I was dizzy, but remembered my teachings. *Meditate. Stay focused. Outwit your opponent.* Sometimes the simplest solution was the answer. Suki approached me, backing me up to the wall. I looked over to the table at my belt and knives next to the surgical bed. Kiril and the guards stared in amusement at what seemed to be my final moments.

Suki lunged forward. Her hand was about to crush my face. I ducked to the side. She hammered the wall and a crack shot toward the ceiling. Suki let out a shriek. I jumped over her head, the blade in my boot thrust forward and I planted it in her shoulder, pushing off with my toes. I landed close to the table,

The Matriarch

barrel rolling across the floor as I grabbed my belt. I heaved one of the knives in Suki's direction. It sunk into the back of her leg, sending her hobbling to the ground. I dashed for the hole in the wall, heaving another blade into a guard's jugular. He dropped his weapon, clutching his throat.

"Kill her!" I glanced back to Kiril. He looked nice and pissed off. *Fucker*. A barrage of gunfire exploded from the guard's weapons. I dove through the opening as bullets seared over my head, hammering into the wall around me. Once through, I took off in a sprint down the hall and burst through a pair of double doors into the cool night.

Where the fuck did he come in?

Fifty yards away, a small swath of chain link rattled with the wind from a hole cut in it.

The Matriarch

The Matriarch

chapter thirty
cody powell

My vision was blurry but began to focus. A man in a mask was carrying me up a set of steps to a mansion. *Where the hell am I*? I tensed up.

"Shit, sorry about the mask, buddy. I'd take it off but you're pretty fuckin' heavy."

My eyes darted around the expansive grounds before an old man opened the front door.

"He gonna be okay?"

"Yeah, but he's pretty damn beaten up."

"Mags know?"

Who the hell is Mags?

"Bek—" My jaw and face throbbed, stinging pain tore through my cheek and I groaned. The old man jumped at my voice.

"Take it easy buddy. We gonna have to fix you up." He turned to the man in the mask. "Can't get hold of her."

"Why aren't you taking me to the hospital?" My cheek throbbed and stung, but I needed answers.

The taste of blood was still in my mouth. I pressed my tongue to my cheek, grunting as it opened the cut in my face.

"I said take it easy, son. Rebekah should be here soon."

"Why haven't you called the cops?"

The masked man carried me to a room and set me down. "Try and get some rest. The bleeding stopped. You'll be fine. Cops can't be trusted. Or the hospital. Kiril will be looking for you. You're safe here."

My eyelids were like anchors when I hit the bed.

The Matriarch

I woke a few hours later and my eyes were still heavy. I heard the two men speaking but couldn't understand what they were saying at first. I looked over at them, sitting in ornate, decorative wooden chairs smiling at one another.

"I'm so glad you're here." The old man grinned.

"Good to be home. See family."

My ears perked up at the word 'family'. Who was this guy? Rebekah said her family was dead. All that remained was her grandpa.

"Bekah is going to have a heart attack when she sees you. Too bad you weren't here a few days ago. We had some fine ass women running 'round here."

My eyebrows twitched as I eyed the other man, assuming he was the one who wore the mask.

"You haven't changed since I was a kid. Only now Grandma isn't here to slap you around, keep you in check."

"I know, I know, god rest her soul."

I groaned and the men turned.

"You awake, boy?" Rebekah's grandfather grinned at me.

"Water." I moaned, still having trouble with my words.

My rescuer scurried through the house to grab a glass.

"You're a demanding little bastard, ain't ya?" Her grandfather chuckled. Attempting to grin, pain flooded my face.

"Take it easy, son. You took a hell of an ass whipping."

I pointed at him. "Rebekah grandpa?"

"Yeah, that would be me. Mostly a blessing, sometimes a curse."

The Matriarch

He walked over and eyed me close, pressing on my arms and legs, searching for tender spots.

"Cody." I tried to point to myself.

"Pleasure. Charlie umm, Balfour. People around here call me Grandpa though. You need to rest up, okay?"

"Rebekah?"

"She's out. Went to see her private investigators. Guys she knows she can trust. We are trying to reach her. I promise. She's probably on her way."

The younger man swung the door open, holding a glass of water and a bottle of pills.

"Try to call again. I found some pain pills in the cabinet."

Grandpa snatched the bottle from his hand and read the label.

"Oh yeah, this is the good shit right here. You'll be feeling nice real soon."

My rescuer helped me up and took two of the white tablets from the bottle he snatched from Grandpa.

"These might make you groggy, but they'll help with the pain. I promise."

He put them on my tongue and held the glass of water to my lips. I swallowed the pills, letting out a squeal when the water oozed down my cheek through the open wound.

"Fuck me. That guy is an animal."

I nodded and pointed to him.

"Family?" I was still confused.

He stood still for a moment and nodded.

"Rebekah's brother, Kyle."

The Matriarch

The Matriarch

chapter thirty one
maggie madison

Intense, sharp pains pounded at my jawline. My head turned, looking for anything familiar on the street. *Who the hell blew up the wall and tried to rescue us?*

Cars peeled out of the compound, patrolling the area. I zigzagged through the trees and bushes, and found my bike. Shifting it into neutral, I rolled it next to the road about a hundred yards from the guards. I took in the cool city air. My lungs were on fire and a million thoughts ran through me. A set of cars passed and I straddled the bike.

"Fuck it."

I turned the key and the motorcycle started to fire up and then sputtered silent.

"Goddamn it!" I gritted my teeth.

I turned the key again. Same result. Men yelled and raised their guns in my direction. I heard the crackling of handheld radios and orders being barked.

"There! There!"

The men howled and ran toward me. I beat on the gas tank of the motorcycle.

"Start you fucking piece of shit."

To my surprise, I flipped the key and it came to life, purring between my legs. With a twist of the wrist, I hammered the throttle. The back wheel slid sideways, trying to gain traction.

The men opened fire. Bullets peppered the trees and bushes around me as I tore up the grass, before finding pavement. The bike howled as I shifted the gears, my body wrapped tightly around it. I looked back as the men and their guns grew smaller, the sound of gunfire fading. I stared straight ahead at two black cars blocking the street. Men in uniform pointed weapons at me.

They opened fire. Bullets ricocheted off the plexiglass shield that curved in front of my face.

Thank god Grandpa installed this shit.

I looked around for any means of escape. Hammering the brakes and flipping the handle bars, I spun to my right as the back end of the motorcycle slid and my foot planted on the ground. My forearm flexed, hammering the throttle as I rocketed toward a side street. A steep, man-made irrigation ditch appeared between me and the road.

I leaned into the bike and cocked my wrist on the throttle, pegging it to red. I ramped a small hill in front of the creek, soaring through the air. Bullets sliced past me. I floated over the creek bed and braced myself as the tires slammed into the asphalt.

The bike corrected and I sped down the road with a smile on my face, thinking about Kiril's bandaged face and his reaction when he learned of my escape. I laughed to myself.

I rolled into the driveway, parking a ways from the house. I skulked through the garage and down the hall to the secret room leading up to the closet.

I quickly concealed most of my wounds with makeup and I dressed the rest of them quietly. *Thank god Cody is too beat up to touch me.*

I pressed the corner of my eye and cringed. On the desk sat my notebook with printouts of Kiril's plans. They confirmed my suspicions all along. *Suki received injections.* The thought chilled my core. I had to stop him. Soon.

The Matriarch

I exited the closet, looking as presentable as possible. The house was quiet as I retraced my path to the front of the house. I had to make it look like I was just coming home from meeting with my security team.

I idled in front of the door for a moment, composing myself for the events to come. I'd have to look at Cody's beaten body and lie to him in the process. I knew I'd be scolded by Grandpa, but he was usually good about waiting for the right moment.

I fidgeted with the door handle, pretending to unlock it and pushed it open. I stepped through.

"Hello." My voice echoed up the staircase and vaulted ceiling.

"In here," said Grandpa.

I strolled around the corner to the guest room. Cody was on his back in bed.

"Oh my god." I ran to his side.

He was half awake. I ran my hand along his bruised arms and lightly traced his face, careful not to press on his dressed wounds.

Cody managed a smile, then groaned when the wound in his cheek peeled open.

"Shh, sit still." I brushed his hair from his face. "Don't say anything."

My head snapped back to Grandpa and the acting continued.

"What the hell happened?"

"Ask him." Grandpa looked at the man sitting in a chair against the wall.

I looked over to a mop of sienna hair atop his head, familiar brown eyes rounding out his lean, muscular face. His grin sent goosebumps down my arms. I knew the grin. I knew him. He looked like — Dad.

I stared for what seemed an eternity.

"Hey, umm, Beks." He stared at me and I froze.

The Matriarch

The acting ceased.

"*Kyle*?"

I sprang from the floor, tackling him into the wall with a giant bear hug. Grandpa smiled from ear to ear, before pulling out his suture kit and strolling over to tend to Cody.

"What? How? I don't care!" I squealed and smothered him with all the strength I could conjure up.

"Missed you too, sis."

Grandpa cleaned up Cody's face and started stitching him as Cody watched us from the bed.

I pulled back from my brother, warming my palms on his cheeks. "I want to know everything."

Cody napped in the guest room, trying to regain his strength. Grandpa, Kyle, and I sat around the table, telling tales from childhood. I nearly followed Kyle into the restroom a minute earlier, intent on never letting him out of my sight again.

"So you rescued Cody? How? Why?" My senses were still shocked.

Kyle smiled.

"I escaped from Kiril's prison a while back. Been keeping an eye on him ever since. Something is going on."

"Why don't you go to the authorities?" Grandpa looked to Kyle.

Kyle chuckled.

"They're on his payroll. They won't do shit."

I twitched when my forearm bumped the table.

Kyle looked down to my arm, then back up at me. "You alright?"

My head shot up to his face.

The Matriarch

"Yeah, I'm good. Just overwhelmed. Sorry for being so overbearing. Don't mean to hover over you."

He and Grandpa smiled at each other. My teeth clenched and my jaw tightened.

"So, how did you know to bring him here?" I turned to Grandpa. He looked away, humming some old show tune. He'd have made a terrible poker player.

The two of them sat in silence.

"How long?"

"Beks look—" Kyle stared at me.

"Grandpa?" I turned to the old man. "How long?"

Kyle interrupted when Grandpa started to speak. "About a week."

I glared at the old prick. A look he was all too familiar with.

"Does he know?" I gestured to Kyle.

Their heads dropped.

"What the hell were you two thinking?" I growled at them through my teeth. "You could have killed us with that blast."

"He was looking out for you. That's what brothers do, Bekah. Don't be ungrateful. You flew out of here, emotional, chasing after your boyfriend—"

"I just wanted to help. I know that place in and out." Kyle's eyes cut into me. I couldn't help but think it was some kind of trick. That it wasn't really him. Grandpa sat there, thankful to be interrupted.

I gave both of them a cold stare.

"I didn't need help." I looked away, muttering to myself.

"We care about you. We know you care about the guy lying in bed." Grandpa's voice was stern. Maybe I was too hard on both of them. They cared about me. It was understandable.

Kyle reached over and took my hand.

The Matriarch

"I missed you." His grin was the same as I remembered.

I smiled back at him as old feelings and memories ran through every inch of me.

"I missed you too. I love both of you assholes so much."

I motioned to Cody. "What'd you tell him?"

"You were meeting with your security team. What we discussed on the phone. Nothing more," said Grandpa.

"I wasn't compromised?"

"Secret is safe." Kyle nodded, trying to reassure me.

I sat in my room, eyes squinting, pushing a needle through my skin. My brain beat on my skull. I tried to recall ever taking a punch that hard. Toes first, I slid under the cool, cotton sheets. Motorized curtains opened to reveal a curved glass window encompassing half the room. From atop the hill where my house sat, the skyline of Bathory filled the view. I stared. It gave me comfort, reminding me when I was a child staring up at the large skyscrapers sprouting to the clouds. The pillow was soft against my cheek. Memories and thoughts of childhood flooded back. Fatigue overwhelmed me and I tumbled into a deep sleep.

I bolted upright in bed, saturated with cold sweat, panting and gasping for breath. My stitches ripped at my skin, stinging as I scratched at them. When I realized my dark visions were only a dream, I drew in huge heaves of air, sending my chest rising and falling. The nightmares were frequent. They'd plagued me since the night I escaped.

I swept the sheet to the side, reaching for the glass of water on my nightstand. I gulped down half of it.

I need something stronger.

I pulled a cloth robe over my naked, battered body. The wool in my slippers tickled my toes as I slid them on and crept through the bedroom door. I eased past Grandpa's room in time with his snores. When I made it halfway down the staircase, I heard rapping on a keyboard, and saw a light filling the living area from the couch. *What the hell is he doing out of bed?*

I assumed it was Cody being restless. When I peeked around the corner I saw Kyle with a serious look on his face, staring at the laptop.

"Hey little brother."

Kyle jolted, nearly knocking his computer to the ground as he clawed at it, clutching it in his arms.

"Jesus Christ, Mags. I mean, umm, Bekah. You scared the shit out of me!" He paused. "You're barely older than me you know? And sorry, I'm still getting used to this 'Bekah' business."

"Can still whip your ass too." I stared at him with my arms folded across my chest.

"Please." He stared at me. "Okay, fine. Superhero. I'm sure you could. Can't sleep?"

"Bad dream. What are you doing up?"

"Just chatting online."

"Ohh. A girl?"

"Maybe." Kyle blushed and looked to his laptop.

I walked over sat next to him on the couch, curling my legs up under me. I propped my head up on my hand. I could tell he wanted to ask, but we'd avoided the topic since he'd come back into my life.

"Kiril?" He tossed his computer aside.

The Matriarch

I nodded, clutching a pillow to my chest. His face held compassion as I let my guard fall, showing him the fear I usually tucked deep inside me.

He reached over, pulling my trembling body close, wrapping me up in his arms. He squeezed my head tight against his chest and we sat for a moment in silence.

"He told me you were dead. That you and mom were both gone." I buried my face in his shoulder.

He hugged me tighter.

"I know. He let me know every day I'd never see you again."

"Do you think mom—"

"No Mags, I saw…" He pulled me face to face. "I'm here now."

I smiled and hugged him again, this time harder.

"I would have come for you. I didn't know." I said it over and over, burying my face back into him. "I should've known. I'm so sorry. I didn't—"

He cut me off mid-sentence. "It wasn't your fault."

He wrapped an arm around my neck and I snuggled into him.

"It wasn't your fault," he said.

I looked up to him as he stared off at the pictures on the wall.

Two days later, Cody was still laid up in bed. We all sat at the kitchen table eating breakfast. Cody was recovering, slowly. I'd been inseparable from Kyle the past few days while Cody was on the mend. Catching up, telling stories from childhood, reminiscing.

My phone vibrated against the oak tabletop. I answered while sipping on a scalding hot cup of coffee. The steam wafted into my nose, bringing my senses to life. My limp was slowly subsiding and I had taken a few days off from work. Well, I hadn't gone in to the office in a few days anyway. I hung up the phone.

"He updated his Twitter." I stared at Kyle and Grandpa.

"Kaos?" asked Grandpa.

This got Kyle's attention. He straightened in his chair. "What's it say?"

"'Greetings from the Capitol. I have a surprise for you, soon.' He signed it. There's a picture of him with the Capitol in the background."

Kyle smirked. Grandpa and I both looked at him.

"What? You have to admit he has a point about some things."

"He's a murderer." Grandpa squeezed the coffee cup tight in his hand.

"He wants justice. Who doesn't? People are fed up."

"He kills children, women, innocent people—"

Kyle stared at me and knew to tread lightly.

"I'm just sayin' the power in this country is out of touch. Out of control if you ask me. Spying on citizens? That's not freedom. It's tyranny."

I examined my brother carefully. He was always strong-willed in his beliefs, even as a boy. But I had studied Kaos meticulously. So had Grandpa. We knew what he was and what he was capable of.

"Well, there are other ways to change things," I said.

"I suppose. Have to admit he's effective. Wonder what his Tweet meant?" Kyle was always curious as a boy. He always had to figure everything out.

The thought of it sent pin pricks down my arms. I needed to find out. Soon.

The Matriarch

The Matriarch

chapter thirty two

maggie madison

Lightly knocking on the door, I heard Cody speaking in his room.

"Come in."

I inched my way in with a glass of iced tea and a sandwich. The swelling had subsided and he could open his eyes. I placed my hand under the back of his head as his hand squeezed my thigh. A warmth rushed into my heart. I pored over the stitches in his cheek. Grandpa had done a good job sewing him back together, but it was going to leave an awful scar.

"What do you mean?" Cody barked into the phone before cringing and placing a hand on his stitches. "No, no, that's impossible. Why didn't you call—"

I heard a dial tone on the other end. Cody clutched his face in his palms, avoiding the stitches.

"What?" I fidgeted with my fingers as I looked at him.

He turned up to me, black crescents under his eyes.

"I lost it. They — they sold the company."

"Kiril?"

"No, some other company I've never heard of. They got to my brother and sister. Made them a huge offer if they agreed to sell their stake. They told me I get to stay on and run the place, but it's not ours. It's not my family's anymore."

"I'm so sorry, babe." I caressed his hair.

"It's all I've got left. I promised them I'd take care of it."

Guilt crept under my skin.

I clutched his head, looking deep into his emerald eyes, ignoring the bruises. "I'm going to go get

The Matriarch

dressed and we're going for a walk. You need some fresh air. Okay?"

Cody nodded and I walked through the room, ignoring the shocks of pain in my abdomen.

"You need to tell him, Bekah." Grandpa sat on a bench in the hallway.

"I can't deal with this shit right now."

"He's going to find out. One way or another. Better to come from you."

I spun around and glared at him, hard.

"I said not *now*." I started up the staircase.

When I got to my room I flung my dresser open and ripped at the clothes in my drawer. The handles rattled against the wood and I stared at myself in the mirror, hating what I saw. I slammed my fist down on the top of the dresser.

"*Goddamn it*."

I threw on a pair of jeans and a white blouse and started back toward Cody's room. Kyle walked past, clearly on his way out.

"Going to see your girl?" I turned to Grandpa when Kyle nodded. "He has a girl he's after."

"Well, is she after you?" Grandpa looked at him, his eyes wide and a smile on his wrinkled face.

Kyle looked up at me, smiling.

"She is. She just doesn't know it yet." He winked at both of us.

The three of us huddled up in a group hug. Kyle walked through the door and hopped into a black car that was arranged to pick him up. He waved through the window as I wrapped my arm around the old man.

Grandpa turned to me.

"Where you off to?"

"Taking Cody for a walk. Hopefully help him clear his mind and focus on his recovery."

"You going to tell him?"

The Matriarch

"Let the shit go, old man."

Cody and I circled around a large pond on the grounds. My house sat on twenty-five acres spanning most of the hill. The skyline grew gorgeous as we reached the top. The end of the pond overlooked every square mile of the city.

"It's beautiful out here." Cody turned to me. He was starting to heal.

"Yeah, I love the view. I used to stare at it as a kid."

He turned to me and moved a strand of hair blowing wayward in the wind.

"I wasn't talking about the buildings." He smiled.

My cheeks warmed as I giggled.

"Take it easy, you need to recover before you try anything frisky." I gave him a playful shove on the shoulder and he winced. "Oh shit. I'm so sorry."

"It's okay. I think I'm up for it." He took a step and grabbed at his hip, arching his back in pain.

I stepped in to let him prop his arm on my shoulder, bearing some of the weight.

"I see that." I grinned back at him. "Sit down and rest for a minute?"

"Yeah."

He hobbled to one of the benches that sat along the rippling water with me at his side.

"You going somewhere today?"

"No, why?" I looked at him puzzled.

"No reason."

I shot him another quick glance then played it off. It must have been the makeup I'd caked on to hide the bruises.

The Matriarch

"Had a conference call this morning. Had to look good from the neck up."

"Gotcha."

Whew, I think he bought it.

We sat and stared out at the city, both with a million thoughts racing through our minds. Cody concerned about the company and his next move. I was trying to figure out how to navigate my life — all the secrets. Lying to him tore me up inside, but I knew things could go south in a hurry and it would only get worse. Now wasn't the time. He needed to focus on recovering and didn't need any distractions.

He moved his hand to mine, sensing something was wrong.

"So much for taking things slow." He smiled.

Both hiding our pain, we laughed. Cody ran his hand up along the stitches and turned his face away.

"It's okay." I turned his head to meet my eyes.

"Have you looked at me? It's humiliating." He looked broken, scared. It ripped me up inside.

I put my hand gently to his face. He tried to shy away but I wouldn't let him.

I pressed my lips to his. It stung, but the warmth rushing over my face outweighed the pain I felt as his lips melted back into mine.

I grinned as our lips parted ways.

"What?" His cheeks were flushed.

"Chicks dig scars. I'm just sayin'."

He smiled at me and we laughed, falling back into each other's arms.

We strolled back down the hill and into the house. Grandpa had made dinner.

"Charles." Cody nodded to Grandpa as he came through the door.

"Charles? What the hell is that all about?" I'd never heard anyone call him Charles.

"Not everyone calls me Grandpa, Margaret."

The Matriarch

My mouth dropped to the floor. I stared at him and played it off. "You'll pay for that, old man."

"Why Margaret?" Cody looked flummoxed.

I cut Grandpa off before he gave away any more of my past. "It's an old family name. Rebekah is my middle name." I shot Grandpa a pissed off look when Cody turned and Grandpa mouthed 'sorry' at me.

"Oh." Cody smiled.

We sat around the table, passing the meat loaf and sides back and forth while one of the Supreme Court justices was interviewed on a national TV show. Cody scoffed at the man's answers regarding his opinion on the case. I bit my tongue, refusing to rock the boat. I'd done enough already.

Grandpa reached for the remote as they were taking phone calls from people with questions. He was about to turn off the TV when we heard the next caller's voice. My fork clattered to my plate.

"Well, Mr. Justice, I do indeed have a question for you."

"Kaos." I glanced to Grandpa and Cody. Then we all turned back to the screen.

Grandpa nodded.

Justice Howard was shaking. The host motioned to his production crew. Howard was a middle-aged man of about fifty: short salt and pepper hair, stocky build, brown eyes, wearing a navy blue designer suit with a smoky gray tie.

"What do you want?" Howard brushed his hands across his pants.

"What do I want? Well, let's see...great question by the way. I thought the caller asked the questions on this program? I guess you make your own rules.

So I can understand the confusion, Justice. See, here's the thing...I happen to know the reason you did what you did." Kaos paused and the host stared at Howard, mouthing 'I'm sorry' repeatedly. Howard held his hand up to stop him. He attempted to look composed, but even a child could see he was scared shitless.

"But..." Kaos drew out his syllables. "Well...I want to hear you tell everyone. Don't want to spoil anything for our viewers."

"I did what I did because it was in the best interest of the..."

"Enough!" The host and Howard flinched in their seats at his outburst. Kaos quickly composed himself and returned to a slow drawl. "Perhaps, since you're a...what word am I looking for...umm, coward. Maybe, just maybe, I should give you a little incentive, Your Honor."

Muffled screams of a woman and boy rang through the TV speakers.

"Shh, we're on national television. You can't be screaming in my ear like that, dear. I tell you what, Your Honor. I don't know how you hear yourself speak at home with these two loud mouths yapping constantly."

Howard jumped from his seat. "Suzanne! Mikey! Are you okay?"

"Oh, they're just fine, Your Honor. I'm keeping them entertained. This show on the TV we are watching is just delightful."

"You son of a bitch. You had better not touch a hair on their..."

"Shut. Your. Mouth. How does it feel? You don't like not being in control, do you? It hurts to see the things you love being threatened, doesn't it?"

The Matriarch

Cody's hand was soft as it intertwined with mine. I squeezed back, a little too hard. All three of our hearts pounded as we watched the events play out.

"This man is a monster. I can't watch this." Grandpa grabbed the plates and stalked into the kitchen.

I couldn't peel my eyes from the screen. The fork on my plate rattled back and forth as I pawed at it, trying to grab hold.

"Now. Do you care to amend your answers to our gracious host this evening?"

"I haven't said anything I don't believe in. You're trying to coerce me into convincing people your agenda is legitimate. It's disgusting. You're a sociopath."

"Oh, no. You see, Your Honor. It's unfortunate that you feel that way. Being blind to reality is a bad thing. Greed seems to have clouded *your* reality. I think it's time we brought you down from the clouds though. You see, the people, they want accountability. They want to know the real reason you voted to strip them of their freedom. They will get the truth. And if you don't give it to them, well, I'm going to, umm, carve up your wife. Right in front of your son. And he's going to know that it was all daddy's fault. For the rest of his life. Sure, he may believe whatever story you tell him for now, but one day...one day, Your Honor...see, he's gonna get curious. He's going to start digging, and researching. What's he going to find? See that's the beauty of this ordeal, I only have to kill one person, but you will lose two. It's like a *sale.*" Kaos' sinister laugh rang through the phone and the speakers of millions of viewers.

"You're a monster. I don't deserve this."

"Oh, but you do. It's our decisions in life that define us. You have a chance to make things right with the world. Now go on. Tell 'em. Tell 'em, tell

The Matriarch

'em." Horror ran through my body in waves, in time with his evil laugh.

Screams and thrashing on the other end of the line had me cringing. Kaos screamed at the woman in the background. The boy whimpered.

There was rustling on the line and Kaos picked up the phone. "Sorry about that. Nag nag nag, how do you put up with her? She just *never* shuts up, does she?"

I could picture Kaos on the other end of the line smiling. He loved holding power over people. He got his rocks off beating women and kids.

"Okay, okay." Howard's face was red. He clutched it in his palms. "Please, just don't hurt them. Please take my son out of the room. I'm begging you."

"Ohh begging. That's good. Don't beg to me though. You beg the people for forgiveness for what you're about to tell them."

There was a lull.

"Well go on, *beg them*."

Howard looked into the camera screen. Huge tears and regret filled his eyes. "I'm sorry. I'm so so sorry."

"What did he do?" Cody's fists clenched on the table.

"Oh man, your face is priceless." Kaos could barely speak through the laughter. "Mikey, come here. You gotta see this buddy. You have to see your dad. I think he's pissing his pants." Kaos continued to laugh as Mikey's cries grew louder.

"Say hi to daddy."

"H-hello?" The boy sounded scared for his life. I wanted to choke that fucking clown until he died in my hands.

"Son! Are you okay? Is he hurting you?"

"No. He kicked mommy."

The Matriarch

"It's going to be okay. I promise buddy. I promise." Howard cried at the sound of his son's voice.

"Tell them!" Anger grew in Kaos' voice. "You look in that camera and you tell your son what you did."

"I'm sorry, son. I'm sorry." He looked at the screen. "I, I, was paid to issue an opinion on the ruling."

The host gasped, Cody and I along with him. Grandpa was still in the other room. He refused to come in and watch.

"That's better...And what on earth did you receive? Surely, it was something spectacular, if it was worth subjugating the population's liberty? What did you get in return, Your Honor?"

"I, I received tuition for my son's school, ten million dollars in government contracts for my company, and a few various gifts from political donors."

"But, but, how did you get government contracts? Isn't that some kind of conflict of interest? I mean, I'm not a lawyer, but I didn't know you could do that?"

"The Senate attached it to a bill a few weeks ago, and..."

"Go on."

"They passed it through during a busy news week. It received little coverage in the media."

"Well, there you have it folks. Your hard-earned tax dollars at work. The very courts...those who take oaths to uphold the law, provide a check against congress, well, they all just sit back and laugh at you. They mock you and do as they please. They abuse the power you gave them. Now, if you'll excuse me, Your Honor. I have some guests to entertain. Mikey, Mikey, buddy, you may want to step back a little. This might get a little messy."

The Matriarch

Mikey shrieked. The dial tone rang through the phone for the nation to hear. Howard fell to his knees on the set of the interview, the host still staring in disbelief. The program immediately cut to commercial. Cody turned and stared at me, neither of us knowing what to say.

The Matriarch

THE BATHORY DAILY NEWS

JUSTICE HOWARD'S WIFE SLAIN ON LIVE TELEVISION

BY: JIM BRISTOL

CAPITOL CITY - The wife of Justice Howard was found in their home in a suburb of Capitol City last evening. Millions witnessed an exchange between Howard and Kaos on national television shortly before the killing occurred. The details are being withheld due to their graphic nature. Howard's son witnessed the killing and is cooperating with authorities. Minutes before it happened, Howard admitted on national television under threat of harm to his family, that he accepted various forms of consideration in exchange for his opinion on the case. He has resigned and is currently being held in protective custody by the Federal Bureau of Investigation pending an investigation. Public sentiment is mixed, many people decrying the killing of Howard's wife, but also believe Howard should be held accountable for his actions. Many are calling for his prosecution.

Despite the killings, the number under Kaos' influence seems to have grown and the rioting has spread to the Capitol and across major metropolitan areas in the United States. Curfews have been installed in some cities along with some jurisdictions banning the white makeup worn by Kaos' followers. The National Guard has been deployed to several areas in order to help restore peace and curb violence. It seems to have had little effect and has bred more distrust. Kaos has released several

The Matriarch

propaganda videos, showing police brutality coupled with a message of liberation, and in some instances, anarchy. He is urging his followers not to give in and not to relinquish their freedoms. He maintains they have every right to riot and bring justice to those who seek to steal from them and their families. We will keep you updated as the story progresses.

The Matriarch

chapter thirty three

maggie madison

"You two need to get out of this house and go on a date. Seriously. That's what he wants. He wants people hiding in fear. He preaches freedom, but it's all about control." Grandpa was livid, clanging dishes into the dishwasher.

"I don't know. It's pretty bad out there." Cody frowned.

"Bunch of damn hoodlums and thugs. No respect for people's property."

I sat and watched Grandpa's passion as he spoke about the riots. They'd spread through the city like a wildfire and while it was relatively safe during the day, night was a completely different story. Cabin fever was setting in. We'd been cooped up in the house for a week. Cody being there at night meant I couldn't get out, couldn't get any work done. I was worried about my business interests. I'd postponed meetings all week and investors didn't like uncertainty.

They also didn't like being blown off as their assets were being ransacked by thugs in makeup.

"I really need to take some business meetings today, and yes, a date would be nice."

I smiled at Cody, trying to win him over.

"I don't have a good feeling about it."

I knew he was scared and I didn't want to emasculate him. He was far too kind, and after the beating he had taken who could blame him? I had to remind myself he wasn't used to this kind of situation. He'd grown up in a happy home and lived a normal childhood. Some of us weren't afforded that luxury.

The Matriarch

"Come on...It'll be fun." I begged him.

Grandpa mumbled to himself. I caught something about the younger generations and ungrateful bastards. He was obviously still caught up in thinking about the riots.

"We could go out to lunch, or for a walk?"

I could see the apprehension, but convinced myself it would be good for him. Being stuck in the house kept me thinking of what I'd done, the secrets I was keeping. My fingers were starting to bleed from picking at them.

"Fine, but we need to get back before the sun sets."

My heart raced. A million ideas popped into my head.

"I'll go get ready." I squeaked and clapped my hands together. *Jesus, Maggie. Maybe you're a girl after all.*

Grandpa turned to Cody, intent on keeping him in a state of perpetual fear.

"Now, I know you need to get out of the house in principle. But you take care of that girl. She's all I've got."

"I swear, sir. I won't let anything happen to her."

"Mmmhmm." Grandpa gave him the stink eye.

I walked up to my bedroom and stripped, rifling through my closet. I needed something that would be good for an afternoon date, but could also pass as business attire in case I needed to meet with clients.

I settled on a pair of black slacks and a light sweater. The chill air from the ceiling vents felt amazing against my warm skin, but I quickly noticed the bruises and cuts on my body. I'd managed to conceal my facial injuries from Cody, but what if things went to the next level? The thought of it brought up everything else I was hiding. I wanted to crawl into a corner and die. How could I tell him though? In my mind it was unforgivable. It would

The Matriarch

bring everything to a crashing halt. *The old fucker is right*. I didn't want it to end though. I'd never had a fairy tale romance. While this was anything but a normal way to start a relationship, it was the closest I'd ever come to one. I couldn't risk it.

Grandpa whistled as I walked out to greet two of my three favorite men.

"Looking good, sweetie."

Cody gazed at me as I came down the stairs and grandpa stared him down.

"Don't get any bright ideas, boy."

"Yes sir." Cody straightened up real fast.

"*Grandpa*. Be nice." I slapped him on the shoulder.

"I'll be watchin' ya."

Cody's face went pale.

"Come on." I wrapped my arm around Cody's. "Don't listen to him."

"Four medals in 'Nam. I've killed dozens for far less."

Grandpa chuckled to himself at the table.

"Oh my God, he was a hippie, let's go." I grabbed Cody by the hand as he stared back in horror at grandpa. Grandpa gestured like he was cocking a shotgun and pointing it at him.

Autumn was beginning to show its face in Bathory as we strode to the car. The trees were changing colors and it was beautiful.

"Thank you." He always looked mesmerized when he stared at me. I could get used to it.

"Umm...you're welcome. Not sure what I did."

"Thank you for taking care of me."

The Matriarch

The words made my skin crawl. Somehow, I managed a fake smile.

"You're welcome."

Cody stood in awe when he saw the garage for the first time.

"Sorry, I have a thing for sexy cars." I smiled.

"I should say so. Hope you don't have this same fetish for sexy men."

I blushed.

"Which one should we take?"

"Man, what a nice problem to have." Cody looked around like a little boy in a toy store.

"What's that?"

"Deciding what to drive. It must be exhausting."

I slapped his shoulder, gently. He grabbed it and frowned.

"Oh my god. I'm so sorry."

I started to kiss his cheek, hesitating before moving to the other instead.

"It's hideous, isn't it?" He looked away.

"What?" I tried to play it off.

"You know what."

His face warmed my fingers as they ran along the stitches. I stared at the closed wound running from the corner of his mouth up his cheek.

"It's not hideous. Nothing about you is hideous. You're perfect. Please, do not let this change you. There aren't a lot of good people left in the world. Trust me, I know."

"You're not so bad yourself." His hand in my hair sent a shudder down my spine.

What should have been the ultimate compliment was like a knife in an open wound. I rocked back on my heels, but feigned a smile. I kissed him apprehensively.

"Are you going to choose?"

The Matriarch

Cody's grin grew wider and it made me happy to finally see those perfect white teeth again.

"Mustang." He nodded at the Shelby.

"Ohh...A great choice." I grinned and grabbed the keys.

Walking up to it, the light perfectly reflected its lines and curves. It was white with blue racing stripes running bumper to bumper. I brushed my hand along the cowled hood. The rocker panels were painted blue with "GT500" in white lettering. I started to get in when Cody shouted, "Wait!"

He walked over to my side of the car, staring at me with a look of contempt. My stomach tightened and my lips pursed, wondering what I'd done wrong. His eyes beat down on me as he neared and then reached out for the door handle and opened it.

"One day you'll learn."

I felt lighter than the air I breathed. He opened my door as I floated down from the clouds. *Chivalry isn't dead after all.* It all came crashing down as he walked around the car. *And I'm going to lose him.* I promised myself as soon as this ordeal with Kiril was finished I would come clean, tell him everything. If he would just listen to me he'd realize my intentions were pure. He was a kind and reasonable man who always thought everything through. I clung to any bit of hope I could muster.

When Cody sat down in the car I could see the anticipation in his eyes as I inserted the key into the ignition.

"So, what are we working with here? If you know your cars and didn't just buy it because it's pretty." There was a cocky, humorous tone to his voice. If it were anyone else I would show them *pretty*, but I playfully dropped my jaw and my eyes narrowed.

"Four hundred and twenty-eight cubic inches, four on top tranny, aluminum intake, zero to sixty in six point five seconds, three hundred and fifty-five base horsepower, four hundred and twenty foot pounds of torque, and it gets an eco-friendly nine to eleven miles per gallon." I looked over at him and smiled. "We'll be getting seven today."

Cody's mouth dropped and he adjusted in his seat.

I fired her up. The garage walls shook in rhythm with the raw power that awoke under the hood. The red brake lights illuminated the wall behind us as the car rumbled in neutral.

"If it were stock." I glanced to the surprised look on his face.

I shifted into first gear and assaulted the gas pedal. Releasing the clutch, the tires squealed as we blew past the garage door and down the drive. Cody gripped the seat tight with his right hand. He gripped my forearm with his left, cutting off circulation to my arm.

It hurt like hell, but it sent a wave of heat down between my thighs.

"So, what's really under the hood?" He tightened his grip.

"A little supercharged upgrade." I hammered the gas to the screams of the engine.

I sped into the first curve, jerking us sideways. Cody grunted. I could feel the force taking a toll on his body. He still smiled like a child on Christmas morning. I hit a turn going the other direction and Cody brushed against my shoulder.

"Holy shit." His breaths were short.

The car roared down the hill, kicking up dust and rocks as we swept through each curve, the impressive skyline growing larger every second.

"What do you want to do today?" The motor rumbled as I grinned in his direction.

"Run away with you." He smiled.

The Matriarch

He always said the perfect things. I had the same wish in my mind and even contemplated it briefly, before snapping back to reality.

"I'm serious."

"How about...a light lunch, maybe a cruise through the countryside in this beast?" He tapped on the dashboard like he'd made a new best friend.

"It's a she." I smiled back at him.

"You might have some competition." His eyes darted around the interior of the car.

"She would never steal my man. She knows better."

"Is that what I am? Your man?"

Ohh, he was good. My stomach tightened. This was the first time we'd hinted at defining the relationship. Hell, it was the first time I'd ever defined a relationship.

His hand trembled as it ran on top of mine. My insecurity told me it was his injuries. I gripped the wheel with clammy palms, trying to sound confident in my response.

"Are you asking me to be your girlfriend?"

He admired my face as I clutched the wheel, turning to lock onto his eyes. His gaze swept over me and his fingers slid down between mine.

"Yes."

Cody exited the car in the parking lot of a small diner, nestled in a shopping center on the corner of a main intersection. He walked over and opened the door, grabbing hold of my hand while I stepped out of the car. I started toward the entrance when he stopped me.

The Matriarch

He held both my hands and leaned down a little, inches from my face. I broke free from his eyes, studying the stubble that dotted his chin, following it down where it disappeared under his t-shirt.

"Will you be my girlfriend?" His look was heavy and intense.

It seemed like a cheesy question, but butterflies riddled my stomach. He had no idea how happy his words made me. I looked over and saw my twelve-year-old self in the window of the car, before reality smacked me in the face. The backdrop was perfect. The skyline was visible. The old buildings full of character filled the canvas. My heart palpitated into a drum roll, the tempo increasing with every moment. His hands trembled in mine and his knees knocked together like they might give out at any moment.

"Yes." I looked up to his emerald eyes and grinned.

Lips locking onto one another, both of our cheeks turned pink and flushed. His eyes sparkled. Colors grew vivid as we twirled slowly, wrapped in each other, heated lips bound to one another in the parking lot of the diner, oblivious to the cars whizzing past on the busy roads. We came to a stop and my lips rested on his, never wanting to part from him.

We eventually walked through the door of the diner, taking a seat in the corner. We quickly realized we were the only patrons. It was perfect. The waitress brought a few plastic menus over and we peered over the selection. I opted for a club sandwich. Cody ordered a bowl of soup.

We sat googly eyed for most of the meal, permanent grins affixed to our faces as we held hands, rarely pausing to eat. I became caught up in the moment. Thoughts of terrible things I'd done disappeared from my brain. For once in my life, I forgot my past and all the anguish that accompanied it.

The Matriarch

Looking at my boyfriend, I finally broke the silence.

"I don't have a fucking clue what I'm doing." I laughed as his back stiffened in the chair.

"No, no. I don't mean that it's a mistake. *No.* I just mean, I have no clue how to be a girlfriend. What do I do?" My question was sincere but Cody grinned.

His face relaxed. Relief wafted over him as he breathed a heavy sigh.

"Damn, thought it was over before I said a word. Don't worry. We'll figure it out. But for starters, you just sit there and look beautiful while I stare at you."

He released my hand reluctantly to sip his tea. A lemon wedge hung off the side. Some of the tea spilled down his chin when the ice met his wound. I moved my napkin to wipe it from his face, noticing the disappointment in his eyes.

"Have you never let anyone take care of you?" I stared at him, serious.

"No. I've always taken care of myself."

"Isn't being a team what this relationship stuff is all about?" I didn't get the smile out of him that I expected.

"I guess. It's just not supposed to be this way." He looked to the checkered tile floor.

"What do you mean?"

Cody shook his head and stared out at the street.

"I just feel helpless, you know? I'm supposed to be the strong one, take care of you. You're so independent and I respect that. I like that about you. I just..."

"Just what?" I was in a trance. Caught up in his eyes.

His brow furrowed, eyes narrowing.

"The way I was raised, the man is the protector. He takes care of the woman he lo..." He stopped himself.

The Matriarch

My heart erupted and my stomach cramped simultaneously.

"You know what I mean. A man should treat a woman with respect, but he should be the man. She relies on him. Sorry, I'm screwing this all up. I sound like an idiot."

"No, babe. I get it. I think. Yes, I own a big company. I grew up raising myself. I'm in the media and they portray me as being powerful, influential..."

I stopped for a moment. Cody looked uneasy and I didn't want it to sound like I was gloating. He fidgeted with his thumbs and glared back at the floor.

I reached across the table and smothered his frigid hand, warming it with my touch.

"Look at me."

His eyes slowly rose as I unconsciously batted my eyelashes at him.

"I'm still a girl."

I couldn't believe those words left my lips, but they were true.

"And when you hold me...it's the safest place in the world."

Shallow breaths escaped my tightened lips. The words sunk in. A new, strange feeling radiated through my body. My brain realized my words were the absolute truth. Cody smiled at me.

The elevator rose as I felt his fingers locked between mine. I was surprised we hadn't encountered any rioters. I knew that would change when the sun went down.

Cody's apartment looked the same as before. He quickly offered to cook for me. I didn't want to decline. This was the first time he'd felt up to doing much, but I didn't want to overwhelm him.

"That sounds fantastic." I wrapped my arms around his neck.

"But?" He stared at my eyes.

"But, we just ate and you need to take it easy. Let's get some rest. Hang out for a bit and go back home."

"What are you thinking?"

I batted my eyelashes again, this time aware of my actions. *What in the hell?* I snapped back to my fairy tale, intent on keeping it alive as long as possible.

"Would it be a total cliché if I said I wanted to lay on the couch and snuggle?"

"Yes."

I slapped him gently on the arm, laughing. "Jerk."

He held out his hand and I took it. He led me around to the couch and he sat down. I climbed up next to him, tucking my feet underneath me, nuzzling my chin on his chest while I turned on a movie. Before long, I was asleep on top of him.

Sometime later I woke. Briefly in a daze, I scanned the room before everything clicked. Cody was focused on my face. I stared at his familiar smile. The smile that caught my attention in his store the first time I saw him.

Surprisingly, I had no missed calls or messages when I peeked at my phone. Arms stretching for the ceiling, I peered out the window.

"Fuck, it's dark out!"

"What? Sorry, I nodded off too."

"Shit. *Shit.* I have to call Grandpa and make sure he's okay."

"I'm sure he's fine. You live in the most guarded house in the city."

I knew he was right, but hated being away. I could already see fires starting to dot the streets in the distance.

The Matriarch

"Do you want to try and make it? We may still have time."

"Let me call him real quick."

I walked to another room and pressed his name on the screen. I looked around at the scattered pictures on the wall. Cody's nieces and nephews were always smiling and laughing with their uncle. Grandpa and I spoke. He told me to quit worrying and to have a good time. "I've got four medals from 'Nam for fuck's sake." I started to choke from laughing.

"You are too much. You call me if anything happens."

"I will, sweetie. You tell that boy Big Brother is watchin' his ass...and his hands."

"Oh hush."

"Mags?"

"Yeah?"

"Enjoy yourself. You deserve it, baby girl. It's okay to be happy."

"I love you."

"Love you too. 'Night."

I walked back to the couch and curled up next to my boyfriend.

"You can say it."

"I'm not saying anything." He looked straight ahead, grinning.

"Yeah, yeah. You were right, okay?"

"Not saying anything."

I tickled his ribs and he winced.

"Oh my god, *shit*. I'm so sorry."

"It's okay." He groaned. "I promise. I'm fine."

"I suck at this being a girlfriend thing."

He tilted my chin up with his index finger.

"Come here." He pressed his lips to mine.

My lips tingled at his touch. The feeling migrated south as the butterflies in my stomach intensified.

I worked my way from his lips around to his ear.

The Matriarch

"Let me make it up to you." I breathed heavy in his ear.

I straddled him gingerly, careful not to hurt him as I placed my palms on the sides of his head, parting his mouth with my tongue. I felt him growing underneath me and I slowly began to grind my hips on him.

His hands moved to my ass, massaging it over my pants as the kissing turned to a passionate embrace.

Synapses fired into my inner thighs and radiated through my body. Cody nibbled along my neckline, up to my earlobe, running his fingers through my hair and tasting my neck.

"I want you." His warm breath penetrated my ear.

I cooed, taking in his lips once more, grinding along his cock that was now fully erect. My panties grew moist as I bit on his bottom lip playfully.

"Follow me." He took my hand.

The Matriarch

The Matriarch

chapter thirty four

maggie madison

Cody led me through the bedroom door and I sat down on the bed. He hovered, nibbling up and down my neck. His solid frame pressed into me. I wasn't sure how long I could hold out before tearing his clothes from him.

"The lights." I stared into his eyes.

"I don't care if you see me."

Fuck. That wasn't the problem. I couldn't let him see me. My body was bruised all to hell. It would ruin the moment. It would ruin everything. "The lights, please." I ran a hand along his cheek and moaned.

Cody scurried over and flipped the switch on the wall.

"It's really okay..." He leaned over me and my finger interrupted his lips.

"I don't want anyone below to see the light on and know we're home." I breathed a sigh of relief. *Good one, Maggie.*

"Right, right."

"Shut up and kiss me." I grabbed his shoulders and pulled him into me.

My breasts pushed into the ridges of his pecs. His neck was tense when I wrapped my arms around it. I spread my legs, inviting him closer. His erection teased against my clit as I moaned into his ear, dragging my nails delicately over his scalp before throwing my head back to the bed. His left hand ran down to my breast, massaging it gently, his palm on my tight nipple. I grabbed the sides of his head and leaned up.

"My turn."

The Matriarch

I ran my hand up his shirt, feeling his smooth, chiseled abs under my fingers as my hands neared his chest. I dragged my nails back down his stomach, staring up into his eyes, and lifted his shirt over his head.

I flipped him over and pinned him down on the bed, his legs hanging over the side. I moved my feet down to the floor. A hand on each knee, I spread his legs, inching between, kissing him deeply.

I grabbed a handful of his hair as I rose from his lips.

"Mind if I take care of this?" I caressed his dick, stroking it slowly. His eyes rolled into his head at the slightest touch as the moon lit his face. I turned around and pressed my ass to his cock, grinding up and down against it as I slowly unbuttoned my blouse and slid it from my arms. My hands ran over my lacy white bra that corralled my breasts, tweaking my nipple as it grew hard between my fingers, breathing heavy for him to hear.

My pants slid to my ankles and I kicked them aside. Reaching back and clawing at the sheets, bits of light traced the outline of Cody's face as I watched his reaction. I smiled, teasing him with my body.

I continued grinding my ass on him, nothing between us but his jeans and the thin lace of my panties. I turned and massaged his shaft, staring at him, logging every reaction in my memory.

I wanted him so bad, but I wanted to make our first night memorable.

I ran my fingers up his stomach and chest, all the way to his shoulders before moving them back down, feeling every curve, every muscle, every inch of detail on his body. He tried to sit up and I shoved him back down.

"Not this time." His legs tightened at the sound of my whispers.

The Matriarch

My hands passed his lower stomach, feeling down the v-shaped muscles in his hips. I unbuckled his belt and heard him groan as I pulled the leather strap to the side. Unbuttoning his jeans, I kissed his stomach and my fingers grazed his muscular thighs, up to his ass to grip the top of his jeans from behind. I dropped to the floor and his pants came down with my body, revealing a tight set of boxer briefs concealing what I ached for. My panties were soaked against my hand when I reached down into them and my clit swelled between my fingers. I rubbed small circles around it as I kissed the tip of his cock. It jerked as I exhaled down the shaft, teasing it delicately with my teeth through his briefs.

Shudders in his torso brought a smile to my face. I wanted to please him more than anything in the world. Not for money. Not for power over his actions. Not out of fear of what would happen if I didn't. I wanted to please him because I cared for him. I wanted to please him because he cared about me. Because he was a good man. Because he deserved it.

I pulled my hand from my panties and felt the bulge in his briefs as I gripped the waist band with both hands. I pulled his briefs down and released his cock. He moaned when it wobbled free in the air before halting, lined up with my salivating, eager mouth. I tossed his shorts and they flew against the wall.

I wrapped my small fingers around the base of his dick and felt his hips jerk. Waves of ecstasy heated inside me as I explored him. His head tilted back as I caressed it. His cock grew rigid in my hand from the friction against my palm.

I adjusted my position and touched the tip of my tongue to his throbbing, swollen head.

I swirled my tongue around it, eyeing him eagerly, stroking him at a rhythmic pace. My velvet tongue

The Matriarch

pressed to one of his balls, warming it with my breath.

Licking to the top, my lips took him whole. His hips hammered down into the bed but I followed, guiding him into my mouth. I slid halfway down, teasing. Then a little farther. He grunted when I repeated, and sucked my cheeks around it.

As I went down on him, I felt his hand work into my hair. It did something for me. I gripped one of my breasts firm, my other hand exploring my thighs, taking him deep in my throat. A leak of pre-come only made me hungry for more.

Two of my fingers parted my soaked folds and caressed my clit. Synapses fired down my thighs to the tips of my toes as I increased the tempo, sucking him and stroking my fingers back and forth against my throbbing, wet pussy.

Two of my fingers slipped in, plunging to my core. I hummed on his prick, pounding my fingers into my slick cunt, but they weren't enough. My aching pussy yearned for more. I had to feel him.

Staring up at his face, I pulled him from my mouth.

"I need you inside me."

He nodded, scooting to the middle of the bed. He leaned to a nightstand and pulled a condom from the drawer. I crawled on all fours to him. Our eyes met as my tight nipples teased at his stomach and chest. I took the condom from him.

Biting the wrapper with my teeth, I ripped it open and threw the wrapper off the bed. I smoothed the condom down his stiff cock in delicate strokes. Hands on his shoulders, leaning down for a kiss, I lifted my leg and straddled him. His hands inspected my soft, creamy skin, kneading my ass. I moaned into his ear, breathing down his neck, whispering to him.

The Matriarch

"I need to feel you in me. Over—" I bit at his ear. "—And over—" I grabbed a fistful of hair. "—And over."

He nodded as I eased onto the tip of his cock. I rocked my hips back and pressed down on him, pushing him deep inside of me as I moaned up to the ceiling.

I leaned down and our foreheads met. I stared deep into his eyes, and felt his heart beat in his dick deep inside of me. My head angled to the ceiling, back arched, my breasts flattened into his chest as I slid back and forth on him, pushing onto him harder in time with each thrust of his hips.

I sampled his neck and his collar bone, then nibbled on his lower lip, careful not to irritate the stitches in the side of his face. My eyes a few inches from him, I pulled my hips up so the head of his cock barely parted my slippery entrance. I sunk my hips back onto him. His hands squeezed each of my breasts. A light moan escaped my lips.

His face tensed as he fucked me harder. Our bodies timed each thrust perfectly. I squeezed every inch of him inside of me.

His palms went to the side of my face and he stared into my eyes.

Tension built in my clit. I leaned back from his face and sat up on him. My hands spread my cheeks, grinding his balls against my puckered asshole. My pussy completely filled. His fingers dug into my thighs as he grunted, trying to push his cock even farther inside.

My moans grew loud as I rocked my hips faster and harder. Cody clawed the sheets and my legs as the headboard rapped lightly on the wall. The oak bed frame creaked beneath us in rhythm with my grinding hips.

The Matriarch

My hands found his chest and I squeezed my breasts together with the inside of my arms.

"Fuck me. Fuck me hard, Cody."

He gripped my ass and began to thrust into me. I moaned. He thrust again, this time harder. His knees bent and his weight shifted to his feet. He went into me harder, a steady rhythm as my moans grew louder. I was on the edge, so close to taking the fall and coming all over his cock. My right hand went to my pussy, fingers circled my clit. He drilled into me.

"Oh my god, just like that." I gasped. I could feel his cock against my clit with my fingers on top of it.

He increased the intensity with each push into me, soon pistoning me with everything he had. My moans turned to screams and then to uncontrollable panting as he hammered into my cunt. I'd never been so hot and wet in my life. My vision started to blur. Smacking sounds echoed through the room as my pussy streamed into the bedsheets and down his thighs. He grunted, pounding me harder than I'd ever been fucked in my life.

"*Fuck, Cody*. I'm gonna come." My voice hitched. I started convulsing on top of him, my mind numb. It was too much to take. Sensory overload. Waves of pleasure rushed through my whole body as I shuddered on his dick. I came once as he kept fucking me hard and then again. I clamped down on him and his cock grew inside me. I seized on him for a moment, frozen in time. My hips tried to push away and my vision blurred. I stared down to his closed eyes and clenched jaw, his cock still pumping into me and I knew he had to be close. I leaned in, pressing my forehead to his. His eyes opened.

He nodded. I buried my hips down onto him as he fisted my hair, wrapping his other arm around my back, thrusting balls deep. With a grunt, he unleashed his hot seed, clutching me tight against his

The Matriarch

chest. His hips and legs jerked. He thrust again as I felt his toes curl stiff and his breath grow shallow.

His arms went limp and then his hands ghosted across my back. Our lips met, sticky naked warmth between us as he pushed sweaty strands of hair from my face.

I stared at him adoringly, my mind floating in the clouds from the intense, intimate orgasm.

"Hi." I stared in his eyes a few inches from his face.

His lips curled and a sheepish grin formed.

"Hi." He drew in deep breaths and wrapped me up tight. I rolled onto his shoulder and fell asleep almost immediately.

We woke up the next morning entangled in each other. Flesh on flesh. I ran the tip of my index finger down Cody's arm, watching him sleep peacefully.

Sunlight poured in from between the curtains as I rose up out of bed. I slipped on a pair of his boxers and one of his t-shirts before walking to the kitchen to make a cup of coffee. I examined myself in the mirror for any bruises he might question.

Good to go.

I rifled through his cabinets, giving up when I found the large, overwhelming assortment of imported organic coffee beans.

"What the fuck? Where's the Folgers, man?"

"Maybe I better take care of the coffee." He stood in the doorway. Even battered, bruised, scarred, he was still the sexiest thing I'd ever seen. His body may have been beaten, but it was a sight I could wake up to every morning.

The Matriarch

He walked over and reached to the coffee-filled cupboard and shifted bags around. I took my time, working my gaze from his ass up to his back and shoulders. "This should be nice."

He turned around and caught me ogling his body.

"Eyes up here. I'm not a piece of meat."

I shook from my schoolgirl crush and smiled.

"You are if I say so." I muttered under my breath.

"What's that?"

"I said quit being a tease and get me some fucking coffee. Jesus."

He laughed.

I looked at the giant stainless steel contraption he fidgeted with.

"Yeah, I would have broken that. This is certain."

Cody lit the gas stove and walked to the refrigerator, pulling a few eggs out. He threw a few slices of bread in the toaster. I sat at the table, looking at the hills etched with trees, roads snaking through the middle of them. My mind went to Grandpa.

"What's going on today?" I glanced back to Cody.

"Relaxing."

I snuck up behind him as he cracked the eggs on the side of the pan and wrapped my arms around him. I ran my palm across his abs for my own enjoyment.

"And a lot of this." He turned around in my arms and kissed my forehead.

"That sounds amazing. I need to check on Grandpa. Can we do it at my place?"

"Sure."

I turned back to the window. Thin wisps of smoke rose from smoldering fires down in the streets.

"Is it bad down there?" Cody asked.

"Could be worse."

The Matriarch

After breakfast, we loaded into the Mustang, taking off for the foothills. I let Cody drive. He grinned, driving the speed limit the entire way, ignoring my constant urging for him to "hammer that shit".

When we got home and walked up to the front door I inserted my key but the front door pushed open. There was no sign of struggle. I assumed Grandpa was being careless as usual. I hollered for him but there was no reply.

"Probably sleeping." I looked at Cody like nothing was wrong, but I had a bad feeling.

After a few minutes of shouting for him throughout the house, I began to pace. I ran out to the garage and counted the cars. Everything was where it usually was, nothing out of the ordinary.

I called Kyle, pacing back and forth in the living room as Cody tried to console me.

"Hello."

"Grandpa is missing! I don't know what the fuck to do!"

"What do you mean he's missing? What are you talking about?"

"He's not here, Kyle! I'm freaking out!"

"Meet me at the cafe at Eighth and Crossway. We'll figure it out.

The three of us sat in the cafe, waiting for our drinks to reach the table. We didn't plan to eat. Not while Grandpa was out there somewhere.

We watched on a TV in that hung in the corner as riots broke out in downtown Bathory. Police had lost control of Blythe Park in the center of downtown. The

The Matriarch

park seemed an easy center of refuge for rioters, now openly plundering stores in broad daylight.

"Animals," said Cody.

Kyle and I nodded in agreement.

Cody had sentimental attachments to the park and his store was only a few blocks away. It wouldn't be long before it was hit.

"At least I don't own that damn place anymore."

"Sorry to hear that, bro. I have a couple things I have to take care of. Bekah, are you okay? I can stay as long as you need me to." Kyle stood from the table.

"No, no, it's okay."

"Should we go to the cops?"

"No, I have people looking into it. I don't trust them to do a damn thing."

Cody fidgeted with his fingers. I could tell I was making him uneasy. I was worried I'd already exposed him to too much. It's why I didn't date. I reached out and grabbed Cody's hand then looked to Kyle.

"I need to make a few calls to clients. We need to run by and let Cody get some things out of the shop too. Just be careful, okay?"

"Okay, but you call me as soon as your guy calls you back. I mean it. If he calls, you call, got it? I won't be long."

I nodded but Kyle didn't seem convinced.

"You make sure she calls me." He turned to Cody.

"I will."

I followed Kyle as he walked away.

"I like him, Mags. He's good for you."

"He makes me so happy. Happier than I've ever been."

"Hey." Kyle smiled at me.

"Hey yourself. I got you and him both back in the same week. I should have known something would happen to ruin it. Things never do go right with us, do they?"

"It's made us stronger. We'll get through this and we'll find him. And sure...things got bad. Bad things happen. It's part of life."

I stilled for a moment. I couldn't believe my twin was all grown up, talking like an adult. It saddened me that I'd missed out on so many years with him. He was so put together now: full of goals, purpose. I remembered how much I used to worry about him.

"I, I can't lose him. I just can't. It's not an option."

Kyle wrapped me up in a hug.

"You'll find him. We'll find him. It's in our blood. We found each other after all these years, right?"

I smiled and latched onto him again.

"Okay."

Cody and I stood in front of the shop. It was the first time he'd been there since it was sold. I was trying so hard to be strong for him. It was obvious he was an emotional wreck. Who wouldn't be? He tried to play it off and kept asking about Grandpa. I couldn't think of anyone more selfless. He'd lost everything he cared about, but all he wanted was to comfort me. It warmed my heart and baffled me at the same time. Selfless people rarely get ahead in this fucked up world.

"You coming inside?"

"I really need to make a few phone calls. Is that okay? If you need me I will go with you, babe."

"Nah, it's okay. Give me a few minutes. Probably better I do this alone anyway."

"Take all the time you need. We're safe now. If it looks like it might get bad I'll run in."

The Matriarch

"If it even smells like it will be bad, you get your ass in here. Got me?"

I liked when he was forceful in the way he wanted to protect me. My entire life I was vulnerable, always to someone or something. Even now with Grandpa gone, I felt exposed. The guilt flooded back when I realized the whole reason we were at Cody's shop was my own fault. It ate at me inside. Grandpa's words kept ringing in my ears. As soon as he was found, Cody and I were going to sit down and have a discussion. After last night, I didn't want anything between us. If it meant losing him, well, at least I had one night to remember.

My pocket buzzed and a strange number appeared on the screen. I answered.

"Hello?"

"Bekah? Bekah?"

"*Grandpa?* Where are you? Everyone is looking for you."

His voice disappeared.

"Hello Bekah. It's been a while."

I squeezed the phone tight. I hadn't heard the voice since the night Kyle came to our rescue. The night this sick fuck cut open Cody's face. The night he had us beaten senseless, and probably would have killed us had we not escaped.

"You motherfucker."

"Don't talk. Just listen."

"Let him go."

"You know I'm not going to do that."

"What do you want? You win, okay? What do you want for him? I'll do anything."

"That's quite a proposition for me to think about."

"*What do you want?*" I cried into the phone as I heard a groan in the background. Knowing Kiril it could be anything, but I feared the worst.

The Matriarch

"I know you're friends with her. I'll trade your grandfather, for her."

"Who?"

"This isn't the time to play stupid." His voice was eerie and commanding as ever.

"*Who*?" Tears ran down my face.

"The Matriarch."

"Nobody knows who she is."

"You do."

"Why the hell would I know her? I have no business interest with her."

"She stole from me. You used the information. One hour in the park by the main stage. You get her for me, and your grandfather lives. You don't...well, I think you have a good idea of what I'll do."

"Hey fuck you, buddy. Fuck him, Bekah. Don't listen to Scarface's bullshit."

"Quiet!" Kiril sounded royally pissed.

Grandpa could drive the calmest person mad in a matter of hours. If he wasn't making jokes, then he wasn't seriously injured. It gave me comfort.

"This guy ain't shit, Bekah. You hear me? Don't you make a deal with his sorry ass."

I heard Grandpa groan.

"*Okay.* I will get her. As soon as you see her, he goes free. Just don't hurt him anymore."

"One hour or he dies."

The phone clicked and they were gone.

I flipped around and Cody was still in the store. I sprinted to the Mustang. I had to. It would look bad, but I had to protect Cody.

The tires screeched under me and I saw Cody sprinting toward the door. My heart dropped as I watched him clutch his face, growing smaller in the mirror.

The Matriarch

The Matriarch

chapter thirty five

maggie madison

I typed a text to Cody as fast as possible.

'So sorry. I have to do something.'

I got one back immediately.

'Come back. I want to help.'

I gripped the phone tight in my hand. If Kiril wanted the Matriarch, he would get the Matriarch. I quickly typed out one last text.

'Have to do this alone. Sorry.'

'Okay. Be careful.'

I nearly lost it in the car. Cody trusted me. Even when I left him stranded in the middle of riots downtown. I was the worst person in the world.

The more I played his words in my head, the more they sank in. The more real they became. It was that moment, I realized I was in love with him. It was also the moment I realized it wouldn't possibly last.

Grandpa.

I needed to focus. Grandpa was all that mattered right now. I would deal with the fallout when the time came.

I punched the gas and flew through the gates into the driveway. I sped around to the garage and parked in the middle, hopped out of the car, and flew to the room that held my weapons. The garage door closed behind me, in case any of Kiril's little Family minions sat in the trees with a sniper rifles. I flipped the light switch, my tools of death and suit on display.

I stretched the top over my head and smoothed it down.

Grandpa.

I brought the wig up to my head and pulled the leather pants up over my ass. My knives looked

The Matriarch

hungry for blood as I strapped them around my waist. I reached up in my boots pressed the buttons inside to test the blades. They were good to go as I pulled them on. My mask sat in my hand and I brought it up to my face and tied it in the back. I turned around slowly to the mirror. Each time I put on the suit I became a new person. A person for criminals to fear.

"Fuck this motherfucker."

My hand unsheathed a throwing blade and I whirled. It shot across the room and hit the garage door button, sticking into it as sparks flickered to the ground. The garage door rose slowly. The setting sun illuminated my feet first and slowly radiated up my suit as the skyline came into view from the top of the hill.

Grandpa.

I flew around the curves in the Mustang when my phone rang.

"Did you get what I want?"

"She'll be there. You better let him go motherfucker."

"And when will she be here?"

"When you see bodies start dropping."

I hung up the phone as I skidded around a corner. The car hugged tight to the road, engine screaming as nightfall set in.

I parked a few blocks from downtown, hiding the car in the shadows of an alley. I crept along the side of the wall, poking my head around the building. Heat from the raging fires rushed around my face. Four men busted the glass out of a store and crawled inside. Mayhem was everywhere. People were wearing ski masks and makeshift disguises. Many of them weren't even affiliated with Kaos. The police were barricaded behind patrol cars a few blocks

The Matriarch

down, hollering at rioters over loudspeakers as the rioters ignored their warnings.

I blended with the cityscape, running around cars and trees, hiding when anyone neared.

"These fucks will do."

The main stage was in the distance and appeared deserted. All the rioters hung out in the streets. Most of them looked younger, in their teens or twenties. They wore the Kaos makeup, clad in tattered jeans and boots. A few sprayed graffiti on the walls of the shops they robbed.

Roughly fifty of them stood there as I emerged from the shadows. They were all hell bent on creating anarchy. One of them spotted me and froze, staring. His friends noticed, too. They looked scared, afraid to make a move.

"The CEO of Salzberg Industries is in the park. Follow me if you want real justice. Or you can keep burning innocent people's stores like a bunch of fucking pussies."

The men looked at each other. Anger and hatred filled their faces. They walked to me with purpose. If I had to kill all of them, it was fine by me.

"You really her?" One of them stared at me. I couldn't tell if he was scared or wanted to fuck me.

"The fuck do you think dummy?"

Some of them snickered.

"Alright, we'll follow you over there. Lead the way, baby."

"You don't do shit until I say so, or I'll filet your scrawny asses. Understand?"

"Fuck you, bitch! We don't take orders." I looked over to the punk fuck leaned against a brick wall, smoking a cigarette.

Without looking, my arm whipped and a knife impaled his hand against the bricks. His half-smoked cigarette fell to the street.

The Matriarch

"Smoking is bad for you, dipshit."

All of their jaws hit the ground. The doubt vanished from their eyes.

"Now, when I give the word...have your way with these cocksuckers." I grinned at them.

"Yes ma'am." One of the younger ones smiled at me.

"Well, aren't you just cute." I pecked him on the cheek as I walked toward the stage. "If you see an old man with them, get him out of there. I'll reward you later." I winked as the men smiled and ogled my ass.

We neared and I could see Kiril's guards. *Family fuckers.* When we were within a hundred feet of Kiril's men, I motioned for my new recruits to be quiet.

There was one lone gunman hanging out on watch. I flashed past with lightning speed, quickly dismantling the man's gun. I dropped the clip to the grass, cutting his throat as blood sprayed the tree next to the Kaos boys.

"Fucking hell." My little crush stared at me, whispering. I shot him another wink.

I crept in closer looking for my target.

Grandpa.

I could see Kiril pacing the stage. I assumed Suki held Grandpa somewhere nearby.

He had at least seventy-five guards all forming a large semicircle around him. My patience ran thin. I motioned to the men to follow me.

A backdrop of burning buildings lit the night sky as we marched toward the stage. Kiril's men took notice, their eyes growing large when they saw the gang behind me, cracking their knuckles. They had bats, chains, guns, any weapon suitable for a massacre. Kiril could order the guards to fire at any time but I knew him. He was bloodthirsty. He wanted

The Matriarch

to torture me, kill me slowly, savor the moment. Show my death to all of humanity.

He also didn't want to draw attention with gunfire. That was a sure way to give the cops just enough courage to rush the place.

I picked up the pace as we neared his men, working to a slow jog.

Kiril tilted his head sideways to crack his neck. "Kill them!"

The two armies of men sprinted at each other, weapons drawn.

Mayhem and gore ensued when we collided. Blood painted the sidewalks, screams and the ripping of flesh filled the night air. I drew my knives from my belt and began dicing up any motherfucker in my path.

I twirled, running up the side of a tree to dodge a man's attempt to stab me and came down on the back of his head, impaling his skull with the blade on my boot. "Sorry. That has to be a splitting fucking migraine."

Kiril grew impatient. He began moving through the crowd. He grabbed a man with a painted face and crushed his larynx, dropping him to the ground. His white, linen-wrapped face floated through the crowd, eyeing me, avoiding punches and returning the favor with superhuman strength. I could hear bones crushing in faces from fifteen yards away as I stabbed into one man's jugular with a kick, then spun back and swept a guard's feet, sending him to his back.

He rose to his knees and I grabbed him by the back of his hair.

"You want to eat this pussy?"

I shoved his face between my thighs, furiously slashing another man's chest, before stabbing my knife into his heart and ripping it back out.

The Matriarch

"You don't eat pussy for shit." Fear clouded his eyes. He put his hands up to defend, but I twirled two knives in my fingers. One knife stabbed into his stomach and yanked upward, the other spilled his throat to the ground.

Kiril was now ten feet away. He bludgeoned one of the teens with a bat he had grabbed from someone in the melee.

I focused on him, trying to make my way when a familiar foot struck me in the face.

I tumbled across the ground, clutching my head as the rioters and guards stared in astonishment. I looked up to meet Suki's face. Glaring street lights sent needles into my temples. One of the rioters ran up and Suki caught him with a backhand, pulverizing his throat as he flipped, landing lifeless on his back at my feet.

"Why are you doing this?" I stared at Suki, praying she was in there somewhere.

Suki's eyes were pale white. She looked possessed by a demon. She strode toward me, death in her eyes, clenching her fists, breathing heavily. Everyone stilled. They all watched the girl stalking the Matriarch. I scooted across the ground on my ass and my back rammed into a tree.

Suki's leg shot to the sky and came straight down towards my face. I rolled out of the way moments before being struck. Suki's leg crashed into the tree, the large oak shook as leaves fell around me. I sprang to my feet, shuffling around, taking in my surroundings as Suki continued to walk toward me like a robot.

Guess this bitch wants to get to business.

I told myself it wasn't her. That wasn't the little girl I knew. I feinted left and whipped a knife out, flinging it at her.

The Matriarch

Suki's head veered sideways. She caught the blade in mid-air. Blood from her hand trickled down to the handle. She tossed the knife aside, raising her hand to her face, and licked the blood from it. She stalked toward me, an unstoppable zombie. Kiril watched. I could feel his stare beneath the shrouds.

Suki's face grew intense as she neared. A shriek pierced the air and she went on the attack, a flurry of fists and kicks. I dodged them, countering with a blow blocked by Suki's forearm. Each blocked strike felt like my bones were shattering. Her power was supernatural, backing me to another tree. Suki's fists unleashed into a fury, pummeling my bruised arms until they dropped. She throttled my rib cage. I shook against the tree, held up only by the blows that kept coming.

When the barrage of flying arms finally ceased, I floated like a puppet held up by strings, like a boxer trying to make the ten count. Suki smiled, grabbing me by the throat, watching the life drain from my eyes. I gasped for air that didn't come. My field of vision darkened. The last thing I saw was the top of Suki's head as it slammed into my face.

I returned to consciousness, my heart beating against my skull, a bright light in my face. It felt like a knife was plunging into my scalp as I looked around, processing my surroundings. Most of the rioters were gone and I wasn't sure why. Why hadn't they just overtaken them? Perhaps they weren't really as interested in the Kaos message as everyone believed. Maybe they just wanted to rob people of their hard-earned money.

The Matriarch

I looked up and my questions were answered. Behind Kiril stood twenty young girls, Suki in the front. They all held the same evil stare. They had the pale look in their eyes.

"They're insurance. In case you have other plans."

I looked past him, refusing to acknowledge his presence.

"What? You have nothing to say?"

He bent down to me, pretending he might lift my mask and reveal my identity.

"Oh, I'll show you to the world soon enough. Don't worry."

"Let the old man go."

"I don't think so."

"You got what you wanted."

He stalked back and cocked his head sideways. Wielding his knife, he teased the blade along my neckline. I felt the cold steel against my skin and didn't flinch as the sharp tip pressed into me. A drop of blood ran down to my top.

"I'm not gonna let him go. I know who your friend Bekah is. Or should I say, Maggie Madison? We've known each other for a long time."

Fear gripped my spine. How the fuck did he know this?

He smirked. "We have a history together." He touched my hair." It made me shudder. Memories came back. "Her grandpa will die, tonight. With you."

I struggled against the rope and pain shot through my arms from the beatings.

"No, I won't give you an easy death. Cowards don't deserve an easy death."

Laughter built in me and I bent over at the waist. My laughter grew and rang through the park. Kiril attempted to hide his anger. He spun quickly, his pale eyes narrowing.

"What's so funny?"

The Matriarch

I died at this point, doubling over my stomach every time I looked up at him.

"It's just. I'm sorry. You just said coward..." I squealed as his fists clenched tight.

Kiril laughed with me, looking like I'd gone mad. He sauntered over and grabbed me by the hair, yanking my head to the sky.

"Is it still funny?"

My cheeks puffed out, trying not to laugh in his face. His grip tightened. He leaned down, inches away. I felt his breath on my face and tried not to lose it.

"*Y-y-yess.*"

"What's so funny about you dying?"

My voice grew stern as I stared at his hideous face.

"You talk about justice for cowards. How about cowards that kill their sister? You worthless fucking cunt!"

A deep scream roared through his teeth, echoing through the park. He pounded my face. Left, right, left, right — then he crossed with everything he had and plowed into my jaw. I groaned as I spat blood all over the stage. My face hadn't completely healed since our last encounter. I couldn't think and could barely see. He had knocked my mask sideways and my head slumped over my shoulders. Blood dripped down my nose from lacerations on my forehead where the mask had split me open.

He turned away and then heard me giggle. It turned into a chuckle, then a deeper laugh. I could tell the pain and anguish was raging inside him and I liked it. He turned to my bouncing head, laughing as my blood pooled the floor beneath.

"You think you can goad me again?" He laughed once more. "Yes. I know Zak trained you. You know, it's too bad what happened to him. Just too bad."

The Matriarch

My feet kicked at the ground. I glared at the smug bastard who hid behind his mask.

He snapped his fingers and Suki brought out Grandpa. Grandpa's face filled with horror when he saw me bloody and beaten.

Still, he acted like he didn't know me. "Who's the girl?" Too bad he couldn't lie for shit.

Kiril smiled as I writhed in pain, glaring at him.

He motioned to Suki who retrieved a rope with a noose tied on one end of it. It stretched up to the lights that hung overhead on the stage. I panted, anger surging in the depths of me. I lunged, and was immediately thrust back into the pole.

"*Let him go.* We had a deal."

"I don't think so. I think I'll kill you. Then I'll take the only thing Rebekah Balfour, umm, I mean Maggie has left."

He looked at Grandpa and wrapped the noose around his neck, tightening it in the back. Suki brought him the other end of the rope.

"I'm so sorry. It's just business." His mouth formed a grin.

Kiril looked away and Grandpa mouthed "I love you" to me, then closed his eyes.

Kiril yanked the end of the rope. I wailed and screamed, kicking at the floor as Grandpa hung suspended in the air, legs flailing in all directions. Kiril stared at me. Blood saturated the rope around my wrists as I fought at it.

Grandpa's legs kicked. He clawed at the rope around his neck.

His face paled, lips turning blue, and urine ran down his legs.

His limbs finally dropped, hanging there without a fight.

The Matriarch

Kiril dropped the rope and Grandpa crashed to the ground. He twitched. His eyes didn't open. I refused to scream his name.

I focused my anger on the man who'd stolen everything from me and was doing it again, slowly, right in front of me.

"You're a fucking coward. You prey on those weaker than you. Your sister was twice as strong as you. A few scars and you showed the world what a bitch really looks like."

He snapped the rope and Grandpa shot back in the air. His legs barely kicked this time.

"No!" I screamed and cried this time.

He handed Suki the rope, smiling, eyeing Grandpa. "But you're a hero. Why don't you stop me? Why don't you save him?"

He turned, his fists cocked like pistons, and throttled Grandpa's stomach. Blood erupted through Grandpa's mouth, running down his lips and chin. His face turned pale blue, his fingertips, lips, and eyelids were a light purple.

Kiril cocked his fist back to deliver the final blow. Everything went into slow motion.

I tried to scream but no words escaped my lips. Suddenly, I heard a loud boom. Everything went hazy and my ears rang. Grandpa fell to the ground, seemingly lifeless. Suki clutched her thigh. Blood oozed around her hand. She fell to the ground and arched her back, groaning.

Kiril's eyes darted around to the shadows. He took cover behind a temporary wall that looked like it was once a stage divider. My veins bulged from my sweaty skin around my wrists, tugging against the ropes with everything I had, trying to make my way to Grandpa. Muscles in my arms and neck tightened and I screamed for him to stay alive. His ribs expanded and contracted. Relief overwhelmed me, but I knew he

The Matriarch

was barely holding on. He had yet to open his eyes and his fingertips were still a faded, pale blue.

"You okay?" I heard the voice come from the shadows.

"Kyle?"

I saw Kiril's large pupils as he squatted behind the wall. Specks of blood seeped through the cloth wrapped around his face. He stood, staring, the hate filling his eyes with a fiery red. His fists clenched repeatedly.

"He's still here!" I looked around for Kyle.

Kiril roared as he burst toward me. A bullet sparked at his feet and he stopped in his tracks. The blast echoed through the park.

The cyborg girls scurried as Kyle opened fire above them. The bullets whizzed over their heads. Kiril dove back behind the wall. Kyle turned and fired at him. The bullet struck the top of the wall, a good five feet from its target. *He is a piss poor shot.*

"Kyle!" There was pain in my voice.

"Coming." I could barely make him out as he worked his way to the stage.

Kiril laughed behind the wall. "Yes, hurry. It'll make killing both of you much easier."

"I'm going to put a bullet in your fucking head, bitch!" Kyle ran behind me, drawing a .45 Beretta from his waist.

I don't think so. He is mine.

Kyle pointed the gun at Kiril and his other arm shrugged the rifle over his shoulder. He pulled out a knife, sawing the ropes from my wrists. Aiming the Beretta at Kiril, he held him hostage behind the wall.

"Don't worry. I'll bury both of you next to the old man."

"You buried me a long time ago. It won't happen again." I hadn't seen Kyle this angry, ever.

The Matriarch

My arms were finally freed. Cool air soothed the rope burns on my wrists and forearms as I flipped to my feet.

Kiril emerged from the wall, more menacing than ever. Blood streaks lined the cloth on his face. His eyes widened. He popped his neck with one hand and opened his stance, goading me to come after him. He smirked at Grandpa, who was still struggling to breathe.

Kyle raised the gun and moved his index finger to the trigger, ready to finally bury the nightmares we'd endured. My arm flew from my side. I wrapped my fingers around the barrel of Kyle's gun, lowering it.

"We have business."

Kyle started to protest, but saw the look in my eyes. No was not an option.

He lowered his weapon and eased away. My feet shifted to a fighting stance as I found my balance. I drew blades from my belt and spun them in my fingertips. A glint of spotlight flickered off the shiny surface of my weapons. My blades stopped in front of me. Kiril motioned to one of the girls who brought him a large samurai sword.

"I've been waiting to use this."

I turned to Kyle. "Get him out of here." I looked over at Grandpa.

My lungs fully expanded as I stared at the man who had stolen my life. *Don't let emotions cloud your judgment.*

Zak's words of wisdom sent a calm over me as we circled each other. Kiril twirled the sword with little effort. I was certain every technique in my arsenal was in his as well.

"When I'm done with you. I'm going to carve up your brother, and then finish off your Grandpa. You played me well, Maggie. I respect you for that. But now I'm going to punish you."

The Matriarch

I stiffened. *How does he know it's me? What the fuck?*

"You are confused—"

"Enough with the games, little girl. Your actions told me what I needed to know when you saw him." He nodded to Kyle. "You're still the same whore that didn't bow."

"Fuck you! I never will either."

He lunged, narrowly missing my cheek as I spun away. He followed with another swing of his sword. I deflected with one of my blades and swiped the other at his head as he ducked, avoiding it.

"You're fast for a whore. Faster than Zak was."

He attacked from every angle. Steel clashed together and sparks flew. Every step he took was impeccable. I hurled three knives hard at his face, but he rolled along the floor, launching to his feet as they embedded the wall, splintering the wood, causing cracks to spider web through it.

Kiril growled. He lunged with both hands drawing the sword overhead and slashed downward on me. I blocked it with my knives scissored, catching his steel between them.

He forced the knives toward my face, grinning through his blood-stained bandages. I dropped to a knee, grunting at the mounting pressure. We locked eyes. I fought back, shifting his blade up a few inches.

He released and came across with a right hook, hammering my jaw. Blood spewed from my mouth, splattering on the ground. He spun, his sword slicing through the flesh in my shoulder, spraying the wall with a coat of my blood. Fatigue overwhelmed me as I tried to fight back. I hobbled to him, refusing to cede, clutching my shoulder. Kiril swept my legs and my breath left me as my back slammed to the floor of the stage. He stood over me, blade drawn up with both hands, ready to finish me off.

The Matriarch

"Maggie!" My head rolled to the side, watching Kyle pumping his hands on Grandpa's chest as he stared at me.

Kiril's face tightened, pausing for a split-second to smile at Kyle as he reached for one of his guns.

I drew a blade from my hip and plunged it with everything I had into his foot. Blood bubbled from his shoe.

Kiril let out an agonizing scream and thrust the sword down at me. I rolled and sliced the heel of his other leg, severing the Achilles tendon. I whipped to my feet with a second wind, knives twirling in my hands. I thrust one into his rib cage, the other across his right shoulder. His sword clanged on the ground.

I stared at him with all the hate I'd pushed down inside me. Zak's lessons played in my mind again. *Revenge or justice?* I drew a knife back, but then slowly lowered it. I thought about Zak smiling as his words resonated in me. I was going to have this motherfucker locked up for good.

I hollered to Kyle from the side of my mouth. "He okay?"

"I'm not sure. Help should be on the way."

I panted, staring into Kiril's pale, lifeless eyes once more.

"They're going to lock you in a hole. You'll never hurt anyone again, ever." I clocked him in the jaw with a right cross. Blood pooled in his cheek, saturating the linens with bright red.

I turned around to walk away and then heard him laugh.

My knuckles whitened on the handle of my blades. Anger blazed in my body. "Something funny?" I turned to face him.

"You're a coward. Just. Like. Your. Father. Right before I put him in the ground. A peasant with no spine."

The Matriarch

My jaw clenched tight and rage overcame me. Time halted. Hatred penetrated my skin. Kyle's jaw gaped open.

"No!" I saw Kyle's lips move but didn't hear his words.

I reeled like a cyclone and my blades cut through his neck from both angles. A geyser of blood spewed from his headless body. I caught his head mid-air by the bandages. It was still shrouded with linens. I held it in front of me and stared into his sunken eyes. Screaming into his face, I hurled the head out into the dark off the stage. His body suspended for a moment, heart pulsing blood from the neck, before his headless corpse collapsed into a pile on the ground.

I stood dazed, covered in both of our blood. Sirens blared, and red, white, and blue lights flashed in the distance as I shook back to reality.

I glanced to Kyle. His mouth was wide as he worked on Grandpa.

"Run!"

That's exactly what I did.

The Matriarch

part three

The Matriarch

The Matriarch

chapter thirty six

maggie madison

Below the shower head, I stood as cold water turned copper, sweeping down my body. I scrubbed on raw skin, tearing open my semi-healed wounds. The blood and dirt stung the cuts and burns. The pain was an inconvenience as I tried to wash away everything I'd done. My tears blended with the water. Murdering Kiril gave me satisfaction. Nothing but torment followed.

I finished up in the bathroom, toweling off my beaten body. I covered my bruises with makeup and dressed my wounds, old and new.

Making my way down the staircase, I found Cody and Kyle waiting on the couch.

"Ready?" I faked a smile for Cody.

"Yeah babe."

We walked into Grandpa's room in the ICU. He was hooked to ventilators and a feeding tube. Wires were sprouting from his fragile body. He was comatose and the doctors didn't know the extent of the brain trauma. Asphyxiation is a tricky thing, they'd told me. We wouldn't know anything until the swelling subsided and they could determine how long his brain was deprived of oxygen.

Kyle picked up a bag. He had to leave again, but promised to be back soon. I curled up in Cody's arms as Kyle gathered the last of his things.

"Aren't you two lovebirds adorable?" He smiled, staring at us.

The Matriarch

I gripped tighter around Cody's neck, never wanting to let go. He winced a little, but he never complained. I gritted my teeth, staring at his face. His wounds were healing. A scar had started to form on his cheek.

"We are in fact." I kissed Cody and then released his lips.

He tilted my head up to his.

"I love you."

I floated toward the ceiling.

"I love you too." I didn't think through any of the ramifications before responding. I didn't care. It was true, but the guilt was going to eat me alive. I planned to tell him the truth, soon.

"Sorry, bad timing. I couldn't help myself. There aren't many opportune moments these days."

Kyle walked over, wrapping his arms around both of us.

"I love you guys too."

Kyle tightened his hold on our necks as the laughter subsided.

"I'll be back soon."

"I'll walk you out." I stood up to follow.

Kyle rose, walking over to hospital bed. Placing his hand on Grandpa, he took his limp hand in the other. "Be back soon, old man."

He turned to Cody and me.

"Call me if anything changes."

He strode through the door, and I followed him to the hallway.

"Gonna miss you, sis."

My gaze dropped to the ground.

"Thank you," I said.

"For what?"

"Saving my life."

Kyle shrugged. "It's what brothers do."

The Matriarch

I wrapped him in a bear hug. The same hug I'd welcomed him home with. My face planted in his shoulder and I sobbed.

"I'm sorry."

He stared at my eyes and palmed my cheeks. "You didn't do anything wrong."

"I murdered him. I should have waited, let the police do their jobs."

"Mags, listen to yourself. He was a monster. You know what he did to us. To the others. He deserved everything he got."

I relaxed just knowing someone was on my side.

"Please come back soon." I couldn't fight back my tears.

"Be back before you know it. Besides, it looks like I'll have to be in a wedding soon. Dropping all them 'L bombs' in there."

I slugged his shoulder.

"We're taking it slow, asshole."

"I see that." He smiled big. The same smile from when he was twelve.

He started down the hall.

"Hey Kyle?"

"Yeah, Mags."

I paused, trying to find my words. "If that day comes, if you know...Grandpa can't be there...or even if he is...will, will you walk me down the aisle with him?"

Kyle retraced his steps to me and put a hand on each of my shoulders.

"Nobody would be able to stop me."

The Matriarch

I sat in Cody's arms, crammed against the tiny sofa in the hospital. Grandpa was in the bed next to us. I kept getting up to make sure he was breathing.

The news played on the small television suspended near the ceiling. Cody watched while I paced near the bed. He reached for the remote, turning it up. They were reporting the riots in Bathory and the death of Kiril. Kaos hadn't Tweeted in over a week and the riots were losing steam.

The reporter clutched at his ear piece and his face was white as a ghost. Cody nudged me and increased the volume.

"Folks, we have just received some disturbing footage. We haven't verified, but the owner claims to be Kaos, saying it reveals the truth about the Matriarch."

My heart nearly stopped. I leaned in toward the TV. "Turn it off, please, I can't watch."

"C'mon, I wanna see this." Cody gave me a weird look.

"Please, I'm begging you."

"Why not? This might show something about what happened to your grandfather. Don't you want to know?"

I knew it was a losing battle. He knew me well enough to know I would want the information. I couldn't tell him what had actually happened. He thought I'd been called to an emergency client meeting in front of his shop. My chest drew in tight and my breath grew shallow. *Why now?*

Kaos appeared on the screen. His orange hair and white makeup crawled under my skin. I reached for my elbows, squeezing my arms into my chest, waiting for the worst.

"Oh, hello." Kaos appeared looking surprised. "I hear my message is dying. That people have moved on to the next best thing. Well...let's just hold off on

The Matriarch

that for a moment. Now...I'm a fair, objective guy...you know?"

I scoffed.

"And I too, was caught up in the mystery of the Matriarch, and her umm...good deeds. Hell, I think every city needs someone like her defending the poor, protecting us from all those evil, you know, what's the word I'm looking for here? Rapscallions." He laughed to himself. "Great, great, word. But, I just happened to stumble on to a little secret. See, the umm Matriarch...see she fights evil, right? You might say, 'Oh Kaos, but that's a good thing' but...there is a difference between justice, doing what's right, and cold-blooded murder. See...you see Kiril was an evil man, a villain so to speak. But in a country with liberty, even the villain gets a fair trial. Even evildoers get a fair shake. Now I know what you're thinking, 'but hey, don't you kill people, Kaos?' A fair question, but the people I use to send a message have openly admitted their wrongdoings. They have publicly displayed their disdain for you and the underlings they step on."

"As far as I know, Kiril never got a chance to explain. He never committed those crimes he was accused of in front of anyone. He never admitted to doing anything wrong. And yet the Matriarch, she, she mowed him down. There is also evidence of her whoring around with these bad guys, wait oh—" He turned to someone off camera and mouthed something inaudible. "—okay, okay, so I can say whore on TV? Okay. She *whores* around with these men. For all we know she could be in collusion, and then—" He laughed to himself.

"To top it off, she has him captured, ready to face the music, and she cuts his head off." Kaos was now laughing uncontrollably. He then grew stone cold and silent, a horrifying demeanor came across his face.

The Matriarch

"No, no, my friends. That is not justice. That is someone who kills for fun. That is someone with no sanctity for freedom and basic human life. A human has the right to live in this great country. So without further ado, I give you, your hero of Bathory. The Matriarch!"

The feed cut to the reporter. It warned the audience that the video contained graphic sex and violence. That it was not suitable for children. A video popped on the screen and I could immediately tell it had been edited. My face dropped into my palms, peering through my fingers. I caught a glimpse of me riding Damon Sabbath, then snapping his neck. It showed the park, a close up view of my fight with Kiril. *How in the fuck did he get that angle? How did I not see the camera?*

In the video, Kyle could be seen working on Grandpa as I stabbed Kiril in the foot, then plunged my knives into him. The audio kicked on when Kyle screamed "*No*" after Kiril had goaded me. Then it showed me in slow motion, severing his head, catching it with my hand. It zoomed in to my face as I stared at the head, holding it and screaming. The sound was slowed. My deep scream like a serial killer's voice as I slung the head out into the darkness, blood from his neck spraying in the air and raining down on me like a fountain.

I pried my eyes open, praying it was all a dream but thankful none of it gave away my identity. I looked to Cody, sitting there, shocked with his jaw on the floor.

"Cody?"

He didn't budge.

He sat there dazed. He had always thought the Matriarch was a good person, cared for the city. His head twitched, snapping out of his stupor.

"Cody?"

The Matriarch

He looked over.
"That woman is a monster."

The Matriarch

The Matriarch

epilogue
maggie madison

one week later

The riots had spiraled out of control, forcing most non-participants from their downtown homes and into the suburbs to stay with relatives. Others lived in hotels or homeless on the streets.

Fires raged in barrels and buildings. Looters controlled all of downtown. There was no hint of police in sight.

I slinked down the red brick wall of an alley in my suit and mask, stealthily melding with the shadows. I remained undetected as I paused at the view of the moon and the towering buildings that soared toward the stars.

Screams invaded my ears and I looked over to see two men surrounding three girls, pawing at their clothes.

Kaos thugs.

I snuck behind them.

I'd been out every night that week trying to help anyone who hadn't made it out of the city. None of it made the news.

I tapped on one man's shoulder, surprising him with a burst of punches as he turned around. The other took notice, stalking toward me.

"Run!" I motioned the girls to the end of the alley.

They didn't hesitate. Their screams carried up between the buildings. The fear criminals once held when I would greet them had disappeared since the video.

"Aren't you supposed to fuck us first?"

The Matriarch

The other chuckled. I kicked a knife into his shoulder, laying him out on the ground. Kiril would be the last man I killed, ever. The other man swung, and I caught his arm, dropping my elbow into it and snapping it in half. I grabbed his cock while he clutched his arm. "I wanted steak. This is a salad course you fucking pussy."

I pulled one of them close to my face and yelled at him through gritted teeth.

"Tell your boss I'm coming."

"Tell him yourself." The man laughed and hobbled off after his buddy. An eerie laugh emerged from the shadows. I recognized it immediately.

The figure stepped out from behind a dumpster, the moonlight glowing on the side of his face.

"Kaos..."

"Very astute observation." He sidled over to me. Blood seethed under my skin. I'd repressed the rage, knowing what it had cost me.

"Why are you doing this? I thought you cared about the people?"

He laughed.

"See, therein lies the rub. The people are a means to get something bigger...something I covet more than freedom and liberty. No, we lost those long ago."

"Who the hell are you?"

A breeze kicked up dust through the dark alley, whipping through a haze suspended throughout the city.

"Oh, search within yourself. Search hard. I'm sure a smart woman like you can figure that one out. See it all makes sense, if you just turn the plans on their side a little and see things from a different, umm, angle."

He stepped closer. I stared hard into his eyes. A smile turned up on his face.

The Matriarch

"Hello, Mags." He stepped closer to give me a better look.

My jaw dropped. I was completely vulnerable and helpless. Thoughts sprinted through my mind, praying it was all a bad dream, the worst nightmare imaginable. A tremble began in my feet, inching north. My body shook at his face paint. His voice and his words carved my intestines with a jagged blade, devouring my entrails.

"Kyle?" I knew the answer.

"Bingo." He tapped me on the nose in a playful manner.

"W-what? Why? I don't unders-s-stand."

"Oh I think you do. I think you really, really do. I think you had this feeling all along and were just afraid to act on it. You were afraid of the truth, because it just might be, well, umm, true."

Every piece of the puzzle started to fit together. When he left my house all those times.

"Well is she after you?"
"She is. She just doesn't know it yet."

Walking downstairs while Kyle was on his laptop. The surprised look on his face, clutching his computer tight.

"You? You worked for Kiril the whole time?"

"Oh Maggie, please. You think that old man could put all this together?"

Turning slowly, he seemed to admire the fires ripping through the city. The screams of the innocent.

"Why?" My face was angry. *"Why?"*

Instantly, his hand clutched my throat. He smiled into my eyes, staring at me. His eyes were crazed like a diseased dog. I slapped at his hand as his voice grew cold and angry.

The Matriarch

"You left me there. My best friend...left me to rot in that fucking place. Do you know what happened when you left? When you escaped? To help these — these whores and lowlifes?"

He released my throat and my lungs rapidly searched for air, panting hard, unable to catch my breath as I felt the bruises around my neck.

"Answer me!"

"I, I thought you were dead." My knees quaked.

"Oh, I died alright." He nodded. His normal voice returning. "I was tortured, beaten, maimed...*raped!* That's right, your brother, nineteen-years-old and scared, fucked by old men, over and over 'til I bled, begging for death."

"I, I thought you were dead. They told me they killed you."

"Did you see my body?" He composed himself. "See, Mags, I never would have given up on you. We had a deal, remember? In dad's classroom? I would have fought for you. When you escaped, I had hope. Oh I had big hopes. I prayed every day for you to show up. And you never did."

"So, after a while I adapted. I made myself valuable to the organization. They gave me a computer to play with, taught me how to fight, taught me the art of warfare. I read everything I could get my hands on. My sister, well...well she was going to college, becoming a billionaire, driving these, these fancy cars. You didn't raise an eyebrow when I telegraphed where all Kiril's info was hidden on William's computer? Just some random, anonymous source. Pfft. C'mon Mags, you're smarter than that." He laughed.

"Why Grandpa? Why would you include him in this?"

"Grandpa? Why, he just let us go. Let Mom and Dad take us to hell. He never even came and looked

The Matriarch

for you. Didn't look for me. Knew Mom and Dad were dead and yet he still stayed behind. Fucking coward. Some family we've got. Some fucking family."

"Please, I can't lose you. This isn't you. You aren't thinking right."

"Oh, I'm thinking clear as ever." He ran his hand up to my face, his index finger tracing my cheek. "This is going to be fun. Playing this little game, you and I. It's going to be simply — delightful. Allow me to get it started."

He pulled a phone from his back pocket and he tapped on the screen.

"What are you doing?"

"Oh nothing, nothing at all...and send." After a final tap on his phone, he smiled at me.

"What the hell did you just do?"

"Oh, I just sent our precious Cody a little something. Great guy that Cody. He deserves a real winner. A woman who will treat him right. A woman who is, what's the word I'm looking for? Umm, tru...no, no, no...integr...no that won't work, umm, honest!" He snapped his fingers at his thought. "Yes, an honest woman. Are you honest with him? Does he know about this, this, persona?" He waved a finger up and down at my outfit, scoffing at the sight. He leaned in to my ear. "Does he know how much you love fucking evil men?" He grinned. "Does he? Does he?" He kept laughing.

"What did you send him?"

"Oh just a little video of you and our good friend William. He's dead by the way. Did you know, well, that you got a married man killed after cheating on his wife with you? Yeah, so that happened. Then, you took information from his computer. I just had to type you a little email and you jumped all over it. What was on that again? Oh, plans for Kiril to buy Cody's parents' business. That was a shrewd one,

The Matriarch

gotta give you credit for that. I mean, I'm the one who told him to do it. But you know, I didn't get any credit for that. Oh well, he's dead now anyway."

"Does Cody know who actually bought his parents' business? Does he know, Mags?"

My head sank and I stared at the ground. "I was going to tell him when the time was right."

"No? So he doesn't know?" My head rose as he faked a look of sincerity, followed with a wide grin. "I didn't think so. Well, good news, he knows *now!*" His psychotic laugh murdered my soul.

"Please, stop this, please. I begged as he smiled, enjoying every emotional scar he sliced into me.

"Stop? Hell sis, I'm just getting started." He began to walk away, stopping with his back to me. "Nice move going to his family. Showing them the loopholes, and whatnot. Business speak always eludes me, but yeah, that was a good one." He wagged a finger again.

"I had to protect him, Kiril was going to..."

"Blah blah blah, you don't have to explain to me, Mags. You'll do enough of that at home later. If, if he's still *there*." His sinister laugh tore me up once more.

My phone vibrated and Cody's picture appeared on the screen.

Kaos walked down the road with his arm held out, like he was escorting a bride down the aisle, his voice echoing off the walls. "Dum dum de dum...dum dum de dum," he hummed, as he disappeared into the night.

The Matriarch

coming soon

Thank you for reading book number one of The Matriarch Trilogy. I hope you enjoyed it. If you have some time please consider leaving a review so I know what you thought. It would be much appreciated. As of publication, I do not have release dates for books two and three but I anticipate them to release in 2016. To be notified of new releases you can follow me on Amazon or sign up for my mailing list at the link below to get an email. You can also get plenty of announcements and more if you find me on one of my social media pages: Facebook, Twitter, or Instagram.

www.sloanehowell.com

The Matriarch

other books

The Panty Whisperer Series

(available in e-book format)

The Panty Whisperer: Volume 1

The Panty Whisperer: Volumes 1 - 5

The Panty Whisperer: Volume 6

The Payne Capital Series

(available in e-book format)

Payne Capital

The Matriarch

The Matriarch

about the author

I spend my days doing the opposite of writing. I crunch numbers. Yes, I work as an accountant and spend most of my time in Excel spreadsheets. At night, I turn into a dirty-minded, erotic romance author. I've also written science fiction and comedy under other pen names. When not reading or writing I enjoy hanging out with my family, watching sports, traveling, and engaging my readers on social media. You can almost always catch me goofing off on Twitter so stop by and say hi. Thanks for reading my books, I hope you enjoyed.

The Matriarch

acknowledgements

I could literally write an entire novel just thanking people. People only see an author's name on a book, but it truly takes a team of people to make these things happen. First, my family, who give up countless hours with me so that I could create these stories for you. I love you and thanks for putting up with me. I need to thank my editor, Celia Aaron. This book would not be what it is today without her. I often joke that she took a complete piece of crap and polished it into a diamond. I'm actually not joking when I say that. Her talents are unreal and I am truly grateful for all the hours and hard work she put in on this book. I couldn't have done it without her and she's as much a part of this book as I am. Her writing is also brilliant and you should definitely check it out. Her book Counsellor is one of my favorite reads of all time.

Next, I would like to thank all of the book bloggers out there. I can sympathize with them because I used to have a book blog and review books, so I know firsthand the amount of time and energy they put in with little to no recognition. They truly enjoy doing it, and it shows, because they give up time with their families simply because they love to read and interact with us authors. I can't thank all of you enough. Thank you to all of my readers, both the ones that I interact with on Twitter, Facebook, and Instagram, and those who read silently and merely purchase and enjoy the stories I write. I am truly honored every time one of you spends your hard earned money and more importantly your time, reading something that

The Matriarch

I have written. I try my hardest to thank you all individually and I will continue to do so as long as I am writing books. But sometimes it's impossible, so hopefully this reaches you.

I would also like to personally thank Cecily Bonney at Cecily's Book Reviews. She is my first fan, the first person I ever interacted with and discussed one of my books with. She still gets the first copy of every single book that I write. I wouldn't be where I am without her. Next, I'd like to thank Rae Daniel aka Smutttt at Getyoursmuton. She has reviewed and been a beta reader for a few of my books. Even when she is swamped she always makes time for me, gives me feedback, and more importantly is a great friend who I speak with regularly. She is about to release her first novella as a writer and I couldn't be more proud of her for going after it and I'm honored to help her out with making it happen. Prepare yourself for tons of promotion on my behalf when it comes out. I have to thank Melissa Garland, or "The Queen of Teasers" as I call her, at Booknerdingout. She makes almost all of the teasers and graphics that you see on Twitter, Instagram, Facebook, etc. She is also a beta reader and provides invaluable feedback for me. She is extremely talented (an understatement) and her hard work is much appreciated. E.J. Robinson, author of Robinson Crusoe 2244 and Robinson Crusoe 2245. He's one of my oldest author buddies from when I started out writing sci fi and he's also one of the most talented authors I know. I don't know anyone who knows how to get the most of out of a plot the way this guy does. He also has pretty good taste in beer and I can't wait to get out to Cali and have one with him. Be sure and check out his books, he writes brilliantly.

The Matriarch

Mardell Bonasso, another beta reader I am truly grateful for. I gave her this story with only a few days turnaround time and she had it read and notes back to me that evening. I am extremely thankful for her involvement in my stories. Margeaux Hendricks at Tropical Mary literary review blog. She is the ultimate beta reader. She gives me extremely detailed and valuable notes. I could sing her praises all day long and if she ever takes her editing skills to the professional level you can expect me to bombard you with recommendations. Last but not least, Katie Ekvall at Underline This Editing. A freelance editor who has sacrificed her own time to give me a ton of sage advice. She's also not afraid to tell me when something sucks, which surprisingly is a great commodity when you're an author. She's extremely talented and can spot continuity issues like a champion. Be sure to check out the Underline This website if you need editorial services. I cannot recommend her enough.

I can almost guarantee I have left someone out. If I have I am so sorry and I will catch you on the next book release. Thank you all for reading and listening to me sing the praises of these people who helped make my book a reality. I am more grateful than you will ever know for each and every one of you.

Sloane

17349510R00178

Printed in Great Britain
by Amazon